LADY OF MISRULE

LADY OF
MISRULE

T. A. PRATT

The Merry Blacksmith Press
2015

Lady of Misrule

© 2015 Tim Pratt

Cover art by Lindsey Look
lindseylook.com

Cover design by Jenn Reese
www.tigerbrightstudios.com

Interior art by Zack Stella
www.zackstella.com

For information, address:

The Merry Blacksmith Press
70 Lenox Ave.
West Warwick, RI 02893

merryblacksmith.com

Published in the USA by The Merry Blacksmith Press

ISBN—0-69242-665-5
978-0-69242-665-4

DEDICATION

For Ginger

Bradley in the Gazebo at the Center of the Multiverse

BRADLEY BOWMAN, FORMER ACTOR, former heroin enthusiast, former apprentice sorcerer, and current overseer of the structural integrity of the multiverse, sat reading a newspaper in his gazebo. The "gazebo" was a replica of one in Fludd Park in the city of Felport, except instead of being made of wood and nails and paint, this one was a thought construct in a little bubble of conditional reality where the temperature was perfect at all times, and as he read, he breakfasted on a plate of scrambled dodo eggs and a sweetly tart glass of juice from a fruit that had gone extinct on almost every version of Earth before humans ever got around to tasting it. He could hear Henry, his boyfriend—dead in most branches of the multiverse, with one instance of him saved and brought here as a companion—humming as he worked in the garden. This job had its perks.

The newspaper was an affectation, in a way, since Bradley hardly needed second-hand reportage. A portion of his vast-but-not-infinite self was constantly operating on a less literal level, monitoring the doings of the multiverse, and he could look in on any bit of any Earth he wanted whenever the whim struck or the need arose.

Of course, in practice, he couldn't bother himself much about individual Earths. He was too busy looking for cracks in the structure of the cosmos, checking for tiny tears in the fabric of endlessly branching space-time. There were little holes popping up all the time, keeping him busy. Civilizations that were technologically advanced enough to cause trouble, but not advanced enough to know better, were always attempting to breach the walls that separated realities. There were particularly adept philosophical entities dwelling in clouds of stardust, performing slow cogitations that might turn into computations that could threaten the integrity of some pretty vital mathematical constants. He monitored places where ancient wars—or

1

the resonances of future ones—fought with reality-altering weapons had made the fabric of the multiverse thin and threadbare in places. Sometimes sorcerers used the brute force of magic to try to change the world in ways more apt to destroy it. Such things were all the routine matters of his custodianship. A tweak of an asteroid's trajectory here to provide more pressing concerns to ambitious scientists, a distracting supernova there to dazzle the deep thinkers, a bit of eighteen-dimensional spackle, or a touch of sewing in the form of applied string theory, and the multiverse was preserved to keep on branching out, ever more vast, every possibility that didn't contradict physical possibility coming to pass, eventually, somewhere.

In a worst-case scenario, he could lop off a branch from the greater tree of the multiverse, and let it wither and die without infecting the rest of the organism. A terrible loss, of course, a ruination of near-infinite possibility, but sometimes you had to amputate a limb to keep infection from spreading to the trunk.

Bradley had been human, though, and not so very long ago, back before every possible version of himself had been squished into a higher-level being with a collective consciousness and the wisdom of trillions of lifetimes, many of those lives broadly similar, but with enough profound outliers to give him an unmatched breadth of experience to go with his vast powers and responsibilities. He liked to pay tribute to that human part of himself by reading a newspaper from a particular city—a past-its-prime place on the east coast of the US called Felport—from one particular version of Earth. One of his iterations had died in that city, before the rest of Bradley ascended to his current lofty position as a meta-god, and he took a particular interest in some of the denizens of that universe. It was pleasant, sometimes, to pretend to be just a man, sitting in the gazebo, reading about local politics, local weather, and national news filtered through the local lens: what does all this upheaval abroad mean for *us* in our unfair city? Nothing in Bradley's life was local anymore, not really. Reading one version of Felport's last surviving daily newspaper was an admirable way of providing perspective—

A siren wailed. Or not a siren, exactly. It was every annoying car alarm, every air raid siren, every test of the emergency broadcast system, every drunk yelling in the 3 a.m. street when you had work in the morning, every air horn a so-called friend used to wake you up for a prank, every grating wail of a toddler inexplicably brought into an R-rated movie, every dying smoke alarm, every sound that had ever annoyed Bradley in every iteration of his life.

Henry looked up from his pots of tomato plants, winced, and shook his head. "That sounds bad!" he shouted.

Bradley nodded and waved his hand, shutting the sound off. It *was* bad. He'd put that warning system in place with no expectation that he'd ever have to endure hearing it go off.

"What's going on?" Henry ambled over to the gazebo. The man moved like a cloud, but his eyes were concerned.

"It's, ah… an incursion." Bradley held up his hands. "From outside."

Henry frowned. "Someone breaking into a parallel universe?"

Bradley shook his head. "No, that's bad too, but this is worse. There are… other universes. Our universe, our *multiverse*, it's… think of it as a bubble in a vast sea of foam. The other bubbles are other universes."

"Ah," Henry said. "Right, you've told me about that. There are things in the spaces *between* the universes, right? Like… monsters?"

Bradley wobbled his hand back and forth. A small portion of himself was talking to H, while the majority of his attention was investigating the incursion and considering various ways to prevent the *thing*, the *outsider*, from destroying all reality. "Those things aren't monsters, exactly. I'm not even sure they're alive. They're sort of like viruses but more like prions—they're just *structures* that are inimical to life. Some sorcerers have learned a way to step outside of our bubble, to pass through the empty spaces, and step back into our bubble at a different point—teleportation, but with a double-digit percentage chance every time that one of those monsters would maim or kill them. Only the desperate or foolish use that trick. But those in-between creatures aren't interested in messing with our world. They aren't interested in anything—they just have a tropism toward intelligent life, you know? They're like a Venus flytrap chomping on an insect, they just spasm around whatever comes into contact with them."

"Oh," Henry said. "So we're talking about something *scarier* than that."

Bradley nodded. "Yeah. See, some of those *other* bubbles, other universes… They have different physical laws. Most of them can't support life, and those that do have life… it's so different from life in this universe that we can barely recognize it. Our universe is a branching multiverse, right? It's a universe that doesn't like to make choices: everything that can happen, from a quantum level on up, *does* happen—it just branches off into a new reality, rather than make a choice. A lot of those other universes aren't like that, though: they're linear, deterministic, constrained. Or they're infinite in other ways. Some of the denizens of those worlds, they're capable of coming to this universe—or being exiled here."

There'd been some trouble with that kind of thing in the past. Bradley's counterpart in another universe hadn't realized Bradley's realm was inhabited—to be fair, it *was* 99.9% empty space over here, dark matter aside—and had sent a parasitic monster into this universe with the idea that it was being consigned to oblivion. That creature had proliferated through the multiverse, a new version of it spawning with every branch of reality, and then it figured out a way to breach the walls between parallel realities in order to join forces with *itself*... and to breed. Bradley had contained that monster, but barely.

Now, apparently, something similar had landed in his multiverse again.

"They're *outsiders*," Bradley said. "Some of them can survive here, even though the physical laws are different. Some of them are stronger here, because the altered physics just work out in their favor—the same way you could jump higher on the moon. Some of those creatures have... call it magic... that's more powerful than any magic the locals can muster. And one of those outsiders is presently on Earth. In... California."

"Not Oakland?" Henry said. They'd lived in Oakland together, in his branch of the multiverse.

"No, it's... Death Valley. But it's moving fast." He shook his head. "I can't figure out where it got *in*, there's not a hole, not a pinprick, it's almost like it's been there all along, and it just *erupted*."

"Maybe it got into that branch a long time ago, and it's just been dormant," Henry said. "Sleeping like a cicada, but on a way longer timescale."

Bradley grunted. "It's possible." He waved his hand. "Well, quarantine is the only option. I'll cut off that branch, stop it from segmenting further, and let this outsider do its worst. I'll turn that branch of the multiverse into a prison for it. Let it destroy and consume everything until there's nothing yet, then let it freeze in the resulting heat death of the universe."

Henry whistled. "So. Billions of humans, trillions and trillions of whatever other creatures live in that universe, just consigned to oblivion?"

Bradley sighed. Oblivion. It was true. In the usual run of the multiverse, if you died in a car crash, or got mauled by a tiger, or tossed into a volcano, there were countless other branching realities where you survived or never got into trouble in the first place. It wasn't immortality—everyone died everywhere, eventually, given time—but it *was* a consolation. If he cut off that branch, all those versions of people from that moment forward would meet their final ends, and if the outsider wrought sufficient damage to the fabric of that reality, even the realms of the gods in that branch would crumble, and any eternal afterlives with them. Everything would become the void. "It sucks," Bradley said, "but it's the only way..." He trailed off, then groaned, crumpling the newspaper between his hands.

"Hell," he said. "It's one of *those* realities. The ones branching off from the moment I died in Felport." He hadn't *just* died there. His soul had been eradicated, in that universe. He'd been consigned to oblivion, too. No afterlife, no resurrection. He had no memories of the realities that branched out from that moment, because he wasn't *in* them, that self had been lost forever, but he had friends in that universe anyway. A sorcerer and part-time god named Marla Mason. A hedonistic but good-hearted psychic named Rondeau. A wise old narcoleptic wizard named Sanford Cole. Sure, those people existed, in various forms, in countless other branches... but he'd taken a special interest in the reality where he'd died, following their lives with interest, even communicating with them from time to time—and reading their paper. Hell, without the Marla Mason from one of those worlds, he never would have ascended to his current lofty position. He owed her, and the others, too.

Could he just let them die, even just one version of them all, at the hands (or pseudopods, or whatever) of the outsider?

"What are you going to do?" Henry said.

Bradley considered, with a lot of minds all at once, and made a decision. It was sentimental, but not dangerously so. "I won't cut that branch off entirely. The outsider is a living cancer, and I can't allow him to spread through the multiverse, but there's a stopgap solution—I can freeze the branch. Prevent it from splitting for a while, but without cutting it away from the world tree. I can't hold it that way forever. A certain kind of pressure builds up when I prevent reality from branching—it's like keeping a lid tight on a boiling pot. But I can give it a month, maybe six weeks, something like that."

"Okay, but who's going to stop this outsider before time runs out?" Henry said.

"With luck, the version of Marla Mason in that branch will find a way to stop the outsider, and if she does, I'll let her branch continue to thrive."

"How is she even going to *know* about this monster?" Henry said.

"She has a good nose for trouble," Bradley said. "And looking back... yeah, this thing was imprisoned in a cavern a long, long time ago, and it looks like it was some of Marla's hapless death cultists who let the creature free. She tends to take stuff like this personally, so I bet she'll be on it." Then he grinned. "But... I think I can spare a fragment of myself to help point her in the right direction."

He couldn't spare much. He *wasn't* infinite, just vast. But he could send a single instance of himself, one that knew Marla, with enough information to give her a hand.

Damn. A little piece of him was going to be on the road with Marla, hunting a monster from beyond the back of the stars, with the fate of an entire branch of the multiverse at stake. "Is it possible, Henry," Bradley said, "to be jealous of *yourself?*"

"Only if you're really fucking cool," Henry said. "So in our case, yeah."

Rondeau in Las Vegas

"THIS WEATHER IS ABSURD." Pelham shed layers of coats and scarves and methodically hung them on the rack by the suite's front door. "There are children in the streets of Las Vegas throwing boiling water into the air and watching it transform into showers of ice. The rather bewildered weathermen expect the temperature to descend as low as thirty degrees below zero today."

The suite was a balmy seventy-two degrees, and Rondeau sat on the couch in a robe, watching anything but the weather on the big-screen TV. "This slop is terrible for business," he complained. "Half the casinos aren't even open. The slot machines out at the airport are literally frozen up, I heard—you can't even pull the levers." He shook his head. "But what are you going to do? It's the weather."

"Business is one thing, but we're supposed to be tracking this monster that Marla's cultists set free."

"What do you want from me? I called up an oracle, and it couldn't get a fix on the thing. Maybe the monster died of natural causes or something. You want us to, what, go door-to-door out in the cold, asking people if they've seen a cultist-devouring monster, and no, we can't describe it?"

"I admit I am similarly unsure how to proceed." Pelham finally removed enough layers to get down to his customary suit with waistcoat and jacket. "I can't believe this weather is natural." He perched on the edge of an armchair and wrung his hands. "Don't you get any sense of… magical interference?"

Rondeau winced. "I drink a lot of champagne specifically to dull my psychic senses, okay? I'm not going to summon up an oracle just to complain about the cold. The weather guys say it's just a thing, anyway, a hyperborean vortex or whatever. Some of that counter-intuitive global warming shit. It's comfortable in here. I say we wait it out. The weather's gotta break eventually."

"Half a dozen tourists have died already," Pelham said. "The locals aren't likely to fare any better. No one is prepared for this kind of cold here. You can get frostbite in *minutes* if you aren't careful. People are already losing fingers and toes, and they're the lucky ones. If it's magical weather—"

Rondeau sighed. "Fine. Let's go ask Nicolette. Chaos witches are good with weather, and she can sense when somebody's playing kickball with natural order too."

"Have you been to see Nicolette since Mrs. Mason returned to the underworld last week?"

Rondeau made a face. "No. Why would I? I just stuck her cage in the bedroom, turned the TV on, and left her to it." Rondeau had pretty much always hated Nicolette, and she hadn't become any more pleasant since she'd been decapitated and had her head endowed with a magical quasi-life and stuck in a birdcage for use by their absent leader Marla as a magic-detector.

They went to Nicolette's bedroom door, knocked once, and went inside. The cage on the bed was empty, the base separated from the top. A folded letter rested beside the cage. Rondeau read the pages with rising dismay before handing them over to Pelham.

"Oh, dear," Pelham said after an interval. "That fellow Squat that Mrs. Mason hired for muscle has absconded with Nicolette."

Rondeau groaned. "We let Nicolette escape. We didn't even *notice* she was gone for, what, almost a week? Marla's going to kill us when she gets back to the mortal world. Seriously. Kill us. She can do that. She's the bride of Death, isn't that what the cultists called her? We've got three weeks to live."

"The situation is indeed problematic, but we are not jailers, and I'm sure Mrs. Mason will understand—"

"She'll understand," Rondeau said. "But understanding won't stop her from *smiting* us. We're gonna get smitten. No. That sounds too pleasant. We're gonna get *smote*. How could things get any worse?"

They both tensed up, because saying something like that was an invitation to the universe reading "Please fuck with us further." Lightning didn't strike, no one burst into flames, and a chasm didn't yawn open at their feet, so they went back into the living room, mildly bickering about the best way to deal with Nicolette's jailbreak.

They stopped talking when they noticed their visitor. A tall, regal-looking older woman in a long black fur coat stood gazing out the windows at the ice-locked streets of Las Vegas below. She turned to them, smiled in a distant and superior way, and said, "Tell Marla Mason that Regina Queen is here to see her. Wait. No. That's not quite right. Tell her that Regina Queen is here to *kill* her."

"Ah," Rondeau said. "Marla's… out of town." Despite the bottle of champagne he'd already had that morning, first mixed with orange juice and then with apple juice when the orange ran out, his psychic senses tingled and twinged in this woman's presence. She was magic, and big magic, too. Something about her name rang a bell, but he couldn't quite place it.

"Then summon her," Regina said. "I'll wait." She sat on the couch and crossed her legs. The temperature plunged at least fifteen degrees wherever her roving gaze fell.

"Oh, right." Rondeau snapped his fingers. "Marla told me about you. She met you on a mercenary job, years ago. You're an ice witch."

"An ice *queen*, really—as my name declares. Twice."

"I heard you were up north," Rondeau said. "Arctic Circle territory."

"I was, for a time. I find humans objectionable. I came south when I learned my son Leland—you knew him as Viscarro—was killed. By Marla Mason. Your employer."

Rondeau winced. "Employer? Lately I've been the one giving money to *her*, but come to think of it, she does still give me orders."

"I do not wish to speak to the valet," she said. "Or the psychic parasite."

"Hey, us parasites are people too," Rondeau said. "Or, at least, we possess people, which is pretty much the same."

Pelham cleared his throat. "Ma'am, if I may." Pelham had lots of training on how to talk to nobility, and he used his best butler's tone. "To be technical Viscarro was already dead, having transformed himself many years ago into a lich, a ghost haunting his own corpse—and, to be more precise, it was not Mrs. Mason who ended his corporeal existence, but a dark duplicate of Mrs. Mason who hailed from an alternate timeline parallel to our own—"

Regina held up a hand, and Pelham stopped cold. "I may be a snow queen, but that doesn't mean I have any patience for fairy tales. I looked upon the charred fragments of my son, and found traces of Marla Mason's aura and flesh and psychic resonance there. She is to blame, and frankly, I don't care if it *was* some alternate dimension version of her, or a clone, or a time-traveler from her own future, who did the deed—I will take my vengeance on the Marla I can *reach*. It's a shame. I was mildly fond of the woman—she did me a favor, once. But some crimes can have only one punishment."

"I thought you hated Viscarro?" Rondeau said.

Regina turned her icy regard on Rondeau, making him shiver. "What does that matter? He was my son. No one gets to kill my children without consequences, except me. Call her."

"Okay, that business is between you two, but Marla is… seriously unreachable," Rondeau said. "For at least three more weeks." Rondeau wasn't about to explain that Marla was a part-time goddess of death, spending six months of every year in the underworld, doing—literally—gods alone knew what.

Regina *hmmed*. "I understand Marla prefers that innocent lives be spared whenever possible. Tell her I will kill one person the first day she makes me wait. I will kill two the next day. I will double *that* number the next day. And so on, doubling the previous day's total each subsequent day. It won't take long to empty the city at that rate, will it? Those deaths will be in addition to any who simply succumb to the weather, which will only get worse the longer I wait. Tell Marla to hurry, won't you?"

"We can't," Rondeau began, and then stood in horror as the saliva in his mouth froze, jamming his jaws closed. He grunted in surprise and pain as Regina strolled toward him. She reached into the pocket of his robe, took out his phone, and diddled around with the screen before returning it to the pocket. His lock screen didn't seem to slow her down any, either. "There's my number. Call when Marla's here. A little hot water will clear out your mouth. Don't say 'can't' to me ever again, all right?" She sauntered regally out the door, leaving it standing open behind her.

"Oh, my," Pelham said after a moment. "I suppose *that's* how things could get worse."

THEY MADE A GOOD-FAITH ATTEMPT to reach Marla. There was a magical bell she used, in her mortal months on Earth, to summon her husband the god of death, but ringing it didn't accomplish anything. The old necromantic rites were no good either—Marla and Death had stopped appearing or letting their underworld minions answer when necromancers made sacrifices, because, as Marla said, who wanted to encourage that kind of antisocial behavior, all the vivisection and ritual murder? They even tried the supernatural equivalent of leaving a message, by shouting into a fire full of small animal bones (remnants from the empty kitchens downstairs), and when that failed, they slumped down on the couch in the suite. They didn't know what Marla did during her month in the underworld, but it was vast business, and she didn't have much concern for the mortal realm while she was there.

"Ms. Queen can't mean it literally," Pelham said. "Killing two people the second day, fine, and four the third, all right, and eight the fourth, and even on through sixteen and thirty-two—but before long she'll be into hundreds, even thousands, every day. How is it practical to kill that many? With any precision?"

"You're right," Rondeau said. "She'll probably top out around thirty a day, sure. Or else she'll show a willingness to sacrifice precision, and just kind of kill *roughly* the right number of people." He put a pillow over his face. "So what do we do?"

Pelham shrugged. "What would Marla do?"

"Something clever, and if that didn't work, something violent. She'd stop Regina, anyway."

"Then as Marla's agents on Earth during her absence, we must do the same," Pelham said.

"You're noble. Why do I live with someone noble? Your plan is mostly flaws. You mix a hell of a hangover cure, Pelly, and I've seen you thwack guys pretty good with a walking stick, but you're not actually a sorcerer. And while I've got some psychic powers that came along with this body I stole a while back, they're definitely more on the diagnostic side than the offensive one. I could find out where Regina Queen is hiding, but I can't make her head explode when I do."

"Ah, but you and I possess one great power that Mrs. Mason does not," Pelham said. "We are capable of asking for *help*."

Rondeau took the pillow off his face. "I like the sound of that. On account of how it doesn't involve me fighting Regina Queen directly."

"I KNOW, IT MAKES SENSE, start at the top, call up the big guns first." Rondeau stared at the syringe in his hand, the rubber tubing wrapped around his upper arm, the bulging vein in his forearm. "And Bradley Bowman's more than a god, he's like a *meta* god, he's the scary story grown-up gods tell their little godlings to make them eat their celestial vegetables. But this is the only way I know to get Bradley's attention, defiling this body I stole from him, in this very particular way, and I'm afraid he's going to be *pissed*."

Pelham sat on the edge of the tub, hands laced over one knee. He'd bought the heroin from a dealer who usually supplied Rondeau with different drugs, and cooked up the stuff with the same skill he used to flip crepes. "You don't actually have to inject the vile stuff. Just make Bradley *think* you will—"

"But I have to mean it. I have to really intend to do it. Bradley oversees the multiverse, he can see possible futures or something, I don't know exactly how it works, and if he sees that I'm really going to shoot up, *that's* when he'll come, if he comes at all." Rondeau closed his eyes. He had nothing against getting high, but he did have something against annoying beings of unfathomable power, especially Bradley, since he'd already stolen the guy's body. But here he was. He moved the needle.

"Rondeau, put that shit down," Bradley Bowman—B to most his friends, when he'd been mortal enough to have those—called from the living room.

Rondeau exhaled in relief, put down the syringe, untied the tube, and walked unsteadily into the living room.

Bradley wasn't there in person—if he even had a person anymore. His face loomed on the TV screen, in extreme close-up, his tropical-ocean-blue eyes calm, his former-movie-star features as scruffily handsome as always. "Don't pull anything like that again, all right? Heroin, hell, man, you know my one true love died of a heroin overdose. I get it, that was the point, to get my attention, but that's *cold*, Rondeau. Next time you want me, go to Oakland, down by 38th Street and Telegraph Avenue, and yell my name into the sewer grate. I'll lodge a fragment of my attention there. But make sure if you call it's more important than *this*."

"Sorry," Rondeau squeaked. Bradley had been a nice enough guy once, but now he was something far beyond human, however normal his face looked.

Pelham cleared his throat. "Mr. Bowman, sir, we have a terrible problem—Regina Queen has threatened to kill—"

"Hey, Pelham, yeah, I know. This isn't the only universe where she pulls this crap, and it doesn't look good for you, but there are a few paths where you come out the other side intact, basically. You'll work it out. My job is watching out for existential threats to the fabric of reality, incursions from hostile universes with inimical physics, stuff like that, not... fighting ice witches. I sympathize, but I've got an exiled outsider from an especially nasty bubble in the quantum foam increasing his ontological mass on your Earth at an exponential rate, and I'm a lot more concerned about him than I am about Viscarro's mom going around killing people." He paused. "Can you believe Viscarro has a *mom*? Who's still alive? I figured the dude was hatched from a spider egg or something."

"If you can see worlds where we don't fuck this up," Rondeau said, "maybe a little guidance—"

"Rondeau, if you need guidance, you can summon oracles. I know— you use the brain that used to belong to *me* to do it. Take care of my body, would you? It wouldn't hurt you to get on a treadmill every once in a while, lay off the all-you-can-eat buffets a little. As for this Regina thing, keep doing what you're doing. There's a good sixty percent chance you won't even die."

The television turned itself off.

"Hmm," Rondeau said. "Keep doing what we're doing. So. Next witch on the list?"

"**YOU'RE SURE THIS WILL WORK?**" Rondeau said.

"Mrs. Mason told me it would attract Genevieve's attention." Pelham was methodically slicing his way through a bag of lemons from Rondeau's bar.

"But you make lemonade all the time. And lemon chicken. And lemon drops. Lemon meringue pie. You slice lemons a lot, is what I'm saying, and it's never tempted a reweaver capable of altering the nature of reality to come out of the pocket dimension where she lives."

"The element of intentionality is necessary." Pelham picked up a lemon and sniffed it, eyes closed. "I have to call her, with my mind."

"Not fair. Why did you learn this summoning trick? Did you ever even *meet* Gen? I was actually there, when she was turning Felport into a hallucination amusement park. I even helped stop the nightmare king who tormented her. At least, I mean, I was *around* at the time..."

"Hello, Rondeau," Genevieve said. One end of the kitchen had turned into a pavilion of white silk, and a woman with violet eyes and caramel-colored hair stood shyly, half-hidden by a curtain. "Did you need something? Is Marla all right? It's only, I shouldn't stay too long. Just being in the world like this, it makes thing start to go... soft... around me..."

Rondeau suddenly regretted suggesting they call Genevieve. She'd developed some control over her powers, so her worst nightmares didn't just pop into being anymore, but she was still dangerous, and she *knew* it—that's why she chose to inhabit a little pinched-off bit of reality, where she could reshape the landscape to suit her whim without damaging a place where regular people actually *lived*. "Uh," he said. "The thing is...."

Then he blinked, or didn't even blink, but it was like *reality* blinked, and he was on his back underneath the glass-topped coffee table in the living room, wearing only one shoe, with a terrible headache, and Pelham was sitting up groaning beside the frosty balcony door. "Wha?" Rondeau said. "Did Gen... do something?"

"I think she left," Pelham said. "I think... she might have been annoyed? That we called her for this?"

Rondeau squinted. Had there been yelling? His memories were like those of a dream, fading from his short-term memory as he came awake. Something about how if Genevieve meddled, she might cause a drought that would consume the world, or bring on a new Little Ice Age? About how you didn't bring a thermonuclear bomb to a knife fight? "Oh. Right."

He turned his head. His beautiful big-screen TV was gone. In its place rested a single yellow lemon.

"Damn," he said. "I liked that TV."

"**WHAT?**" Rondeau held the conch shell to his ear. "You—okay, I get that, I know, Marla owes you a favor, you don't owe anyone any favors, I'm saying, maybe I'll owe *you* a favor if you come help. I don't know, you're an ocean witch, that's basically the same as weather magic, and anyway, won't this hyperborean vortex mess up the Gulf Stream or something—Huh. That's—right. Okay. Uh, no, yeah, I'm still gay, not planning to hit the coast soon anyway—right, sure, thanks." He hung up, if that was the right terminology to use for putting an enchanted conch shell back down on the table.

"That didn't sound good," Pelham said.

"Zufi was in a pretty lucid state of mind," Rondeau said. "Not having one of those days that's all non sequiturs or talking in rhyme or making dolphin noises, so at least I got a straight answer, even if the answer was 'no.'" Zufi, the Bay Witch, was one of the more powerful sorcerers they knew from their old days in Felport, and she'd given them a hand in Hawaii not long ago, so they'd had hopes she might intercede this time too.

"Did she say why she can't help?" Pelham said.

Rondeau shrugged. "She's an ocean witch. Nevada is landlocked."

"There are *planes*," Pelham said. "Rivers, too, if she insists on swimming. Lake Mead isn't entirely frozen over yet."

"You ever try arguing with Zufi via conch shell? It's even more pointless than arguing with her in person." He sighed. "Who's next? And what will we have to sacrifice or chant or *en*chant in order to call them?"

"I suppose we could try Hamil," Pelham said. "He actually answers his phone."

Rondeau nodded. Hamil had been Marla's consigliere when she was chief sorcerer of Felport, and he was still a big deal there, second-most-powerful figure on the council, and a master of sympathetic magic. "I don't *think* he has any particular reason to hate me," Rondeau said. "And at least he's extremely unlikely to turn either of us into a lemon."

Marzi in Santa Cruz

MARZIPAN MCCARTY, known as Marzi to everyone other than her whimsical parents, gasped herself awake in the tiny apartment over the café she co-owned. She rolled out of bed, her boyfriend Jonathan grumbling beside her at the disturbance. He knew she was a light sleeper, and had long since grown immune to waking up himself just because she had a nightmare. She had them often: mostly about mudslides, earthquakes, wildfires.

But this dream hadn't been one of the usual sort. This one seemed meaningful in a way that was familiar, and unwelcome. A few years earlier, her dreams had contained messages from powerful forces dwelling among the hidden machinery of the world, and she'd done what was necessary to stop the evil those dreams had revealed, but damn it, she was *done*. No more visions, please.

She went to the little round window in their attic apartment, the one that looked down onto Ash Street. Santa Cruz streets in summer were rarely entirely deserted even this late at night, and a chattering group of twenty-somethings went by laughing and babbling, probably a little drunk. About as normal as normal could be. Dreams didn't *have* to mean anything—

A shadow detached itself from the wall of the hot tub place and spa across the street, and Marzi stared, waiting for it to resolve into the form of a drunk, or a homeless guy, or even a mugger. She'd be grateful for a nice mundane mugger.

But it just remained a shadow, even when it entered the pool of light cast by a streetlight: a swirling coil of darkness, like a long black chiffon scarf twisting in the wind... or like a sea serpent, undulating through an invisible sea, moving gracefully toward the four people walking.

Was she dreaming still? Because she'd dreamt of something like this. Only in the dream it had been a rippling shadow drifting across the sky,

17

growing larger and larger until it hung over the world like a veil, blocking out all the light, plunging the world into a somehow carnivorous darkness.

She rubbed her eyes. It had to be a trick of the light. Or, okay, it didn't *have* to be, she knew better than that, but she was out of the monster-slaying business, so she *hoped* it was.

A coil of the floating darkness reached out toward the streetlight, and the light blinked out. In the sudden darkness, Marzi couldn't tell exactly what happened—there was some motion, perhaps, and maybe a muffled gasp, but that was all. She kept watching, waiting for the group to appear again in the light cast by the streetlight on the next corner, but they didn't. The darkness wasn't *that* complete, but… she couldn't see them at all.

She put her nose against the window, trying to get a closer look, but her breath just fogged the glass. Cursing under her breath, Marzi picked up the black silk robe Jonathan had given her for their fourth anniversary and pulled it on over her pajamas. She slipped on her flip-flops and started toward the door, then paused and picked up the revolver resting beside her drawing table. It was a toy, a vintage cap-gun from the '50s… except once, in a showdown, it had been more than that: a more potent weapon than any mortal firearm. If there was any magic left in the thing, it wasn't evident, but holding the pistol always made her feel stronger, more brave, capable of anything. After all, hadn't she once done the impossible, and slain something very like a god?

She tucked the gun into the pocket of her robe but kept her hand on the grip, then unlocked the door. Their little apartment—they called it "the pigeonhole"—was technically the finished attic of the café she co-owned, Genius Loci, but she didn't have to go through the café to get outside; there was an outside entrance with a set of wooden stairs leading down to the street, so she stepped out onto the landing and looked down. The extinguished streetlight was back on now, and its light revealed absolutely nothing. No shadow, no twenty-somethings walking along, no signs of anything… except, was that something glinting in the gutter? Probably just broken glass or the shiny inside of a torn potato chip bag, but…

Marzi went down the stairs, hand on the toy gun's plastic grip, and continued over the sidewalk, across the street, to the far side.

The thing glittering in the gutter was a set of keys, and now that she looked there were three other sets, too. Among other things. Several debit and credit cards and driver's licenses, but no wallets, except for one made of duct tape, and it was falling to pieces. What looked like the rivets and buttons and zippers from a couple of pairs of jeans. A set of eyeglasses, and a four-ounce stainless steel flask engraved with the initials RF. A couple of rings, a pair of hoop earrings, a silver necklace with a tiny leaf pendant, and a scatter of coins.

"What's up?" a voice said, and she whirled, drawing the gun.

Jonathan, wearing his own robe, held up his hands and raised an eyebrow. "Don't shoot, marshal, I'll go peaceful-like."

She tucked the gun away, shook her head, and pointed into the gutter.

Jonathan squatted, peered at the litter without touching it, and whistled. "Well. That's weird. People drop stuff, but… is that a zipper? How do you drop a zipper?"

"I had a bad dream," she said. "Woke up, went to the window, and saw some people walk by. There was this thing… a shadow, but moving, swimming through the air like a sea snake… then the streetlight went out, and…. I think the people disappeared. Or something. I came down, and found this stuff. Now you know what I know."

Jonathan grunted. "And your hypothesis is… killer shadow?" He didn't sound incredulous, and she loved him for that. Then again, he'd seen a few impossible things in his time with her. They'd met in the midst of that nightmarish summer when she'd discovered the true malleability of reality, after all. She'd very nearly lost him to it.

"The thought crossed my mind. Maybe they did just drop this stuff. Maybe it's, I don't know. An art piece. Art students are always doing stupid bullshit."

Jonathan snorted. He'd been an art student, and had a PhD in critical theory to show for it, which he said was a great qualification to run a café. Marzi had been an art student once upon a time, too, until she dropped out to focus on making comics instead. "So what we'll do is, we'll call the cops," he said. "We'll tell them we heard a commotion, and when we came out, we found all this stuff."

"Declining to mention our killer shadow hypothesis."

Jonathan shrugged. "That would be my advice. There are heaps of ID here. If the people did just drop this stuff, the cops will find them, and cite them for littering or something, and all will be well. If something else happened…. We learned a few years back there are some things cops aren't capable of dealing with."

She groaned. "But *I* don't want to deal with it either, Jonathan. This whole normalcy thing—I like it."

"Maybe it's nothing we'll have to deal with. Maybe it's just… I don't know. Sometimes, every once in a while, a shark eats a surfer. Maybe, if something did this… maybe it's just something like a shark. Just passing through." He looked around. "Though staying in shark-infested waters doesn't sound like a great idea. Maybe let's pick this stuff up and go inside, huh?"

"If it's a crime scene we shouldn't disturb it," she said.

"I'm pretty sure killer shadows don't leave fingerprints, and if we leave it all here unattended, somebody will wander by and take the credit cards… but okay. Let's at least go up on the porch, okay? We can keep an eye on the stuff from there."

She nodded, and they withdrew to the steps, the ones leading up to their huge wraparound porch covered in tables and benches, one of the café's great attractions when the weather was nice, which it was more often than not here on the coast of central California. Jonathan went upstairs to get his phone, then came back down and called the cops.

Marzi watched the sky, looking for shadows cast by nothing at all.

Rondeau and Pelham in (and Under) Vegas

Hamil had been Marla's consigliere when she was chief sorcerer of Felport, and though their relationship had soured when he voted with the rest of the council to send her into exile, Rondeau still considered the man a friend. He'd bought Rondeau's nightclub, admittedly a site with interesting magical properties, for stupid amounts of money, laying the groundwork for Rondeau's subsequent life of leisure.

Well, mostly leisure. "I don't know," Rondeau said. "You're a master of sympathetic magic. Can't you just, like, create a sympathetic magical link between someplace really warm and Las Vegas, and kind of balance things out?"

"Possibly, possibly." Hamil's deep, rich voice was uncharacteristically distracted. "But I'd need to go to Vegas, and things are frantic here right now. Don't tell Marla I said so, but the city's gone a bit to hell since she left—just now we're dealing with a rash of inexplicable cases of spontaneous…" The rest of the sentence was indistinct, as if he'd turned his head away from the phone, and Rondeau heard him shouting orders at someone.

"Did you say spontaneous combustion?" Rondeau said. "We could use some of that around here."

"Hmm?" Hamil said. "No, no—spontaneous *decapitation*. Four cases so far, none of our people, only the ordinaries. Very mysterious, and I'm tracing the sympathetic linkages and—I'm sorry, I can't be of any help today, Rondeau. Under other circumstances I might, but it's impossible now."

"But—"

"May I offer a bit of advice?" Hamil said. "If you were in Felport during the days of Marla Mason's reign, and a strange witch arrived and began causing problems, would you call up someone thousands of miles away for help?"

"Of course not," Rondeau said. "Marla was the chief sorcerer, so she'd take care—Oh."

"Quite," Hamil said. "I would have to consult the latest edition of *Dee's Peerage* to find out who is currently chief sorcerer of Las Vegas, but in a city that ripe with human emotional energy and the power of random chance, I'm sure *someone* is in charge, and likely someone powerful. Find the local magical authorities and tell them you know who's causing the cold snap, and you may even be rewarded for your information."

"Thanks, Ham—" Rondeau began, but the big man had already hung up. He turned to Pelham, who was hanging up the other extension, where he'd been listening in. "Hamil makes a good point. I was thinking of this as Marla's problem, and by extension our problem, but it's also the *city's* problem, so we should go see the chief sorcerer here."

"Do you know this person?" Pelham said.

Rondeau nodded. "If you're going to do magical business in Las Vegas, the smart way is to get permission from the guy in charge, and make sure it's a good deal for him, too—which is to say, you make regular payoffs. So we've met. Most people call him Mr. Amparan. Some people call him the Pit Boss. He holds court in a secret casino underground, accessible from various places around town by a series of hidden tunnels. They play games for creepy stakes down there. Weird, dark stuff, I'm talking Korean-horror-movie freaky—roulette with eyes for balls, tables where you can wager your gall bladder or your sense of smell for a chance to win your heart's truest desire. Mr. Amparan is the real deal. He might be able to do something about Regina."

"Then let us make our way to his… pit," Pelham said.

"Yeah," Rondeau said. "It's almost time to drop off this month's tribute anyway."

"How much do you pay him?"

Rondeau grinned. Pelham probably had a better sense of the financial situation in the casino Rondeau co-owned than Rondeau did himself, and was clearly curious about this unrecorded monthly expense. "I don't pay him in money," Rondeau said. "I pay him in luck."

THEY WENT OUT INTO THE COLD, dressed in bulky ski gear that still failed to protect them entirely from the viciousness of the dry and frigid air. Pelham informed Rondeau that there were portions of the planet Mars that were warmer than Las Vegas on this particular day. The streets were not piled deep with snow, because there wasn't enough moisture in the air to produce such drifts, but there was a thin dusting of the stuff, and many patches of ice. Pipes had burst all over town, and some of that water had bubbled into the streets and over the sidewalks and formed treacherous slicks.

They made their way to a trapdoor two blocks from Rondeau's hotel, in the corner of a trash-strewn parking lot. The trapdoor was frozen shut, of course, and they had to go back and get a tire iron to pry it open before descending down an iron ladder—the rungs so cold Rondeau was sure he could feel the chill even through his bulky might-as-well-be-for-an-astronaut gloves.

They walked along an icy brick-lined tunnel to a shining round vault door, which stood wide open and unguarded. "That's bad," Rondeau said. The leather bag full of luck squirmed in his pocket. He harvested the luck from the losers in his casino, every bad turn of the cards or disastrous roll of the dice a tiny piece of luck sliced away from them without their knowledge, collected in special crystals secreted in the ceiling, used to pay the monthly tribute to Mr. Amparan, AKA the Pit Boss, greatest probability-mage and stochastic magician in the western United States.

Rondeau and Pelham went into the underground casino, which was just as cold as the streets above. The gaming tables (with shackles at the corners, for advanced play) and the wheels of fortune (with their possibilities that ranged from the sadistic to the sublime) and the steel cages where the living collateral were usually housed, all dripped with icicles, and the recessed circular pit in the center of the room where Mr. Amparan usually sat with his cronies and held audiences was filled with frozen water, like an ice-skating rink.

Most of Mr. Amparan's upper body was sticking out of the ice, his dark skin tinged blue, his mouth open in surprise, arms lifted up to fend off an attack.

"Hello, boys." Regina Queen spun around on a bar stool in the lounge. A frozen statue of a bartender stood on the other side, holding a by now *very* chilled martini shaker. "Is Marla home yet?"

"Not as such, ma'am," Pelham began.

"Ah. You came here hoping to get help, didn't you? Some of Mr. Amparan's men tracked me down and brought me here to meet with him. First he tried to threaten me. Then he tried to pay me off. Then I got bored and killed them all." She shook her head sadly. "How is it you still don't take me seriously? I supposed I'd better kill one of you, too, to drive the point home." She lifted one long-fingered hand, almost lazily.

Rondeau pulled out the squirming bag of luck and threw it on the ground between Pelham and himself, where it fell open and spilled forth an aromatic smoke of concentrated good fortune. (It smelled a bit like smoky poker rooms, a bit like horse shit, and a bit like the gasoline stink of a NASCAR track.) Regina's aim was off, thanks to their burst of good luck, and a potted palm two feet to Rondeau's right turned to ice and shattered. Rondeau and Pelham ran for the exit, gaming tables and chandeliers turning to ice and shattering in their wake, and scuttled up the ladder to the street above.

Regina didn't follow, but they didn't dare return to the suite, just in case. They found a bar, one of the few that was still open, with half the tables supporting humming space heaters, and a handful of dedicated drunks at the bar wrapped in winter coats and, in one case, a stinking old horse blanket. The guy under the blanket was muttering about how this was wrong, all wrong, Las Vegas was Hell, and Hell wasn't *supposed* to freeze over.

Pelham and Rondeau ordered hot toddies and sat in a corner, sipping, close to one of the heaters.

"We have to kill her now," Rondeau said. "I mean, I'm as civic-minded as the next guy, let's do our bit to save the people of Las Vegas, for sure, but—she'll kill *us*, is the thing. It's personal now." He sighed. "I was hoping to make this someone else's problem, but we'd better find an oracle and ask it how we can stop Regina."

Pelham nodded. "It seems the only sensible path."

"No, getting in a car and driving until we're south of the equator is more sensible, but I like it here, at least when the city's not frozen over, so let's try this other thing first."

They lingered over their drinks, though. Oracle-hunting was cold work.

"THERE'S ONE HERE," Rondeau said at last, his voice muffled by the scarf wrapped around his face, despite the heater in the car running full blast. Pelham doubted the car would have started at all if it hadn't been enchanted to run with magical efficiency.

Finding oracles was always a tricky proposition. Rondeau could sense likely locations for them, but only in a hot-and-cold sort of way, so they'd driven around for a while on the deserted streets. Now they were parked in front of Bally's Las Vegas, one of the most decidedly un-magical places

Pelham could imagine, especially on this icy night, with only a few of the windows in its hotel towers lit. Just about everyone who could get out of Vegas had done so by now. "Why here?"

"Fire," Rondeau said. "This used to be the MGM Grand. There was a terrible fire there back in 1980, killed 85 people, injured close to a thousand. This oracle… I think it likes fire."

"Seems promising, given the nature of our adversary," Pelham said.

They got out of the car, stepped into the brutal moonscape, and walked slowly toward the covered moving sidewalk that ferried tourists from the street to the casino entrance… except the sidewalks weren't moving, and the neon lighting was shattered, and there was no music playing.

Rondeau paused in the entryway and grunted. "It's… this is a big one…"

A sheet of flame erupted from the ground, a curtain four feet wide and eight feet high, and that curtain parted to reveal a…

"Demon" was the only word Pelham could think of. Roughly human in shape, over seven feet tall, skin like flowing magma, eyes black and shiny, and a maw full of glittering obsidian shards. "Speak," it said, in a voice of crackling flames.

Rondeau's voice was strained. Summoning oracles always took something out of him… even before the time came to pay the individual oracle's idiosyncratic price. "How much to answer a question?"

"Mmm. Burn something you love here, so I can smell the smoke."

"An object or a person?"

It chuckled. "Just for a question? An object is fine."

Rondeau nodded. "Okay. How do we kill Regina Queen?"

The demon shrugged. "Easy. Throw her in a volcano."

Pelham winced, and Rondeau sighed. "Right. Okay. Helpful. Thanks." He started to turn away.

"Wait," the demon said. "I'll kill the ice queen for you, if you're willing to pay a little more."

Rondeau and Pelham exchanged glances. "That's… not usually how this works," Rondeau said. "Usually you oracle types just tell me stuff, and make me do stuff in return. I mean… can you even do *anything* by yourselves, without me summoning you up?"

"Hey, this is Vegas. Land of opportunity. I'm just trying to get ahead."

"My understanding regarding the prevailing theory is that you oracles don't have any independent existence or agency," Pelham said, trying to ignore the fact that he was talking to a seven-foot-high magma monster. "That you are essentially externalized manifestations of Rondeau's mind, projections he creates, which allow him to receive psychic insights that are too profound for him to access in a more straightforward way, such as through dreams or meditation. That there are locations of inherent latent power, or places infected with ghost-residue, which serve to boost his psychic abilities and give a particular shape to a given oracle's appearance and manner, but that you are ultimately just aspects of Rondeau himself."

"Yeah," Rondeau said, voice weak with the strain of calling up the oracle. "What he said. Though some of the things I've talked to, I have trouble believing they came out of my own head."

"I don't know about any of that," the demon said. "That's philosophy or psychology or maybe even religion, and that's all outside my area. I'd sure like to kill somebody though. Say the word, and I'll help you get rid of your witch."

"Uh," Rondeau said.

"Perhaps if you agree it will become a sort of tulpa," Pelham said. "A living thought-form. A projection of the mind that manifests in a physical body."

"Whatever," the demon said. "Do we have a deal, or what?"

"Maybe," Rondeau said. "What's it going to cost me?"

"More than burning your favorite baby blanket, that's for sure."

"I'm not burning a person. No murder. Not even mercy killing."

"Understood," the demon said. "How about you just... owe me a favor."

"That's not how this *works*. It's not all open-ended."

"Your call," the demon said. "I can't force you to take the deal."

"Shit. Okay. A favor. But look, I'm not doing anything that violates my, like, personal moral code."

The demon laughed. It was a pretty normal laugh, considering the mouth it emerged from. "That should be fine, given the state of *your* morals." It rubbed its hands together. Sparks flew. "Here's what we do."

THE MIRAGE HOTEL was just as deserted as Bally's, and the fake volcano out front wasn't doing its hourly eruptions. Rondeau had spent enough time in Hawaii, close to real volcanoes, to find the fake rock structure totally unimpressive, more like a pile of cobblestones than a real cinder cone.

But here they were, dressed in bulky coats, standing on top of the damn thing, waiting for Regina Queen. Rondeau was terrified some automatic switch would click over and make the fake volcano start barfing jets of flame.

Regina appeared without making a grand entrance, just suddenly standing with her arms crossed, frowning, on the volcano's edge. Rondeau and Pelham had been forced to find the route the maintenance guys used to get on top of the volcano, but Regina had floated up on a cloud of snow or some shit, probably.

"Where is Marla?" she said. "Wanting to meet at midnight, on a fake *volcano*? I can appreciate the showmanship, but I don't like to be kept waiting."

"About that," Rondeau said, and then grabbed Pelham and jumped off the volcano, down to the pool of frozen water surrounding its base. They landed hard and rolled, flopping onto their backs and looking up at the volcano looming above them.

"What was that in aid of?" Regina peered over the edge at them. "If you're wasting my time—"

The demon loomed up behind her, wrapped her in its arms, and then pulled her backward. The volcano flickered. For a moment, it wasn't a hokey collection of fake stones and pipes and gas and hidden speakers with an ornamental lava flow down the side. It became the cone of an active volcano, dribbling molten rock, rumbling, spitting cinders and acidic smoke, its heat so tremendous that Rondeau was afraid his coat would burst into flame.

Then, in an instant, the volcano was just fake rocks again, and the demon and Regina were gone.

"Is it getting warmer?" Rondeau asked.

"I think these things take time," Pelham said.

They high-fived, weakly, though it didn't make a sound because of their gloves.

THE AIR WAS DEFINITELY WARMER by the time they got back to the hotel—still a cold desert night, but no longer killing cold. They went upstairs, both too exhausted to celebrate, and collapsed into their respective beds.

Some time later, the demon appeared by Rondeau's bed, emerging from a wall turned into a curtain of flame. "I want that favor now."

Rondeau groaned. "Can you turn down your fiery glow? I'm trying to get some sleep here."

"It's time to get up. And get out. I want your share of the hotel and casino. And I want all your money. And all your stuff. Well, no. You can keep, say, ten grand, I'm not a monster. Seed money for your new life someplace else."

Rondeau sat up slowly. Maybe this was a nightmare. "I don't think giving you all my worldly possessions counts as a *favor*, exactly."

The demon growled. "It's not mercy-killing anyone. Or violating your moral code. A young thought-construct like me has to look out for himself. There's a power vacuum in this city. I've got the right look to be the new Pit Boss of Las Vegas—I just need the resources to grease a few wheels. That's where you come in."

"Look, I'm kind of like your… creator, or father, or something, right, so maybe we can work something out."

"You *are* like my father. I want my inheritance early. And I want you to move far away. Who wants to live in the same town as his dad? I talked to Pelham, he's already getting packed. He says you can live with him in his RV. Nice, huh? You've got a good friend there."

"I did not think this through." Rondeau put his face in his hands. What was he losing here? The twenty-four-hour-concierge service. The hot and cold running cute boys. The good booze. The not ever having to actually do any work. Oh, gods. He'd have to do *work* again. "There's a reason I don't get put in charge of killing ice witches. I fuck it up."

"Who said Regina's dead? She's in a fiery little pocket dimension I made. She's not happy in there, either. Fulfill your end of the bargain…" The demon leaned forward and exhaled sulfurous breath on Rondeau's face. "Or I'll let her *out*."

"Is a cashier's check okay?" Rondeau said.

Marzi in Genius Loci

A **DEAD MOVIE STAR** came into the café and ordered a mocha chai. Marzi stared at him: his tropical blue eyes, his affably scruffy two-days-past-shaving face, his easy smile, his curly black hair. As she went through the motions of making the drink, she kept casting glances at him, and said, "You know, you look a lot like—"

He nodded. "Yeah, I know. I get it all the time. But, hey, you can do worse than looking like one of *People*'s Sexiest Men of the Year... even if it was quite a few years ago."

Marzi didn't think he was flirting—for some reason he struck her as gay, though now that she thought about it, maybe it was the dead movie star who'd been gay. What was that guy's name? Bradley something. He'd been a big deal for a little while, starring in quirky independent movies and then a couple of big-budget ones that hadn't even sucked. Marzi didn't particularly follow the tabloids or the celebrities-behaving-badly TV shows, but as she recalled he'd had some kind of breakdown on a movie set, gotten into drugs, dropped out of the public eye, and pulled a serious vanishing act, of the without-a-trace variety. Maybe he wasn't even definitely dead—his boyfriend had died, though, in an overdose, maybe? Had they both died? Could be the real actor was just living like a recluse in Mexico or something. She'd have to check Wikipedia later.

Marzi passed him a pint glass full of mocha chai and reached out to take his proffered ten dollar bill. Their fingers brushed, and he sucked in a surprised breath and then grabbed her hand tightly. Before she could yell at him or pull away, he released her, running a hand through his hair. He had the kind of hair that made him look even cuter when it was mussed. "I... sorry about that."

"Right. Here's your change." She put it down on the counter, not giving him a chance to touch her again. She hadn't had to throw anybody out of the café in ages, and if he behaved from here on, he wouldn't *necessarily* make her break that streak.

"Hey, look, do you have a break coming up? I think... maybe I need to talk to you."

She shook her head. "I own the place. No breaks for me. Heavy lies the head that wears the crown."

"Don't I know it," he murmured, then squared his shoulders and looked her in the eye. He said, "We should talk about gods and doors, okay?"

Marzi let out a little involuntary groan. Tessa came around the corner lugging a full bus tray, and Marzi said, "Take over the counter for me."

Tessa grunted. She was tiny physically, though she seemed bigger because of the many piercings and the bad attitude. She was a pretty good employee, attitude aside. Had Marzi ever grunted her way through a workday back when she was just an employee here, working for the old manager Hendrix? Poor Hendrix, who'd been killed by the acolyte of something like a god, that came into this world through something like a door. Speaking of.

"Come on." Marzi led the guy into the Teatime Room, one of six rooms in the café—formerly a rambling old Victorian house—painted with murals by local artist and noted malcontent Garamond Ray. This room featured life-sized paintings of animal-headed Egyptian gods seated at little round tables, like a Parisian street café. The room wasn't usually crowded, having fewer power outlets than the other rooms, and on this particular weekday afternoon it was entirely deserted.

"Wow." The man leaned over a table to peer at a painting of a lion-headed woman pushing down the plunger on a French press, crushing the human heart inside. "This is wild. What great paintings."

"Yeah, we're famous. There was a spread in *Art Review* a few years back, you can buy a copy online. Sit."

He complied, dropping into one of the mismatched wooden chairs across the wobbly rectangular table from her. "Did you paint it? I get, ah, kind of an artistic vibe off you."

What did that mean? Her hair wasn't even pink anymore. She'd dyed it brown before she went to the bank to get a business loan to take over Genius Loci, and had let it stay that way. By Santa Cruz standards, she looked appallingly conservative. "Nope, these aren't mine. They've been here since the late '80s."

"Oh. I could have *sworn* you were an artist—"

"I do a webcomic. Look. Gods and doors. You got my attention. Who are you? What do you want?"

"I'm… my friends call me B."

"Fascinating," she said. "What should *I* call you?"

"Bradley, then. And you are?"

"Marzi." She frowned. "The dead movie star you look like was named Bradley."

"True enough. Bradley Bowman. And who says he's dead?"

"I don't know," she said slowly. "I thought I heard he OD'ed or something. Or fell off a boat and drowned. I don't remember."

"Boy, you drop out of sight for a few years, and people consign you to the dustbin of cinematic history. No, I'm alive. Just… keeping out of the public eye."

"Shiiiit." Marzi drew out the syllable appreciatively. "I knew a girl in college who had a poster of you on her wall. You were pretty good in that one movie, about the musician who got hooked on crack."

"*The Glass Harp.* Thanks. I never had much trouble playing addicts. Method acting and all that."

Marzi snorted. "You look pretty straight to me now, apart from talking about gods and doors."

"I never said I didn't *almost* die, and you can overdose and live to regret it. I hit rock bottom, dug my way down a little deeper with pickaxe and shovel, then finally started dragging myself out of the hole. Kinda like crawling out of your own grave, zombie-style, but here I am, up in the sunshine again." He leaned forward. "Now I'm in a different line of work. The pay isn't as good as being a movie star, but at least it's dangerous and the hours are lousy. See, sometimes… I have these dreams." He searched her face, and though she tried to betray nothing, he nodded like she'd given everything away. "Yeah. You know about those dreams, don't you? You're sensitive, like me. In kind, if not degree. My dreams got so bad I did a lot of drugs to keep them quiet, but I've learned to live with the visions. They don't just come when I'm sleeping, either. When I touched your hand, I saw doors, and mud, and cracks in the earth, and scorpions, and… a cowboy? Some kind of Old West outlaw?"

Not some kind of outlaw—*the* Outlaw, a godlike spirit of destruction that Marzi had perceived as a villainous gunslinger. "That was a long time ago," she said. Granted, some days, it felt longer ago than others. "Nowadays I draw comics and make drinks, and those are the only jobs I'm interested in. I'm out of the saving-the-world business."

Bradley nodded. "I've had the urge to quit myself, but sometimes the job's gotta be done, and there's no one else around to do it." He sighed. "Or the person who *should* be doing it is taking a long-ass nap. But anyway. I saw something else when I touched your hand, something that felt fresher— something like a shadow, but also like a snake?"

Okay. Marzi had tried the denial thing the last time weird stuff had infringed on her life, liberty, and happiness, and it hadn't done a bit of good. In fact, putting her head in the sand (the dry desert sand) had probably made things a lot worse back then. But still. "I'm not joining your posse or whatever, all right? I'm an upstanding businesswoman these days. My days as a metaphysical gunfighter are way behind me, and I want to leave them there. But, okay. I'll tell you what I saw, a few days ago. If you want to do something about it, that's on you." She gave him the story, about waking from a bad dream and seeing the shadow in the street, watching those kids disappear, looking over the things they'd left behind.

"The police didn't find any trace of them?" Bradley said.

Marzi shook her head. "Not as far as I know. They asked us a bunch of questions, but they believed our story, as far as I can tell—at least, they don't seem to think we chopped up the kids and hid them in the crawlspace, which I'd sort of worried about. I'm not quite old enough yet to think of cops as a force for *good*, you know? In my mind they're just the people who hassle you for loud music or public intoxication. There was an article in the paper a couple of days ago, about the disappearance of three local students and their visiting friend, but I haven't seen a follow-up about their miraculous return."

"It ate them," Bradley said. "The Outsider."

Marzi suppressed a shudder. The Outsider. That was a little too close to "the Outlaw" for her taste. "The thing I fought, years ago… it didn't look anything like a shadow. It was more… shaped by people's expectations. My expectations, anyway. If that makes sense. The Outlaw looked like different things at different times, but it always appeared in more-or-less human form. Not like a twist of shadow." She paused. "The Outlaw didn't eat people, either. It shot them, sometimes. Tried to turn them into forces for chaos. It seemed more interested in wrecking the world, bringing earthquakes and mudslides and wildfires, than in preying on individuals."

Bradley whistled. "You faced something like that? A spirit of destruction, and you beat it without any training—without any help? Somebody should give you a medal. I wonder if the powers-that-be up in San Francisco even know about the disaster you stopped?"

"Which powers? Never mind. I don't want to be involved with that kind of spooky shit anymore. I was just in the wrong place at the wrong time." She sighed. "And here I am *again*."

Bradley made a sympathetic noise. "I've been calling this thing the Outsider because it comes from… well. Some other universe entirely. I've been tracking it for a couple of weeks. It's been moving across California, eating people. Their clothes, too—it seems to consume anything organic. It eats skin and bone and hair and muscle, leather and linen and cotton, but it leaves plastic and metal and glass. Maybe it can't tell one kind of organic matter from another yet. I think it's trying to learn about the kind of life we have in this universe. What you described, a living shadow, that sounds a lot more substantial than it used to be. Survivors—and you *are* a survivor, if you got close enough to see it and live, you definitely count—described it as a disturbance in the air at first, like a heat shimmer. Then it became a shimmer with dark specks in it. Later people compared it to a swarm of flies, only instead of flies, they were just little bits of darkness, all moving around wildly. Now you say it's a translucent serpent of shadow. It's… gaining ontological mass, or accreting layers of reality, or something. I don't know."

"It's eating," Marzi said. "So it's *growing*. That's what you're telling me."

"Yeah. And I think it's still in town. I follow… I don't know… intuitions. Vibrations. The advice of creatures wiser than myself, sometimes, though they haven't been a lot of help when it comes to finding this thing. I went to a beach outside of town this morning and found what I'm pretty sure was a pacemaker lying in the sand near the water. The thing was dry, so it hadn't been there long—the tide was out—which means the Outsider took a victim earlier *today*. You saw the shadow days ago, too, and that's different. The Outsider has never stayed in one place for so long. That worries me. I thought it was just wandering aimlessly… but maybe it had a destination. If it's lingering here, maybe there's something it wants."

"You say it's from… another universe?"

"It's complicated, but that's about right, yeah."

Marzi had some experience with things that came from other worlds. She chose her words carefully. "In your experience, are there places where reality is… a little squishy?"

He raised an eyebrow, a mannerism that was somehow familiar—maybe she'd seen him do it in one of his movies. "There are. I take some professional interest in places like that."

"I told you about the Outlaw—the god of earthquakes. He came to Santa Cruz through a door. A door that shouldn't have existed, a door that *didn't* exist, at least not before something wanted to walk through it. The room where that door opened, I think it's over one of those squishy places. Reality melts and runs and re-forms in there. It seems to me, if this shadow is a creature from *outside*, it might be interested in places like that." She rose. "Do you want to see it? The room where the door used to be?"

"Not especially." He grimaced. "But I think I probably *should.*"

Bradley in the Wilderness

BRADLEY FOLLOWED MARZI—and her name was so close to Marla's; was that just coincidence, or something else? She led him out of the Teatime Room and around the café's front counter, on through the little kitchen, where the walls were decorated with mutant sunflowers, their stems segmented like the tails of scorpions. She paused in front of a wooden door, put her hand on the knob, and then stood there, head lowered, as if preparing herself for an ordeal. What was waiting behind that door? What would this "squishy" place look like?

Bradley thought he was doing a good job of not letting his panic and bewilderment show. He'd come in here to get a drink and think, and hadn't expected to stumble into another psychic. Marzi didn't have the raw power he did, but she'd apparently stumbled into some heavy shit a few years back and come through intact, which made her just as battle-hardened as Bradley himself, and a whole lot luckier.

"The last time I went in here," Marzi said, head still bowed, "it was just a storage room, with a mural of a desert on the walls, all sand dunes and a big yellow sun and cartoony cactuses."

"Okay," Bradley said. "Doesn't sound too terrifying."

She lifted her head. "Once upon a time, there used to be a door in the far wall. A door with a brass knob. That door should have just opened to nowhere, to the inside of a wall or the alley out back, at best, but instead it opened to... somewhere else. Something terrible came through that door. After I killed it, the door disappeared."

"Ah. And now you're wondering, what if the door came back?"

"You're the one who saw visions of doors, dude." She sighed. "Might as well find out, huh?" She pulled open the door and stepped inside, and after a moment, Bradley followed.

The room filled with blinding yellow light, followed by a black interval that obliterated Bradley's senses. In the darkness, light bloomed: a cartoon-yellow sun rising over a desert that combined the endless rolling dunes of the Sahara with towering saguaro cactuses from the Southwest. Rough stone towers like the spires in Arizona loomed in the distance, and were those pyramids? The ground shimmered and became flat, faintly glittering sand, scattered with scrub brush; then shifted again to dirty white salt flats; then again to a valley, lined with cliffs. As if all the deserts of the world had been jumbled together. As if somehow, in this place, all deserts were the same desert.

Bradley pushed himself upright, the ground gritty beneath his palms. The heat of the sun was implacable, though it still looked unreal, canary-yellow, and he could gaze at it directly without his vision blurring or burning. The landscape continued to shift, and at first, all the variations seemed equally lifeless, but then flashes of movement caught his eye: a snake sidewinding away, something small and furry scuttling under a rock, a scorpion moving in a stately march, pincers raised almost daintily. There was life here: quick, stealthy, possibly toxic, but alive. He turned in a slow circle, and directly behind him, found a door: painted a faded yellow, with a brass knob mottled with age. He put his hand on the doorknob—

And blinked up at Marzi, who had his head in her lap, and looked down at him with something between annoyance and concern. "Ugh." He sat up and got his bearings. They were in the little kitchen, the door to the storage room closed again. "That was… wow. That desert. Have you been to that desert?"

"Once or twice." Her voice was as dry as the place he'd just left. "You know, the first time I went into that room and got a glimpse of that desert, I repressed the memory and basically had a nervous breakdown. You just go 'Ugh.' Are you that much more badass than I am?"

Bradley got to his feet, swaying unsteadily. "I doubt it. Maybe slightly more experienced at having the supernatural dropped on my head. The first time *I* encountered some impossible shit I ran right out and started doing drugs and didn't really stop for a few years. You just had a nervous breakdown? You're made of tougher stuff than me. So, uh… what was I looking at in there?"

She shrugged. "This guy I knew called it the Medicine Lands, but who knows? It's a place where gods, or things that we might as well call gods, live. There was one little god, a spirit of wildfire and earthquake and mudslide, that came stomping out and caused trouble until my friends and I killed it, or at least made it go away for a while. There's another thing living in there, too, a thing I've only seen in dreams, where it appears like an immense scorpion. I think it's the god of… I don't know. Spiders, snakes, things that can survive in the desert, but maybe it's not as literal as that. More like a spirit of survival despite horrible adversity, a god of life in the face of terrible odds."

Bradley grunted. "Sounds like I've got a new patron saint. While we were in there, did you happen to notice—was the impossible door back?"

"Oh, yeah. Same old wood, same brass knob. I didn't try to open it, though. It blasted you pretty good right through the closed door."

"You, uh, might want to throw a padlock on that thing."

"You think?" Her amusement was palpable.

"Every once in a while I do. So this thing I'm chasing, this Outsider, do you think it might be drawn to that room—or to the place that's accessible *through* that room, through that new door of yours?"

"It's not my door. I don't know, man. You have a better handle on this stuff than I do. But if that shadow monster is hanging around here, I doubt it's because of how much it loves my lattes. And that door being back… it means *something*. So what do we do?"

"I'm going to make some calls," Bradley said. "Consult some experts. Can I get your number? I'll be in touch."

BRADLEY SAT ON A BENCH in a little park overlooking the trickle of the San Lorenzo River and burned through the afternoon making phone calls. He had to go through a lot of underlings before he reached Sanford Cole, and it took some convincing to make Cole believe his identity— Bradley had to submit to a lot of personal questions, but fortunately, his home reality had been identical to this one until after he left Cole's service, so all the answers lined up.

Cole was the rather reluctant ruler of San Francisco, a wizard from the Victorian era who'd been awakened from magical sleep a while back when his beloved home city was under threat. Bradley had served as his apprentice for a while before taking up with Marla Mason—which, of course, had led to his death in this branch of the multiverse.

"Bradley! What brings you to our humble plane of existence?" His voice was cheerful and bright, which was a relief. Cole's long sleep had left him with a case of magical narcolepsy, and Bradley had been half afraid the old wizard would be in hibernation.

"Would you believe I'm a tourist?"

"Not for a moment. The overseer of the multiverse doesn't send a fragment of his attention to one lonesome branch of his domain for rest and recreation—at least, the bits of him *I* had a hand in teaching wouldn't. I assume this is something important? No, I'm dissembling—I assume it's something *disastrous*."

"Well… it's something potentially disastrous, let's say. An incursion from another universe. It's just a nuisance right now." Gods. The thing had killed between thirty and fifty people, as far as Bradley could tell, and he called it a nuisance. But when the potential death toll included every living thing in this reality, fifty dead was… It was all a matter of perspective. "I'm down in Santa Cruz trying to get a handle on the situation."

"Do you need help? I can have specialists in various disciplines there in an hour and a half—and that's if they don't hurry."

"It might come to that," Bradley said. "Though at this point, I wouldn't know what kind of help to ask for. I hope I'm here early enough to stop this incursion without too much difficulty. I mostly need information—I don't want to step on any magical toes here, or have someone jump on me with both feet if I start doing big magic in town. Normally I'd pay my respects to the local bosses and let them know about the monster hunting within their borders, try to coordinate with the local talent, but does Santa Cruz even *have* a chief sorcerer, or a council, or a protector, or anything? Because they seem to leave jobs like fighting earthquake gods to twenty-something baristas around here."

"Mmm, I seem to recall hearing something…" The sound of flipping pages crackled through the phone. Cole was not a technology kind of guy. He was probably talking on an antique candlestick phone magically hooked into the cellular grid. "Ah. Yes. There is a chief sorcerer of Santa Cruz and surrounding areas, though he's never attended any of the statewide councils, as far as I can determine. He keeps to himself. I'll give you his contact information, if you'd like."

"Sure, I'll take phone, email, whatever."

Cole cleared his throat. "Ah. No. I mean, I can tell you where you might find him squatting at this time of year."

THE OCCULT RULER OF SANTA CRUZ looked like an aging hippie, and when he grinned, he showed off brown gapped teeth. Bradley felt a moment's doubt—*this* guy? Why would any halfway decent sorcerer let his teeth go rotten? Then again, there were sorcerers who embraced madness, or cut their own limbs off, or their own tongues out; one of Marla Mason's teachers had ritually castrated himself for magical purposes, so maybe there was some benefit in having a mouth full of fuzzy tombstones. The man gestured to a stained Mexican blanket spread out beside him on the beach, displaying a hodgepodge of wares: old engine parts, loose tarot cards, mason jars full of seashells and marbles, a leather rose, a toy switchblade, and a lone plastic scorpion, unevenly painted red.

The scorpion, the switchblade, and some of the engine parts sparkled in Bradley's peripheral vision if he didn't look at them directly: there was something magical about them, some quality inherent or imbued that tickled his psychic senses.

"Is your name, uh, 'The Bammer'?" Bradley asked.

The old man squinted at him for a moment, then threw his head back and laughed a laugh with a lot of wheeze in it. When his hilarity had subsided, he leveled his gaze at Bradley, and his eyes were as dark and watchful as a falcon's. "Is that *anybody*'s name? But it's one of the names I give, sure, and if *that's* the name you heard, you're hooked into that whole wizardly bureaucracy business." He shook his head, as if in patient bafflement at the folly of humankind. "What are you doing here? Is there some kind of big conclave you want to invite me to? Because if it's not held on this beach, or downtown, or on the boardwalk, or up in a redwood cathedral, you can count the Bammer out."

"No, I'm not here on any kind of official business." Bradley sat down cross-legged on the sand. "But I hear you're the guy who runs this town."

"Chief sorcerer of Santa Cruz." He nodded, then took a glass pipe from his satchel and began to pack it with weed. Bradley, being in recovery—he wasn't an addict in *every* universe, just the ones where he'd ever tried any drugs at all—watched him with a mixture of fascination and dread. The Bammer lit the pipe took a deep hit, started to pass the pipe to Bradley, then gave a sad smile and put it down in the sand, on the side farthest from Bradley. He exhaled. "Also chief sorcerer of Soquel and Capitola-by-the-Sea, by the way. Not Ben Lomond, though. There's a woman up there, lives in a redwood tree, she's got that covered."

"Uh huh. So maybe you didn't notice, but you've got a pretty major extra-dimensional incursion here."

The Bammer nodded. "Not so major yet. It doesn't even have enough meat on its bones to pass for human in a dark alley. Give it time, though." He clucked his tongue. "Nasty business."

"Okay, so… chief sorcerer of Santa Cruz… what are you going to *do* about it?"

The Bammer gazed out at the bay for a long while, toward the bobbing boats and the surfers and the distant curves of land on either side. "Murderville USA," he said. "Murder Capital of the World. That's what they called my city back in the '70s. October 1970 to April 1973, there were three active serial killers who hunted around here. Twenty-six dead."

"I remember reading about that. Was it, like, a dark magic thing?"

The Bammer shook his head. "Just an evil human thing. I was an apprentice back then. The chief sorcerer here was a wave mage. He was good when it came to surfing, but pretty crap when it came to anything else. I'm into nature magic myself, I don't specialize quite as much as he did, but mostly what I'm good at is enchanting. When all that ugliness went down, my old boss, he realized he wasn't up for the job anymore, you know? He couldn't protect this place, or not well enough. I was the most qualified, the most talented, the best choice for a replacement, so I took the job, and he paddled off into the sunset, like literally, and nobody ever heard from him again. His failure… it's never far from my mind."

"Which explains why you're so eager to deal with this new murder problem—oh, wait."

"You're judgmental," The Bammer said. "Strange. Psychics are usually more forgiving of human foibles, because they know everybody's got them." He took another hit, and the breeze wafted sweet smoke Bradley's way. He tried to concentrate on the smell of rotting kelp instead. "Anyway, the thing is, I know my *limitations*. A few years back we had a big nasty problem, this spirit of earthquake, wildfire, and mudslide came marching out of… a place beyond this world, where things are more malleable and unreal, where gods are born. The Dreamtime, the Medicine Lands, the crawlspace of the world. I knew *I* couldn't stop something like that. So I appointed a champion. She did a great job."

Bradley didn't gape, but it was a near thing. "Marzi? You made her the city's champion?"

"I gave her an enchanted toy pistol, but to be honest I think a stick shaped vaguely like a gun would have gotten the job done. She's got some of the same kind of power I sense in you, that openness to dreams and visions—I don't have that ability at all, I have to do rituals to see anything like you two see when your heads hit your pillows at night—but she's got other powers, too. A touch of the reweaver's gift, I think. Not enough to be dangerous, she's not going to sneeze and accidentally transform a building into a giant watermelon or anything, but in a place where reality is *thin* anyway, or when dealing with supernatural creatures who can change their form, she can exert some control over them, even if it's not totally conscious."

"Uh huh. Right. Well, it's definitely not totally conscious, because she has *no goddamn idea* you've made her the champion of Santa Cruz."

He shuddered dramatically. "Of course not. What's she ever done to me, that I'd put that kind of pressure on her? She just does what comes naturally, and she does fine. Word got *around* when she beat the Outlaw. People heard we had somebody here who turned a great big spirit of primal destruction into a damn near human little man obsessed with revenge, turned a small god into a guy who got stabbed in the back by a moron. All the big uglies started steering clear of Santa Cruz after that."

"It's not right." Bradley remembered well his own years of confusion and misery, having prophetic dreams, seeing impossible monsters, with no one to teach him how to use his gifts, no one welcoming him into the community of sorcerers, at least not until first Marla Mason and later Sanford Cole embraced him. "She's wandering in the wilderness! Why not apprentice her?"

"I ask you again—what's she ever done to me to deserve such a thing? Marzi doesn't *want* that life, as far as I can tell, and I've paid attention. You know what she wants to do? She wants to draw her comics. She wants to laze around on Sunday mornings with that man of hers. She wants to run the café—and I made sure she got the loan she needed to buy it, too, a few years ago, and put a little come-along spell on the front steps to encourage the passing trade, not that she needs it—she does fine on her own. You want me to throw a hand grenade into the middle of her life like that, show up and say, 'Hey, there's a whole secret society of sorcerers, mostly psychotics, assholes, or thieves—wanna join?' You want me to apprentice her, and groom her to take over from me, line her up for the kind of worry and guilt *I* have to carry?" He shook his head. "No sir. She did her service. Her reward is a good life in this city as long as she wants it."

"Except now you want her to fight this *new* monster," Bradley said.

The Bammer scowled. "I do not. I'd just as soon leave her out of it. But the thing is drawn to the café, is all—there's a thin place, there. A point of access to the crawlspace of the world, to an imaginary desert full of real scorpions. This shadow thing senses it, somehow. Maybe it thinks it's a way to get back to whatever universe shat it out in the first place. Or maybe it's just drawn there the way trees reach out for the sun, or, if you don't mind me getting all cliché, moths to a flame. Nah, I don't want Marzi to have to fight that thing." He picked up the toy switchblade and threw it into the sand in front of Bradley. "There you go. You fight it instead. That's what you're here for, right?"

"Gods damn it," Bradley said. "Yes. It is." He picked up the switchblade, a cracked plastic hilt wrapped with black electrical tape, and a chipped, silver-painted plastic blade that popped out at the push of a button. He tested the edge with his thumb. Duller than pop music. "So what's this thing do?"

"It's a knife. You stab stuff with it." The Bammer took another puff of his pipe, then knocked the ashes out onto the sand. "I don't know if you can keep Marzi out of this mess entirely, though. I halfway chose her, and she halfway chose *herself*. She's got a lot of hero in her, and she might want to get involved. You could do worse than her for a partner if this turns into a shooting war."

"I'll keep that in mind. But I was planning to bring in some heavier artillery anyway. I'm going to see a friend of mine in the morning, and bring her back with me."

"Huh. Must be a tough friend, if she's not scared of getting eaten by a monster made of shadows."

"Scared of what? Death?" Bradley clicked the switchblade open, then pushed it close again. "No, she's not scared of death. She married him."

Rondeau in a Dirty RV Somewhere in Death Valley

"But we're *motherfucking wizards*," Rondeau said, some time after they'd been ousted from Las Vegas. "Right? There's gotta be a way we can make some money."

Pelham shrugged. "I am not especially adept at the magical arts. I have other skills, as you know. Certainly I am qualified to be an executive assistant, or butler, or valet, or even, dare I say, to provide personal security. But I have had only two employers. One of them, I am loath to trouble for a reference. The other is presently ruling the realm of death. I fear I would have difficulty obtaining such a position, even if I desired to undertake such work."

"Yeah, I didn't mean to suggest honest employment." Rondeau rubbed his stubbly chin and peered through the dirt-smeared windshield of Pelham's RV. They weren't entirely broke. They'd been robbed and driven from Las Vegas, but the Pit Boss had left them a few grand so, he said, they could get established somewhere else. They'd tried to reach some friends in Felport, hoping for a loan, but hadn't been able to reach Hamil or the Bay Witch or anyone else they knew—maybe the spontaneous decapitation business was keeping the grand high-and-mighties there occupied.

At a loss for how to proceed, they'd bought gas and food and trucked out to the desert to wait for Marla to wake up, hoping maybe more would-be cultists of the Bride of Death had drifted in—cultists were always eager to give up their worldly possessions to some high priest or another, and Rondeau figured, if the black robe fit, he'd wear it. But the place was deserted. Maybe word had gotten around in the lunatic community that serving a death god had a high mortality rate.

"When Mrs. Mason awakens in a few days, we will have direction again," Pelham said. "She will show us the proper way forward."

Rondeau snorted. "Marla was living off my generosity, you know. But you're right—she's a legit wizard, and she always says sorcerers don't have to worry about money, because they have scarier things to worry about. She's going to yell at us and call us idiots before she gets around to helping us, but I've been through that before, and it'll do you good to get the rough side of her tongue for once, help toughen you up."

"I am sorry that you deem me insufficiently tough—"

Someone knocked on the door of the RV. Rondeau frowned at Pelham. "Did you order pizza? No, wait. Thai?"

Pelham sighed. "Don't be foolish, Rondeau. It is likely a park ranger coming to demand we leave the area. We have no magic at the moment to hide us from such attention."

"Yeah. I just figured the RV being entirely covered in filth would work as desert camouflage. Shows what I know. Still, better safe. Got your sword cane?"

Pelham reached down for his stick and slid out an inch of steel.

The knock came again, harder. "Who is it?" Rondeau called.

"Me!" It was a man's voice, but even muffled, there was something familiar about it.

"Me, who?" Rondeau said, and opened the door.

Someone hit him, hard, driving him down onto his back. The newcomer moved with a leap and a growl toward Pelham. Rondeau tried to turn his head to track the assault, but he was too stunned to make much progress. He'd had the wind knocked out of him, and the earth and fire too. He caught a glimpse of Pelham slashing out with his sword, but the intruder was too fast, and Pelly collapsed from a blow across the face.

The figure turned toward Rondeau. His face was familiar. Just about as familiar as a face could be. "Me," he said, and grinned.

"You," Rondeau agreed, and then the light ran out of the world and he sank into the gray.

Crapsey in a Cave

CRAPSEY STOOD IN THE CAVE, humming to himself and scratching obscene graffiti into the stone walls with a switchblade, his artistic efforts lit by camping lanterns. Pretty soon, he'd have the opportunity to deliver some bad news to a goddess, and he was really looking forward to it. He'd been spending his days and nights in Rondeau and Pelham's stinky RV for too long, and it was good to be *doing* something again. Marla wouldn't be happy to see him, and Crapsey was never happier than he was making other people unhappy. He realized that was probably indicative of some profound psychological problems, but what could you do? He was what he was.

It was funny—back when he'd been the dogsbody/factotum/ confidential assistant/amanuensis/body man/personal slave of a world-conquering supervillain in another dimension, and later when he'd been part of a revenge squad run by a redheaded incarnation of devastation and chaos, he'd wanted nothing more than a quiet place to sit and read comic books, and his big dreams had included eating food that wasn't raw and bloody or scooped from the inside of an expired aluminum can.

But once he got free of his assorted monstrous entanglements, with total liberty in this beautiful reality where you could buy fresh food and diverting literature just about anywhere, and getting money to buy said hamburgers and comic books was as easy as hitting a guy over the head in an alley and taking his wallet, he'd found himself yearning for some of the stuff he'd always thought he hated. Like stepping out of the shadows and giving a grin that made would-be revolutionaries shit themselves. Leaning against a wall in the background playing with a knife while an incredibly dangerous woman tortured victims in the foreground. Chasing guys down and unhinging his enchanted prosthetic jaw and threatening to literally bite their heads off if they didn't behave. Making moves. Fucking shit up. Leaving his mark on the world, and if that mark was a metaphorical (or, often, literal) smear of blood, so what? Crapsey had reasons to want the world to bleed. He'd had a rough childhood, and it had only gotten worse when he'd stopped being a child.

So when his old comrade-in-arms Nicolette got in touch—projecting her image into the cracked mirror of the single-room-occupancy hotel in San Francisco's Tenderloin district where he'd been living—to make him an offer, he'd jumped at the chance. The chance to hit his evil twin Rondeau—the version of Crapsey native to this reality, and a smug and coddled and conniving son of a bitch he was—over the head had been the most enticing part of the offer, of course, but he'd been looking forward to this part, too. Nicolette had promised him plenty of opportunities for organized mayhem once he got Marla back to Felport and into Nicolette's clutches. Nicolette was well on her way to becoming a world-conquering supervillain herself, it seemed—or at least city-conquering one—and while Nicolette didn't have the native power that Crapsey's old boss the Mason had possessed, and she wasn't half the chaos witch their mutual ex-employer Elsie Jarrow had been, she *was* good at breaking stuff, and he'd hang around until she inevitably fucked things up for herself. He tried not to think too far ahead. The future had never been too full of bright and shiny things for him. Better to live in the moment.

The bed of soft sand at the far end of the chamber began to stir. Crapsey grinned and picked up the chrome pump-action shotgun he'd taken from the trunk of a drug dealer in Oakland. He'd been informed that Marla Mason couldn't be killed, that she'd become some kind of half-goddess, but he'd also been told she could still feel pain, and he was hoping for the opportunity to perform a little shotgun experiment.

A woman sat up in the sand, probably naked but so covered in dust and earth that it was hard to tell. She turned her head and spat brown muck onto the cavern floor. "This has to be the worst possible way to wake up." She blinked at him and wiped dust from her eyes. Crapsey had arranged the lanterns to make himself a backlit shadow before her. Super dramatic.

"Rondeau, is that you?" she said. "Where's Pelham? Any report on that monster that escaped from the chamber below? If that thing is still on the loose, at least we know what we're doing today. I should take a shower first, so I hope the RV's tank is full—"

"Rondeau and Pelham aren't here." Crapsey pumped the gun, loading a cartridge into the chamber with that wonderful "ka-chunk" sound so beloved of action movie directors. "Last I saw them, they were tied up in the back of a van, but that was days ago. They're all tucked away, now, probably crying and wondering when you're going to save them."

"Oh, I so do not have time for this bullshit." Marla stood up, shaking off dirt as she did, though she still looked like the avatar of some particularly earthy deity, her hair sending down showers of dust with every step she took toward him.

Crapsey pointed the barrels of the gun at her. "You can keep walking, and I'll blow a hole in your middle, and you can listen to what I have to say while you lay there knitting your guts back together, assuming you can really do that. Or you can stop where you are and listen to me *without* getting major abdominal damage. Personally, I'm not bothered either way—in fact, I'd kinda prefer the bit where I get to shoot you, but I've been instructed to play nice until you force me to do otherwise. So which is it, option one, or option two?"

"I'll go with option C. I'm going to walk over there and get a drink." She pointed to a dusty cooler against one wall of the cavern. "Because you don't know what a dry mouth is until you've woken up from your own grave. Then I'm going to put on one of those black robes hanging on the hooks over there, left by my former cultists, because you're lecherous and I'm not in the mood to give you a free show."

"You've literally got sand in your vagina. You are the opposite of alluring."

"Yeah, you say that, but didn't I hear you fucked Nicolette? If so, your standards are as low as they can be without recourse to bestiality. Anyway, shoot me if you must, but I'll make you eat a bucket of scorpions if you do. That's not an empty threat, either. I'm feeling very literal today."

Crapsey couldn't help but feel he sacrificed some of the initiative by acquiescing, but he let her put on a robe and then guzzle a bottle of water while sitting on the cooler. She poured water on her face, but that just made the dirt streak and darken, giving her a very war-paint sort of visage. Her gaze was calm. She'd clearly faced things a lot scarier than Crapsey and come out of it okay. He knew she had; once or twice, he'd been in the vicinity when she did the facing.

She stretched, rolling her head around on her shoulders. Sleeping for a month probably put quite a crick in the neck. "Who talked you into being an idiot this time, Crapsey? I know you don't have the initiative to kidnap my friends and point a gun at me on your own. You've tagged along after some high-quality monsters in the past—the Mason, Elsie Jarrow—but I'm drawing a blank trying to figure out your current employer. There aren't many big scary people with a grudge against me left." She swished more water into her mouth, then spat it out. The water was still brownish. Marla met his eyes again. "There aren't many left because they're dead. Which you *know*. And yet, here you are, throwing in your lot with someone trying to oppose me *again*. Call it the triumph of enthusiasm over experience, huh?"

"Read this." He reached into the pocket of his blazer, pulled out a folded sheet of paper, and tossed it toward her.

She bent, picked the letter up, and read it aloud, in a showy, declamatory voice. He knew that Marla could make anything sound contemptuous if she tried, and she was trying pretty hard. Crapsey had found the letter in the RV, among Rondeau and Pelham's crappy possessions, and handing it over spared him having to tell the story himself. Nicolette had written it—or rather, since she'd been a conscious severed head in a birdcage at the time, she'd dictated it to a mind-controlled hotel maid who'd done the actual writing—in her usual gloating-and-crowing-and-boasting tone. In the note Nicolette explained how she'd learned that Marla was a goddess. That she'd sweet-talked and lied and turned Marla's hired muscle, a cursed and lethal goon named Squat, against her. That with Squat's help she was going to escape and spend the month Marla was down in the underworld wreaking havoc, or plotting revenge, or researching how to murder gods. And how she was going to *finally* make Marla take her seriously as a nemesis.

When she was done reading—"Thugs and pisses, Nicolette"—Marla snorted and threw the letter on the ground. "Gods, Crapsey. You're working for Nicolette, now? You used to be a henchman for *queens* of villainy, and now you're, like, assistant dogcatcher. You're working for a *head* in a *cage*—"

"I don't think she spends a lot of time in a cage anymore," Crapsey said. "I hear she got herself a new set of legs, and all the stuff in between, too, I imagine. The thing you don't get it is, you've *made* Nicolette dangerous, more so than she ever would have been without you to prove herself against. I get that Nicolette's ambition has exceeded her ability in the past, but you're the standard she set herself against, Marla. All she wants is for you to take her seriously. It's sad, but at the same time, it's pushing her to do great things, for a certain fucked-up definition of 'great.' She's determined to become dangerous enough that you can't just snort and roll your eyes when she comes to cause trouble." He shrugged. "I don't know her whole plan, but from what she's told me… hating you has given her some real inspiration. She's making some moves."

Marla closed one of her nostrils with her finger and blew, spraying dirt and less sanitary things at Crapsey's feet, making him jump out of the way. She cleared the other nostril the same way, then said, "I *really* don't have time for this, Crapsey. Do you know why none of my cultists are hanging around right now, ritually sacrificing you to me? It's because they discovered something in the caves down below, something that *ate* them, and then flew away. At least, we think it flew. It's some kind of serious primal monster from out of deep time, imprisoned here by ancient wizards or some shit, maybe not even human wizards, at that. I told Rondeau and Pelham to get started on trying to track the thing, and now you tell me Nicolette has kidnapped them? I am just *so* not in the mood to make a side trip to smite her." She sighed. "Crapsey, it's *stupid*. Nicolette, by all rights, should be dead. She even admits it in the letter. Elsie Jarrow decapitated her, and her original body is literally fish food now. The only reason she retains her consciousness is because I called in a favor and had death… withdrawn from her. I kept Nicolette alive and conscious because I thought she could be useful to me, as an oracle and a bloodhound for dangerous badness and chaos. I needed her as a compass for my monster-hunting trips, that's all, and there are other options for tracking down big bad beasties. If Nicolette annoys me, all I have to do is let nature take its course again, and she'll get bounced right off this mortal coil. Plus, as she may have mentioned, I've got some connections in the underworld—I don't mean the mob, I mean the land of the *dead*—and once Nicolette's a corpse, she's pretty much entirely in my power. She's lucky I don't take her seriously, because if I did, she might have an eternity of unpleasantness ahead of her, but the fact is, when Nicolette is not actively pissing in my face, I don't even think about her. So, fuck it. I'll just let her die, as soon as I can get word to Death, which will be shortly."

Crapsey shook his head. "Come on, Marla. Even if you think Nicolette's stupid, that she's a joke, you know she's not *that* stupid. She's taken steps to keep you from just letting her die. She said *that* in the letter, too—"

"Yeah, she kidnapped Pelham and Rondeau, and she'll arrange for them to be killed or maimed if I let her die, I get it. I'm going to rescue them, or send people to rescue them, assuming they don't just rescue *themselves*. But I don't have time to deal with Nicolette myself. If that hurts her feelings, tough."

Crapsey shook his head. "I'm taking you with me, Marla. You *are* going to see Nicolette. Rondeau and Pelham, kidnapping them was just to get your attention, and to keep them out of my way while I had this little talk with you—they are *not* Nicolette's dead-man's switch. I don't know what she did, exactly, or what her plans are, but she's pretty pleased with herself. She was straight-up chortling last time we talked, and she wants to give you the big reveal herself, let you know exactly how she outsmarted you."

"I've never gone wrong yet underestimating Nicolette, and I don't intend to start."

Crapsey thought she sounded doubtful, though, or at least concerned. With Marla it was hard to tell how much of her act was bravado and how much was actual bedrock self-confidence. The woman was often wrong, but rarely uncertain. "Fine. You can keep right on underestimating her, just as long as you get in the Jeep I've got waiting and behave yourself on the way to the airfield." He hefted the shotgun and pointed it at her. "You can walk, or I can drag your bleeding and screaming carcass. I don't care which."

"Will you go ahead and do something already?" Marla said. "How long are you just going to stand there and watch?"

Crapsey frowned. "What the hell are you—" His eyes suddenly felt heavy, like they were window shades being dragged down, and he blinked and swayed. How had Marla managed to cast a sleep spell on him? She didn't have anything with her, no charms, she'd spoken no incantation, and she was no more psychic than your average kumquat, so *how*... He yawned as widely as he could—and with his magical jaw, that was very wide indeed—and felt himself falling forward, but was deep asleep before he hit the ground, sparing him the indignity of feeling the impact.

Bradley on the Road

"I DIDN'T KNOW YOU COULD DO THAT," Marla said. "I figured you'd just throw a rock at his head or something, make a distraction so I could take the gun away and feed it to him." She nudged Crapsey's unconscious form with her toe.

"I've learned a few new tricks." Bradley stepped from the mouth of the tunnel where he'd been hiding, into the pool of overlapping lantern light. "I'm not much good when it comes to mind control, and that's kind of a gross and evil thing to do anyway, but making somebody really sleepy is a lot easier, and handy, too." He moved to stand beside Marla, looking down at Crapsey, who was curled up and snoring outrageously. He wore a blue sharkskin suit, perhaps the most impractical desert attire Bradley had ever encountered.

"I'd hug you, but I'm covered in filth," Marla said. "Oh, screw it, the robe is covering most of the filth." She threw her arms around him and squeezed him tight. "I know you're not *my* B," she said into his ear, "but it's good to see you anyway."

"I'm very, very close to being your B," he said. "I'm from a branch of the multiverse just half a degree distant. *Your* Bradley arrived at the scene of a crime in time to get himself killed. Me, I was a little late, so by the time I got there, everything was over."

"Rondeau didn't take over your body, then?" she said. "I mean, demonstrably. So, what happened in your branch?"

"Remember that guy Danny Two Saints, the thug? Rondeau took over his body instead. Nobody much mourned his loss, I must say. I stayed on as your apprentice for a while in that world. Admittedly, from that point on, my timeline and yours diverged… a lot. Where I come from, you're still chief sorcerer of Felport."

She grunted. "Sure. I didn't ruin everything by trying to bring you back to life over there."

He nodded. "I appreciate the effort, though. We all do. Anyway, when Bradley Bowman became the new overseer of the multiverse, I got uplifted along with all the other versions of us from throughout all the branches, consolidated into a single consciousness…"

"So what are you *now*, standing before me? Like, a pseudopod? The Over-Bradley sticking his pinky finger into my reality?"

He shook his head. "I'm more like an autonomous vehicle. A single instance of Bradley, cut loose and sent here on a mission. The reason I'm here—"

Marla cut him off. "I bet I know. The thing my cultists found in the caverns, it's from *elsewhere*, yeah? Something from another, inimical universe? Like my old cloak?"

Bradley shivered at the mention of her cloak, which had seemed like a powerful magical artifact, but had actually been an intelligent parasitic entity from a place with entirely different physical laws. The cloak had caused him trouble, even after he was elevated to his position as overseer of the multiverse. "Like that, but not identical. As far as I can tell, this new creature, this Outsider, doesn't need a host to survive in this universe, but it doesn't have much of a body, either—it's almost ethereal, looks like a creature made of shadow. Probably once upon a time it had a more concrete form, but the centuries or millennia it spent imprisoned took a toll. It's traveling around now, consuming humans as it goes, and its ontological mass—it's *reality*—is increasing with each kill. I think it's building itself a body that can function in this universe. Maybe learning about us by devouring us. Maybe taking memories or other properties from its victims. Who knows? I'm just here to kill it, and since you've always been infinitely better at killing things than I am, I figured I'd ask for help."

"Also because it's my fault the thing got loose." She sighed. "I was trying to keep the cultists out of trouble, because a bunch of unsupervised zealots devoted to a goddess of death is a recipe for trouble. I sent them into the caverns to explore, thinking they wouldn't find anything, that it was a snipe hunt, but the poor idiots found an actual snipe. That thing that got loose is my responsibility. I'll take care of it. But I'm happy to have one of the Over-Bradley's fingernail clippings to help out."

Bradley, fortunately, had been under no illusions about how this was going to work. Just because he was an emissary from an entity elevated as far above the gods as the gods were above humans, just because he was a psychic capable of summoning oracles to answer nearly any question, just because he was well-versed in the dangers of incursions from other universes, didn't mean he was going to be in charge. So what if Marla was currently penniless, without unkidnapped allies, and cut off from the powers she possessed as a god of death during her mortal month on Earth? She was still Marla Mason, and that meant she was going to take the lead.

Bradley was fine with that. He had enough responsibility in his life. Let it rest on someone else's shoulders for now. When it came to killing monsters, she was more qualified, anyway.

He nodded at Crapsey. "What do we do with him?"

"Can you suck his mind dry, and find out everything he knows?"

Bradley frowned. "I mean, in theory, I guess. But I'd rather not. Messing around with people's minds is dangerous. I could turn him into a drooling cucumber."

"It might be an improvement." She sighed. "All right, let's get him tied up in the RV. I'm going to take a shower. You can start driving… wherever we're going. Have you tracked this creature at all?"

"Oh, yeah. It's hovering around in Santa Cruz. There's, well… some weird stuff there. A spot where reality is malleable. Either the Outsider is just drawn to that spot mindlessly, moth-to-flame style, or else it's plotting something. Assuming it has anything we would comprehend as thought processes or motivations, which is a big assumption."

"'The Outsider'? You've been chasing it long enough to name it, huh."

"Gotta call it something, and 'Rover' didn't seem to fit."

"Hmm. Santa Cruz. All right. How long to drive there?"

"Like eight hours?" Marla wouldn't want to do any of the driving, he knew. Driving was something apprentices did, and even though, as the representative of a meta-god, he should outrank her, even taking into account her status as a part-time death god, there was no way he was anything more than an apprentice in her company.

She cracked her knuckles. "Good. That allows time for me and Crapsey to have a chat."

"So… you don't want to go after Pelham and Rondeau?"

"Priorities, Bradley. Extradimensional creatures are dangerous, and this one is extra-dangerous—it must be, or *you* wouldn't be here. I know you—or your higher self—doesn't much care about the fate of any particular branch of the multiverse. There are zillions of them, and some of them are pretty horrible places, worlds where human life was extinguished long ago, or never existed in the first place. Worlds run by evil gods, robot spiders, skin-eating mutants, guys with goatees, who knows what. That means this thing, this Outsider, is a threat to the integrity of the multiverse itself, to *all* realities, so the stakes are pretty high, right?"

Bradley nodded.

"Pelham and Rondeau are capable. Good at getting into trouble, especially Rondeau, but also good at getting *out* of trouble, especially Pelham. So we'll go to Santa Cruz, take care of this Outsider thing, and then, if they still need rescuing, I'll get on that. When it comes to triage, 'reality-destroying monster' trumps 'friends in the clutches of an incompetent severed head with delusions of grandeur.' Even if she has popped her head on top of a mannequin or golem or med-school cadaver or something."

"Can't argue with your logic," Bradley said. He cleared his throat. "There's just… one thing. You're right that the Outsider is a threat. It's such a big threat that this branch of the multiverse has been quarantined. Not cut off, just sort of… frozen. It's not branching anymore."

Marla frowned, then nodded. "I get it. Keep it locked down, so there aren't lots of alternate versions of the monster running loose. So if we get rid of the Outsider here, he's gone everywhere, and we get welcomed back into the multiversal fold? The tourniquet comes off?"

"Right."

"And if we fail… what? Amputation? Like somebody who gets a zombie bite on their arm, and you chop off the arm to save the body?"

She was looking at him so intently, he tried not to squirm. "Basically, yeah. But there's kind of a ticking clock, too. It takes a lot of effort to keep this reality from proliferating and branching. I'm—the *rest* of me—is keeping it locked down, but it's like stopping a volcano from erupting by sticking your thumb in the caldera. The pressure's going to build, and when it gets to be too much, we'll have no choice but to cut this branch free."

Marla opened the cooler and took out another bottle of water. "What happens then? Will we even notice? Most people aren't aware they spawn a new reality every time they make a choice between regular or decaf coffee anyway."

"Ah. No. It's not something we have to do often, but… cutting off this branch from the greater multiverse will be about as good for this branch as cutting a limb off a tree is for the limb. Or an arm off a person is for the arm."

"We're talking about some kind of philosophical rot?" she said. "Metaphysical gangrene? Epistemological maggots?"

"Decay. I think 'decay' covers it. What it would look like, what that means in terms of practical effects… Cause and effect would stop working.

Physics would start to break down. Things would get seriously weird, but most people would die before it got *too* weird, like as soon as oxygen forgot how to oxidize, or when the first couple of laws of thermodynamics gave out."

She frowned. "So basically if I fail I've consigned this entire branch of the multiverse, *my* branch, where all my friends and enemies and also my husband lives, to some kind of horrific oblivion, without even the comfort of knowing that I succeeded in some adjacent reality? Well. I wasn't short on motivation before, but this doesn't hurt. Why do you care, though? We're one universe among trillions and trillions. Why even bother with the freezing? Why not go straight to the amputating?"

Bradley smiled. "You'd laugh, but… it's basically just sentimentality. See, you've got continuity-of-experience with the version of Marla Mason who caused us to ascend to our current position. We feel like we owe you, so we're going a *little* out of our way to keep you from dying a horrible death."

She clucked her tongue. "That's no way to run a multiverse, B. You're soft. But it's to my advantage, so I won't complain. What happens to *you*, this instance of you, if we fail?"

"I'm stuck here, going through all that misery with you."

"And if we succeed?"

"Then I get integrated back into the collective."

She nodded. "Good. Then you have some motivation to bust your ass beyond mere sentimentality, because you don't want to get stranded in a decaying universe any more than I do. You're welcome to join me, then."

"Much obliged." He would have said it sarcastically if he'd thought she was likely to pay any attention.

"How long do we have? I've only got a month on Earth anyway, you know, before I'm due back in the underworld. I could try to get a special dispensation, but the way our deal was made, it's like trying to get an exemption from a law of nature, not a zoning ordinance. Which is to say, it's not impossible, but not easy, either."

Bradley grimaced. "I've been here a few weeks already, tracking the Outsider—I came as soon as it got substantial enough to register as a threat. You won't need an extension on your time in the mortal world. I'd guess we've got ten days before our, ah, cut-off. If we haven't killed or imprisoned or neutralized this thing by then…"

"Yeah. Okay. Let's get going. Now that I think about it, we're going to be on the road longer than I said. We need to make a side trip before Santa Cruz."

Crapsey on the Floor

CRAPSEY WOKE UP TO JOSTLING and bouncing, and once he determined that his arms and legs were bound, he decided he should pretend to be asleep. Maybe just keep pretending to be asleep until he actually fell asleep, and then proceed that way indefinitely, on a cycle of real-sleep/fake-sleep/real-sleep. The only problem would be having to go pee, which he had to do a little bit *already*, and then eventually there'd be an issue with thirst, and also hunger, but those were problems for Future Crapsey, and fuck that guy—

"Your breathing changes when you wake up, moron," Marla Mason said in her usual tones, which were whatever the opposite of "dulcet" is.

Crapsey cracked an eyelid and peered at her. She sat above him on a swivel chair that was bolted to the floor, the floor itself being occupied by Crapsey. The RV's carpet was thin and scratchy and uncomfortable. Crapsey lunged forward, opening his jaws, intending to bite her leg, but squawked when a rope he hadn't noticed tightened around his throat and drew him up short.

"Bad dog, no biscuit." Marla picked up a magazine from the table, rolled it into a cylinder, and smacked him on the nose with it, hard. "You have terrible taste in masters, doggie."

"It's not my fault." His eyes watered from the blow to his nose, and he did his best not to let it show. Marla getting the drop on him and tying him up wasn't exactly shocking—she was a tough chick, and he'd been prepared for the eventuality—but the whole situation still stung his pride. "There are some unsightly gaps in my résumé, and anyway, you weren't hiring."

"Oh, I'm always hiring, but your qualifications don't impress me. A friend of mine got a look into your mind during that business in Hawaii, did you know that? He told me, 'Crapsey's not a bad guy, apart from being a mass murderer.' I guess I'm not as forgiving as he is."

"Nicolette told me you're literally a goddess of death now."

Another smack. "God of death will do. No 'ess' necessary. I don't need a special diminutive. Nobody ever got away with calling me a sorceress or an enchantress, so I don't see why I'd put up with 'goddess.'"

"Yes, okay, fine, but you kill people for a *living* now, and you're going to bitch about me murdering a few people in an entirely different *dimension*? Murders I only committed because my genocidal boss ordered me to? My boss who would've killed *me* if I'd disobeyed?"

"Please. You enjoy the work. I don't kill for fun, or because it's convenient. I rarely kill *anybody*, personally. I just help run the whole life-death-rebirth cycle of the world. I'm like the casino manager, watching things from behind the scenes. I'm not out there on the floor dealing cards. Anyway, I'm off the cosmic clock right now, and concerned with more worldly matters. I've got some important business to take care of shortly, but once that's done, I guess I'll go mop up Nicolette, so why don't you tell me where she's hiding?"

"I wouldn't say she's *hiding*," Crapsey said. There was no reason to keep this part a secret. Nicolette wanted Marla to come for her. "She's in your old stomping grounds, the shithole city of Felport. In fact, I hear she got herself installed as chief sorcerer and protector of the city, with the goal of doing the job better than you did. Of course, as long as she doesn't get exiled for being a monumental fuck-up, she should beat you pretty easily—"

"Bullshit." Marla's voice was troubled, and that was a balm to Crapsey's sore spirit. "She was an acolyte of Elsie Jarrow. Chaos witches can be useful, but they can't run a *city*. That takes order, discipline, control, all things she stands against."

"Oh no," Crapsey said, mock-appalled. "A chaos witch making the trains run on time! Think of the penalties she'll face for acting against her alignment. She'll never hit her level cap at this rate."

"You're a bigger nerd than Rondeau. But it's nonsense. Nicolette was notorious in Felport. She was imprisoned in the local asylum for unstable sorcerers! The council would never accept her."

"I get the impression Nicolette didn't give the council a choice in the matter. It was more of a coup than an election. I don't know the details, but the council's a lot weaker than it used to be—Viscarro is dead, Ernesto is dead, Granger is dead, and wait, didn't that all happen on your watch? The newbies on the council aren't any stronger than Nicolette herself, and the ones who are more formidable, like Hamil and the Chamberlain… well, Nicolette knows them pretty well after all these years. Knows their weaknesses, anyway. She didn't give me the blow-by-blow about how she accomplished her takeover, but I'm sure once you get to Felport she'll want to gloat and fill you in."

Marla looked off into the distance, maybe out the RV's windows, maybe at some inner landscape. "Fuck Felport," she said after a while. "They exiled me. What do I care if they have a maniac for a leader?"

"Very convincing. I'd applaud your performance if I wasn't hogtied. My new boss is pissing all over your old house, and you want me to believe that doesn't bother you? I worked for the Mason for a long time. She was a monster, but she was a monster made out of *you*, based on your personality, and she was jealous of her possessions and territorial as hell. Besides, Nicolette has Rondeau and Pelham, and she'll cut them into little pieces if you don't show up to pay your respects."

"Oh, I'll go, but she shouldn't expect too much in the way of respect when I do."

"That's the whole *thing*, Marla." Crapsey shifted around to try to get more comfortable, which wasn't really possible. At least he wasn't tied up on a bed of nails. "The fact that you disrespect her, that's what drives her. I bet she secretly just wants your approval. You're the big-sister-slash-mother-slash-mean-dominatrix she's always needed in her life. Just go kiss her forehead and tell her she did good, and I bet she'll hand you the keys to the city."

"At least you're still disloyal and like to talk shit about your bosses," Marla said. "I'm glad some things in the world never change. Tell Nicolette we'll be along shortly." She turned away. "Bradley! Pull over!"

"Wait. Bradley? Like... Bowman?" Crapsey didn't know the guy well—just that Marla's attempts to bring him back to life had caused a tear to open between Crapsey's home reality and this universe, and had led to all this subsequent bullshit. Bowman was here? Which version of him?

The RV slowed down, bumping up and down as it pulled onto the shoulder. Marla opened the door, then grabbed Crapsey by the ankles and dragged him toward the opening. "B, give me a hand?"

"You're just going to leave him by the side of the road?" Bowman said, grabbing Crapsey's shoulders and helping to lift him out of the vehicle. Gods, the humiliations just didn't stop.

"We're beside a freeway," Marla said. "Somebody will see him soon enough."

They dropped Crapsey on the sandy earth several feet from the roadway. Marla smacked him lightly on the back of the head, because apparently no indignity was too small for her to visit on him. "No murdering whoever stops to pick you up, understand me? I left half the cash in your wallet and your credit cards and fake ID. You'll be fine. Where exactly is Nicolette holding court in Felport, anyway?"

This was a horrible situation, but Crapsey had been in horrible situations before. Marla had once left him tied up in the belly of a ship traveling from Hawaii to Oakland, and he probably wouldn't be bound nearly as long this time. He sighed. Antagonizing her would only prolong his own misery. "I hear she set up shop in Rondeau's old night club."

"What? Hamil owns that place now, he bought if from Rondeau when I was exiled."

"I understand there was a transfer of ownership." Crapsey grinned. Marla looked genuinely concerned now. She'd been close to Hamil, back before he'd voted to fire her from her job as chief sorcerer and kick her out of the city.

"Did Nicolette kill him? Answer me, Crapsey."

"If she did, she didn't tell me about it, and you know how she likes to gloat. He's probably still alive, though I can't vouch for his circumstances otherwise."

Marla nodded. "All right. Let Nicolette know I'll be there as soon as I can. Maybe in a week or so, ten days tops."

"You'd better show up, Marla. Don't keep her waiting too long. Nicolette hates Rondeau a lot. Not as much as I do, but she won't hesitate to maim the guy just as an expression of frustration."

"I will be there within ten days, or else the world will be doomed, and it won't matter anyway. You can tell Nicolette that, too."

Marla climbed back into the RV, and Bradley squatted down next to Crapsey. "Here, there's not much silverware in the camper, but I found a butter knife." He slipped the hilt into Crapsey's hand. "You can cut your way out eventually. I'd hate to make you depend totally on the kindness of strangers."

"Thanks, man," Crapsey said. "When the time comes, I'll kill you last. Or first. Whichever seems more merciful at the time."

"That's all I ask." Bradley climbed back into the RV.

They drove away, kicking up great plumes of dust into Crapsey's face, and he began sawing through the ropes behind his back. It didn't take long, even with the minimal serrations on the butter knife—the ropes were just thin camping lines, used for hanging food in a tree to keep bears away, shit like that. He rolled over, massaged his wrists, and then untied his ankles.

His feet were all pins and needles, so he hopped and stomped until the blood started to flow again.

Once he felt halfway human he took the phone from his inside pocket and called Nicolette.

"How'd it go?" Nicolette said.

"Pretty much like we expected. She got the drop on me and tied me up, but you were right, her curiosity got the best of her."

"That's Marla all over. Refuses to come when summoned, and refuses to come when she's threatened, but you can count at her to come yell at you for summoning or calling her. Any sense of her ETA?"

"She'll be along. She says she has to go save the world or something first, but I'd expect her at the club in a week or so."

"Saving the world?" Nicolette said. "God, her priorities are so fucking predictable. Come on back to Felport, I guess. If she doesn't show up soon I'm taking it out on you, though." She ended the call.

I wonder what it's like to have a normal job, with vacation time and sick days and shit like that, Crapsey thought. He started walking, stuck out his thumb, and hoped for a passing motorist stupid enough to stop for him and provide him with a vehicle. Marla's admonition not to murder anybody weighed on his mind—she was a death god, so she'd probably know if he disobeyed—but she could hardly complain if he followed her example and left someone tied up on the side of the road.

Bradley in Vegas

"YOU EVER BEEN TO LAS VEGAS BEFORE?" Marla said from the passenger seat as they went by the Welcome to Las Vegas sign, recognizable from scores of movies about people making terrible choices.

Bradley chuckled. "I was in the movies. Vegas is the place where people like that go when Hollywood starts to feel too authentic and down-to-earth."

"I never spent a lot of time here, and I admit it's not my kind of place, but Vegas always struck me as what Rondeau would be like if someone magically transformed him into a city." She sighed. "Him getting kicked out like that, by his own supernatural offspring… it's not right."

Bradley had filled her in on Rondeau's conflict with Regina Queen and the subsequent bad luck with the oracle he'd summoned. Bradley had known Rondeau and Pelham were in trouble—he checked in with the home office occasionally, talking to himself in mirrors, and the Over-Bradley had filled him in—but tracking the Outsider had taken precedence, and he hadn't known Nicolette was going to kidnap them. "I know you want to help Rondeau, but…."

Marla kept staring out the window. "Oh, I know. We've got bigger monsters to kill. Regina Queen came to get revenge on *me*, though, so it's my fault Rondeau's been exiled from his favorite place. I have some familiarity with how that feels. I'm also trying hard to fix my mistakes these days, instead of just moving on to newer and bigger mistakes." She scratched absently at the tattoo on her wrist—the words "Do Better," a message from her goddess-self, etched on her skin. "I'll put off helping Rondeau until after we've dealt with the Outsider, don't worry. But then I'll have a chat with this new Pit Boss about his treatment of his creator. I'll admit I'm tempted to bust this demon's head right now, since we're in town, but I can keep my focus—we'll get my dagger and the rest of my stuff, then head to Santa Cruz."

Bradley nodded. He'd helped Marla search, and her dagger wasn't in the RV, and her motorcycle wasn't hidden under the bed, either. There was about nine thousand dollars in cash wrapped in plastic hidden under the RV's dashboard, so they could have bought new pants and a much crappier vehicle, but the dagger was irreplaceable, and it was the one weapon they could access with relative ease that would almost certainly hurt the Outsider. Her knife had been forged in Hell, and could cut through anything, including ghosts, iron, and memories.

They arrived near Rondeau's hotel, a medium-nice place off the Strip—now part-owned by the oracular demon who'd presumably established himself as the city's new Pit Boss by now. They left the RV illegally parked on a side street, and Bradley waited while Marla drew a simple design on each side to keep cops and thieves from noticing the vehicle, dragging her finger through the Death Valley dust. "I've never seen that keep-away spell before," Bradley said. "It's not the one you taught me—way simpler and more elegant."

She grunted, looking over her handiwork. "There's stuff in my head, now, I'm not always entirely sure how it got there. I'm not supposed to remember any of the stuff about being a goddess when I'm in my mortal form, but sometimes weird stuff bubbles up. Supernatural flotsam."

"I'm feeling pretty estranged from my cosmic wisdom too," Bradley said. "For one thing, I forgot what it's like to be *hungry*. I still eat sometimes, and I can eat anything that exists or *can* exist, which is cool, but it's just for pleasure, not need. What I'm saying is, I'm starving—can we hit a buffet or something?"

"After we get my motorcycle and my knife and my coat. Should all still be in my storage unit."

They went around to the back of the hotel, and Marla magicked open a locked service door and led the way down white-tiled corridors. They found a cargo elevator where she pressed some arcane combination of buttons, smiling at Bradley's raised eyebrow. "There are sub-basements that aren't obviously accessible. Not even wizard shit, I don't think, just skullduggery with blueprints and construction. Old-school gangster shit."

The elevator doors opened on a concrete space broken up by tall metal shelves holding file boxes. They negotiated a few dark corridors until they reached an area filled with steel-doored storage rooms, where Bradley figured long-ago criminals had probably kept cocaine and dead bodies and stolen fur coats. Marla went straight to one door, its ordinary lock supplemented by a heavy padlock that looked like it could stand up to a direct shotgun blast. She hummed over the locks for a minute until the padlock fell open and the doorknob turned in her hand. "There's a cargo elevator over there that leads up to the parking garage, so we can get out that way. We'll make a lot better time going to Santa Cruz on the motorcycle."

"Just don't *drive* like you're immortal," Bradley said. "I'm going to be clinging to your back, and I don't think my over-mind can spare any extra bodies if this one gets all busted up."

"There are anti-crash charms. At least, I think so." She pulled open the storage room door and swore. "Where. The fuck. Is my motorcycle."

A voice of dust and rattling chains said, "The Pit Boss wants to see yous."

"Did you just say 'yous'?" Marla said. "For serious?"

Bradley moved up beside her, looking into the space. No motorcycle in evidence. A suitcase lay sprawled open in the corner, with some of Marla's clothing scattered all over the floor, including a nice long brown leather coat. A figure, who looked like an art student's junk sculpture of a man constructed from wooden boards and bicycle chains and rusty pipes and small appliances, stood in the center of the room.

"Don't make no trouble," the thing said, voice emerging from a mouth that might have started life as a hand-cranked coffee grinder. "The Boss just has a few questions for yous."

"Let me guess," Marla said. "He wants to know why there's a dagger on the shelf over there that nobody can pick up. How about you fuck off and tell him the answer: because it's *mine*."

Bradley craned his neck, and there it was, Marla's familiar dagger, forged in some fiery Hell, blade shining, hilt wrapped in purple and white electrical tape.

"This room belonged to some punk name of Rondeau, and everything that belonged to him belongs to the Pit Boss now. Come on." The creature took a step toward her, its pipe-and-toaster feet ringing on the concrete.

"Look, Bugsy, I'm on a tight schedule here," Marla said. "Tell me where my motorcycle is, and I won't cut you into pieces."

"Think you're some kinda tough broad, huh?" For a golem, it had a lot of personality. "The Boss didn't say you had to walk in on your own two legs. We can do this easy, or we can do this hard."

"Of, for fuck's sake," Marla said. "Who programmed your dialogue?"

She whistled, and the dagger spun from the shelf toward her hand, incidentally passing through the golem's head along the way, taking a chunk of its colander skull and one light bulb eye with it. The blade glittered in her hand, and she stepped forward, making two deft slashes, and sending the golem's pipe-and-chain arms clattering to the floor.

"There," she said. "Did I make my point? I know you don't have a ton of autonomy, being a walking junkheap, but surely you've got some kind of protocol for what to do when you're hopelessly outmatched?"

The golem rather gamely attempted to kick her to death, and once that was done failing spectacularly, there was a mess of broken machine parts on the floor. Marla picked up her long coat and pulled it on, instantly looking at least fifty percent more badass. She sorted through the clothes on the floor, finding a pair of red cowboy boots embroidered with skulls and scythes. "Shut up," she muttered, pulling them on. "They're *comfortable.*"

He grinned. "I'm just impressed you're showing *any* kind of fashion sense. Never expected that from you. It's like a chicken that plays piano. You don't expect the chicken to be good. It's enough that it plays at all."

"Ha ha." She swept the rest of her clothes into the suitcase and thrust it into Bradley's hands. "The silver axe is gone. This new Pit Boss might have it, or Squat might have taken it with him when he ran off with Nicolette. She always felt like it belonged to her, just because she was the person who stole it from the guy who *originally* stole it."

"Craziness. Obviously the proper claim is yours, since you stole it from *her.*"

"Last theft wins," Marla said. "I guess we'd better go see the Pit Boss after all."

Bradley sighed. "We got the knife, you know. And your coat, which I can see is bristling with nifty armor magics."

She shrugged. "Yeah, but I want my motorcycle. It was a gift. I can accept this Pit Boss stealing from Rondeau, or at least back-burner dealing with it, but if he steals from *me*? Don't worry, it won't take long."

Bradley nudged a bit of broken glass with his toe. "If we're going to see the Pit Boss anyway, why chop this thing into pieces? Why not just go with it in the first place?"

"I don't go anywhere under duress. Hell, I'll go to Felport to see Nicolette, assuming we can save the universe first, but I won't go because Crapsey came and *told* me to. You've got to have standards, B. What do you have if you don't have your principles?"

"There is the small difficulty that we don't know where this Pit Boss *is*," Bradley said. "Which the garbage gangster there could have told us."

"True. It's a good thing I travel with an immensely powerful psychic with access to arcane wisdom," Marla said.

Bradley sighed. "Okay. Let's go upstairs. I'll look for an oracle."

A SIMPLE DIVINATION didn't require big magic, and he knew for a fact that Marla could probably do it herself if she got her hands on some old coins and animal bones, but it was easy enough for him to amble along a couple of alleyways until he felt that psychic tug of a nearby oracle. He closed his eyes and concentrated for a moment, and when he looked again, a severed head with grievous gunshot wounds bobbed before him like the world's ugliest balloon.

"I am so sick of talking decapitations," Marla muttered.

"Uh, hi," Bradley said. "I'm wondering where I can find the city's Pit Boss?"

The severed head looked at him for a moment, then said, "He has a secret casino under the city." The head gave directions, which involved going down manholes and walking through sewer tunnels, naturally.

"Thanks," Bradley said. "What do I owe you?"

"Go to the Flamingo Hotel and bet whatever you've got in your pockets on black 13," the head said. "Give any money you make to the Damon Runyon Cancer Research Foundation."

One of the more weirdly specific requests he'd gotten for payment from an oracle, but easy enough to obey. "Consider it done."

The floating head shimmered and vanished.

"Pretty sure that was Bugsy Siegel," Marla said.

"He was… a mob guy, yeah?"

Marla nodded. "Basically the founder of modern Las Vegas. The Flamingo was his casino. Some of his mob buddies put a couple of bullets in his head because he was skimming money from the business. Who knew he had a charitable side?"

"Funny how he wants to give money to a cancer fund. It's not like he *died* of cancer."

"Sure, but there's not a non-profit foundation dedicated to teaching psychopaths to be less greedy. Let's go. We'll stop by the Flamingo so you can fulfill your responsibilities. You don't want the annoyed ghost of Ben Siegel floating around yammering at you because you didn't stick to your bargain. We'll grab a bite to eat, too. You don't brace the Pit Boss in his lair on an empty stomach."

THEY SLIPPED DOWN the appropriate manhole cover without drawing any unwanted attention, and didn't have to spend much time in the darker and squishier bits of the city's underside before they found a door hidden with camouflage magics. Bradley didn't even notice the illusions making the door blend in with the bricks, because they were so transparent to his psychic senses; he only realized the door was disguised when Marla said, "Good eye, I didn't even see that" after he pulled it open. There were no locks, presumably because the Pit Boss welcomed people to his secret casino, provided they were clued-in enough to find it in the first place.

From there, the corridors were more sanitary and well-lit, concrete halls illuminated by the bright white LEDs stuck haphazardly on the walls and ceiling. They eventually reached a door that swung open automatically at their approach, allowing entrance to a plush carpeted lounge. The bartender—another junk golem, this one made mostly of bottles and silverware, so he was at least thematic—nodded something like a head toward them and gestured toward the booths and stools, then toward the wider room beyond, where a variety of gaming tables and apparatuses stood.

The lounge area was entirely deserted, and there were only half a dozen people around the gaming tables. A mostly naked middle-aged man strapped to a huge wooden wheel sobbed quietly as he lazily spun, while four people dressed in everything from guttersnipe rags to fur coats raptly watched his rotations. A junk golem operator stood by the wheel counting stacks of chips. Two other men, wearing sopping tuxedoes, knelt with their hands bound behind their backs plunging their faces into washtubs full of opaque black liquid, emerging with writing, tentacled, clawed things in their teeth, which they spat into smaller buckets at their sides. A golem seemingly made of the remnants of a seafood buffet or aquarium disaster attended them, making occasional tick-marks on a clipboard to tally up... something.

Bradley had no idea how either of those games were played, and no desire to find out either the rules or the stakes.

Marla sidled up to the bar. "Looking for the Pit Boss," she said.

"Mr. Amparan is dead," the bartender rasped through its lemon-zester throat.

"Yeah, that's fine. I'm happy to meet the new boss, different from the old boss. Does he have a name yet?"

"Most people call me 'Yes sir,'" a rumbling voice said. "Come to pay tribute to the new king?"

Marla turned, leaning casually back against the bar, and looked the newcomer up and down. Bradley looked, too, but he wasn't quite as capable of keeping his cool as she was. He'd heard about what happened to Rondeau in the city, but he hadn't *seen* it like the Over-Bradley had, so the molten demon that came strolling across the casino floor was something of a shock. His flesh was mostly black stone, but rivulets of lava flowed here and there on his body, and he stood at least eleven feet tall. Bradley wasn't sure why the carpet didn't burst into flame wherever he stepped, but it was probably just magic.

"I met your predecessor once," Marla said. "He liked to wear pin-striped suits. Diamond stickpin. Ruby pinky ring. Always chomping a cigar. I admired the guy, you know? I have respect for the classics. But… big naked demon guy? I dunno. Lacks subtlety."

"You should know I'm new to this job," the demon said. The players in the casino looked at him nervously, but not as nervously as they *should* have, as far as Bradley was concerned. Then again, you probably had to be a pretty stone-cold type to come gamble in this place anyway. The boss crossed his immense arms over his chest. "Basically, I don't have any sophisticated procedures or mechanisms or flowcharts in place. I just kind of kill people who annoy me. Are you going to annoy me?"

"Oh, almost certainly. My name's Marla Mason."

"Is that supposed to mean something to me?"

"Wow," Bradley said, because he wanted to contribute something. "You *are* new."

"You two would look good if you were reduced to piles of charred carbon, I think." The Pit Boss tilted his head, regarding her like a decorator considering a new set of drapes.

Marla yawned, rubbed the side of her nose, and said, "I'm going to need a couple of things from you. I'd say 'favors,' but that would imply they're something I might have to repay someday, and that's not happening. So maybe we'll call them 'boons.' You'd like that, right? New king, big boss— granting boons is all part of the deal."

"Oh, I give people things," the Pit Boss said. "They just have to *wager* for them, and win."

Marla rolled her eyes. "Ha. Like I'm going to bet with *you*, when you inherited the old boss's stash of luck. No thanks. I know you were born yesterday, or near enough, but I wasn't. Nah, we're going to make a different kind of arrangement. The kind you'll understand."

The creature swelled, the cracks in his body widening, revealing deeper fissures of molten glow. "Oh yeah? What kind is that?"

"Extortion, obviously. Let's go talk in your office. I'd hate to embarrass you in front of your customers."

"What's stopping me from burning you to ashes where you stand?"

Bradley couldn't help it—he squeaked out a laugh. The Pit Boss swung his head, which was now growing something like bull's horns, in Bradley's direction, scowling tectonically. "What's funny?"

"The gulf between what you think you know and what you actually know," Marla said. "You can try to burn me if you want. I know you beat Regina Queen, and hey, that's legitimately badass. But see, you were conjured pretty much to exist in opposition to her. You're like Regina's supernatural antidote. But me… You're not made to match me." She reached out and pressed her palm against his cheek. The sound of sizzling flesh was followed a moment later by a sweet, charred, meaty smell that Bradley didn't find remotely appetizing despite its superficial resemblance to the scent of roast pork. Marla didn't so much as flinch as her hand charred—that kind of stoicism was a formidable trick of the mind, Bradley knew, because she wasn't actually impervious to pain. She drew back the burned lump of her fist and held it in front of Pit Boss, and he actually took a step backward as her flesh healed, flakes of ash falling away as new skin appeared, first pink, then darkening to the same even road-trip tan the rest of her exposed flesh possessed. "Point made," she said. "Let's talk."

"Maybe you can heal, but that won't help if I dip you in concrete and dump you in Lake Mead—"

"B, why does everybody have to push me?" she said. "Don't they know I have better things to do?"

She lashed out, her dagger suddenly in her hand, and in several swift strokes she carved a blocky uppercase letter 'M' into the Pit Boss's molten chest. The streaks of lava he had instead of blood (or lymph, or whatever) tried to flow into the empty spaces, but stopped at the borders of her slashes. The Pit Boss whimpered, and that was strange, because Bradley had never heard a walking volcano whimper before.

"Oh, hey," Marla said. "You recognize this knife, don't you? It's the one you found in Rondeau's storage unit. The dagger you couldn't lift, the one that cut the fingers off anyone you sent when they tried to touch it. And here I am, holding it—the rightful owner."

"You're a friend of Rondeau's," the boss rumbled, rubbing a hand over his scarred chest.

"Oh, yeah. Maybe not his best friend. We've had our ups and downs. But definitely his most *dangerous* friend." She let the point of the dagger drift and weave, making little figure-eights and curves in the air. "I once wrote the first couple of letters of my name on someone's ass with a bullwhip, when he annoyed me," Marla said in a low voice. "You're annoying me worse than he did. Want to continue this in private? If we stay here in front of your employees and customers I'm afraid you'll do something stupid to try and look like a big bad boss man, and then I'd have to write my whole name on you, and maybe Rondeau's, too."

The Pit Boss scowled around the room—the gamblers and human employees were studiously ignoring him, and the golems didn't care anyway—before nodding and walking toward the back of the casino, smoke rising from his body. Maybe that was a sign of irritation, or shame. Reading the body language of demonic tulpas was beyond even Bradley's considerable abilities.

Bradley started to follow, but Marla put a hand on his arm. "Hang out here, all right? I don't think he's smart enough to make real trouble for us, but keep an eye on things, make sure our escape route stays open."

"Sure." Bradley couldn't read minds, at least not without making an effort, but he was plenty intuitive. "But what's the real reason you don't want me in there? You still don't entirely trust me?"

Marla chuckled. "I trust you as much as I trust any living soul, B. But the Pit Boss is the kind of guy who puffs up when he's got an audience, and he's stubborn enough anyway. If I get him alone, with no one for him to impress and no cheap seats for him to play to, I bet he'll be a lot more reasonable."

"Makes sense," he said. "Maybe I'll do a little gambling."

"Just don't bet anything we can't afford to lose." She patted his cheek with her now-unburned hand and went after the Pit Boss, who stood glowering a few feet away, waiting with no pretense of patience.

Bradley skipped the gambling, opting to sit at the bar and sip a caffeine-free cola and look at the long row of bottles reflected in the glass. Sometimes being an addict was a drag. Booze had never even been the problem for him, but booze made stupid ideas seem like good ideas, and he'd learned long ago that, for him, liquor was a door that could easily lead back to heroin. The bartender was no good when it came to conversation, so Bradley tried to empty his mind and feel the vibes of the universe, except the vibes of this particular part of the universe were desperate and squalid and gross.

A pretty young woman in a short red sequined dress and shiny hair the same shade slid onto the stool next to him, turning a practiced and professional smile his way. "Hey there, handsome," she said. "Not in a sporting mood?"

"Not my kind of games."

She put a hand on his thigh. "Oh yeah? What kind of games do you like?"

"Ah. Sorry. Not the kind you play with women."

She tossed her hair, and her features shifted, smoothly changing, becoming no less pretty but decidedly more masculine, the jawline stronger, the chin more pronounced, with just a hint of stubble. The breasts, which had been generous but not shockingly so, receded as her chest and shoulder's broadened. "Sorry about the dress. Unless you like it. I've got other things I could wear, too. We could play dress-up, even."

He looked at her—him—more closely now, and saw blue flames dancing deep behind her eyes. "Whoa," he said. "Are you, what, an incubus? Succubus? Are those just *one* kind of creature, that changes appearance to suit the situation?"

The creature leaned back. "That's a trade secret, handsome. Usually I'm good at reading desires—it sort of comes with the job—but looking into you is like looking into one-way glass, so I took a guess, and guessed wrong."

"I've got some pretty solid psychic armor." Bradley tapped his temple. "It's hell on fortune tellers too, drives them crazy. I'm not in the market for any kind of companionship, though, thanks."

"Ah, well, can't blame me for trying. You're awfully pretty."

"Thanks. If I had gone with you, would you have sucked out my soul?"

"I don't even know what souls are," the creature said.

"Me either," Bradley admitted.

"Your life force, though… well, maybe just a nibble."

The bustle of the casino went silent, and Bradley looked over to see Marla come strolling back from the direction of the Pit Boss's office, whistling "This Old Man." He thought "The Farmer in the Dell" was the more traditional whistlin' ditty for a badass who'd just shown up an enemy, but either way, you couldn't argue with the classics.

"We're good," she said. "We can pick up my motorcycle at—" She stopped dead. "Inky?" she said. "Is that *you*?"

The creature stared at her for a moment and let out a low whistle of his own. "Marla *Mason*?"

She embraced the—Inky?—and Bradley couldn't have been more stunned if she'd leapt up on the bar and started singing the hits of Broadway. She let go of Inky and looked him up and down. "Your taste in fashion has gotten worse."

"You know this… guy?" Bradley said.

"Oh, yeah," Marla said. "We were an item, a million years ago, back in Felport. What, were you trying to hustle Bradley? At least you still have good taste."

The incubus, or succubus, or whatever, looked like someone had hit him over the head with a flowerpot and he was still seeing little cartoon birds circling around. "I didn't think I'd ever see you again." He glanced at Bradley. "When I was with her, *I* was the one who got my life energy sucked out."

"You loved every minute of it," Marla said. "Why are you looking at me like I'm about to cut your head off?"

He cleared his throat. "Ah. You said if you ever saw me again... you'd cut my head off. Also that you'd banish me back to the Hell I came from, and if I didn't actually come from any Hell at all, you'd have a suitable one constructed for me."

Marla nodded. "Oh, yeah, that. Well, you did that thing. You know what you did. But that's all acid under the bridge. Let's forget about it."

"I'd like that," he said. "How, uh. How are things with you? I heard you were running Felport."

"Nah, got exiled. Then... sorta got promoted. Cosmically speaking. Oh, and I got married." She reached into her shirt and took out a necklace, with a simple gold wedding band dangling from it. The only thing she'd been wearing when she woke up from her month in Hell.

Inky blinked at her. "Someone married... I mean, you found someone who... I mean... Congratulations, Marla, really."

She nodded and tucked the ring back out of sight. "Look, we're on a save-the-world sort of timetable, so I can't stay and chat, but it was nice seeing you. Do you spend a lot of time in Vegas? I could maybe find a job for you that's more interesting than lurking in the creepiest casino in town."

Inky brightened. "I... yeah, I'm usually here, uh—"

"Somebody will be in touch. Unless we screw up, and the world ends." She beckoned to Bradley and started to go.

"Wait." Inky touched her arm. "You mean *literally* the end of the world? Not just, uh, not to be rude, but not just the death of humankind or something?"

"Everything that lives and breathes, this time. And everything that doesn't live and breathe. Everything, really."

Inky looked at Bradley, who nodded glumly in confirmation. The creature slouched back against the bar. "Shit," he said after a moment. "Well, if there's anything I can do...."

"You never know," Marla said. "You do have skills I don't, though I don't see how they're immediately applicable. Come on, B."

He followed her out of the casino into the tunnels. "So. You knew that... guy."

"Long ago and far away and not wisely, but pretty well."

"You dated an incubus."

"I wouldn't say we *dated*." She glanced at Bradley and grinned. "Just because I'm a respectable married lady now doesn't mean I was never young and horny and stupid."

"Sure, but he's an incubus who did something bad to you, and now you've forgiven him. No offense, but the forgiveness thing...."

"Respectable. Married. Lady. Forgiveness is one of the things I'm trying to learn. Besides, Inky was just following his nature."

"But... I mean... so does *everything*. Even the Outsider is just... doing what it does."

"I promise if Inky tries to devour the substance of the multiverse I will rescind his forgiveness," Marla said. "And if the Outsider downgrades his mayhem plans to something as mild as secretly fucking alley witches who have supernatural venereal diseases that can cross the species barrier from humans to incubi and back again, I'll take him off the kill list." She shuddered. "Damn, that was itchy. It made my *soul* itchy."

"The incubus was just saying he didn't even know what souls are."

"Then his must not have itched as badly as mine did," Marla said. "Let's go get my motorcycle. We've got places to go and asses to kick."

Bradley groaned. "The thought of clinging to the back of a motorcycle for hours is exhausting, and it'll be late by the time we get to Santa Cruz anyway. I have an alternative proposal. Let's get your motorcycle, then maybe find a nice hotel somewhere and spend the night, and set out for the coast in the morning. We could even take the RV, and get a trailer for the motorcycle. What do you say?"

"I say you're going soft, B. Your job ruling the multiverse is way too cushy. Sleep is for people who don't have magical amphetamines. But it has been a long day since I woke up in the dirt... Okay. But we're getting on the road tomorrow with the dawn."

"Ugh. I guess by your standards that's merciful."

"My greatest weakness," she said, "is that I'm too merciful."

Marzi in a Mood

ONE PROBLEM WITH BEING A LITTLE BIT PSYCHIC was that painkillers didn't do shit to get rid of headaches caused by metaphysical environmental badness. Marzi's threshold for human interaction was so low that she made Tessa do all the work of taking orders while Marzi made the drinks, but at least Tessa had taken note of the boss's mood and wasn't being openly surly. Marzi had snarled at Jonathan that morning badly enough for him to steer clear of her, too, and she felt a little bad about it, but he'd forgive her. He knew something weird was going on. She'd told him about the visit from Bradley Bowman, and after listening quietly his only reply had been, "I knew life wouldn't be boring when I married you, baby."

Marzi was doing inventory in the pantry when her weird-shit sense tingled. She went out to the counter, where Tessa was pretending to clean fingerprints off the pastry case, in time to see Bradley come in with a woman.

She was fairly tall, with short hair, and features that were a little too strong to be called pretty. Something about the way she carried herself made Marzi think of the bikers who came into the café for beer sometimes—some of her best customers, actually. That swagger, that certainty. Plus the fact that she was wearing riding leathers and a leather coat, though instead of a black motorcycle jacket hers was long and deep brown, maybe buffalo leather. She took off her sunglasses and squinted in Marzi's direction, letting out a low whistle. "She's the one," the woman said. "We'll talk in there." She walked off toward the Undersea Room, the one with murals of writhing sea monsters on the walls and panes of blue stained glass in some of the windows.

Bradley came up to the counter. "Hey, Marzi. Got a minute? I want you to meet a friend of mine."

77

"This is the heavy artillery you mentioned?"

"If people were weapons, she'd be an elephant gun. Hell. Maybe one of those guns they have on battleships."

"She drink coffee?"

"You bet," he said.

"I'll bring some in a minute. Herbal tea for you?"

"Like you read my mind."

"That's more your gig, man."

He smiled, that dazzling grin that had charmed moviegoers, and went to the table.

"You've got the helm, Tessa," Marzi said, and the girl grunted, clearly uninterested in her boss's visitors. Marzi got a cup and tea bag for Bradley and poured a big earthenware mug full of good black coffee for his friend.

She found them seated at a table in the corner, underneath the coils of a leviathan. The woman had her back to the wall, facing the entrance, and *that* wasn't a surprise—every cop and soldier and criminal Marzi had ever met did the same thing, and something about this woman made Marzi think she might somehow qualify as all three at once.

She put the drinks down and sat beside Bradley, across from the woman.

"You're Marzi," the stranger said. "My name's Marla. If this were a novel, I'd say the author needed to be a little more inventive with names."

"Reality is such a disappointment," Marzi said.

"Oh, I don't know. It's got its moments."

Marla took a sip of the coffee and grunted. "Pretty good. And I used to drink coffee in Hawaii every morning, so I've got standards."

"I gave you the good stuff," Marzi said. "Blue Bottle."

"The gesture's appreciated." She leaned forward, staring at Marzi's face, her gaze disconcertingly direct. Marzi thought of butterflies pinned down on corkboard; she was the butterfly. "There's something about her, B. What is it?"

"You'll have to be a little more specific, boss."

Marzi twitched a little at that. *Boss*? Was Bradley being ironic, or was she really in charge of him, somehow?

"Something… that *pulls*. Like she's a magnet and I'm, you know, the other magnet. I can't quite describe it. I'm only about one-fifth as gay as you are, B, so I don't think it's that kind of attraction—no offense, Marzi, you're cute and all, but this is something different." Marla inhaled deeply, as if taking in a scent, her eyes closed.

"That's creepy," Marzi said. "You're creepy."

"Sorry." Marla opened her eyes, that pinned-down gaze again. "You've got a light in you. Something gods and monsters can see."

"Marzi's a natural champion," Bradley said. "A little bit psychic. Touch of reweaving ability, probably. And that thing I have, where I… excite supernatural creatures? Help make them *realer*, put flesh on ghosts, make the tenuous more actual? She's got that, too, even more so than me. Reality gets *just* soft enough in her presence that she can twist it to her advantage, too."

"You're a supernatural catalyst, kid," Marla said.

Kid? If this woman was more than two or three years older than her, Marzi would be surprised. "What's that mean?"

Marla shrugged. "There's something in you that supernatural creatures can feed on. Your presence gives them more weight, more strength. You make the world a more wondrous place. Honestly, it's a wonder this place isn't overrun with shapeshifters and psychic vampires and invisible brain-lampreys, all drawn to you. The fact that your café is sitting on a place where reality gets thin *anyway* makes it even more remarkable. I'm surprised you don't have to kick imps off the steps on your way to work every morning."

"I told you she got a tough reputation," Bradley said. "She's the magical champion of Santa Cruz. Defeated a big bad called the Outlaw. Nobody wants to fuck with her."

Apparently I'm badass, Marzi thought. "I don't have a lot of interest in being a champion of anything. I just want this shadowy snake monster to stop eating people outside my front door, and Bradley says you can help me do that."

"Oh, sure," Marla said, like it was no more trouble than helping her get something down from a high shelf. "I'd better go take a look at this room with the door in it."

"I'll show you," Marzi said.

"I'd rather go by myself. You're… distracting."

Marzi wrinkled her nose. "Wait, you said supernatural creatures are drawn to me. Does that mean *you're* supernatural?"

The woman shrugged. "You might say that. A little bit. Some months more than others. It's through the kitchen, Bradley said? Just point me in the right direction."

Marzi rose and they followed her. She pointed behind the counter, toward the storage room beyond the kitchen, and Marla nodded and went inside.

"Can I go on break?" Tessa said.

Marzi glanced at her watch and nodded. "Yeah, sure, I've got it." The girl headed out onto the deck, already deep in her phone, and Marzi took her place by the cash register. She beckoned to Bradley, and he came back there with her. Marzi glanced around the café. It was quiet, middle of a weekday, and though there were a few people camping out at tables and nursing their beverages, nobody demanded her attention. She craned her neck. The door to the storage room was open, and there'd been no screams or thumps of falling bodies, so apparently Marla wasn't as supernaturally over-sensitive as Marzi and Bradley were.

"So what's her superpower?"

"Hmm?" Bradley said.

Marzi lifted her chin toward the storage room. "Her. You can summon oracles, and I'm apparently catnip for monsters or whatever. So what does she do? Shoot fireballs out of her eyes? Hallucinogenic gas breath? Turns her skin into diamonds? Super strength? What?"

"I guess her power is… sheer bloody-mindedness," Bradley said. "She just doesn't know when to quit, so she never does. You know those movies about supernatural psycho killers, the guys who get set on fire and stabbed with machetes and run over by monster trucks, and they *still* get up and keep coming, just pursuing the final girl implacably?" He nodded in Marla's direction. "Now imagine one of those guys is on *your* side."

"I was really hoping you'd say super strength," Marzi said.

"Well, she *does* know martial arts," Bradley said.

"Oh? What kind?"

Marla emerged from the storage room. She was wearing her sunglasses again for some reason. "Screw-you jitsu." She looked Marzi up and down, seemed to catalogue her entirely at a glance, then gave Bradley a grin. "You forgot to mention my amazing sense of humor."

"And your exemplary sense of hearing," he said.

She nodded. "That too." She took her glasses off. "That's some kind of crazy desert behind that door. Brightest sun I've ever seen."

Marzi gaped at her. "You opened the *door*?"

The woman shrugged. "It's this habit I've got. See a magical impossible door, open it up."

"And the padlock I used to seal it shut?" Marzi said.

"Yeah. That. I owe you a new padlock."

Marzi frowned. "You hiding a set of bolt cutters under that coat?"

"Nah. I've got a dagger that can cut through anything." She rubbed her hands together. "Okay, B. You start figuring out how we're going to lure the Outsider into a trap. And you and me, Marzi, are going to make sure the trap is strong enough to hold him."

"How are we going to do that?"

"Well, when I looked through the door, this giant scorpion monster was in there looking *back* at me," Marla said, "so I figure we should talk things over with her, don't you think?"

Pelham Imprisoned

"**Nice of them to let us share a cell.**" Pelham sniffed at some kind of thin, bone-dry wheat cracker before putting it back down on the tray uneaten. Their evening meal was hard sumptuous.

"Stupid of them, you mean." Rondeau paced back in forth in front of the large (but barred on the outside and covered with a metal grate on the inside) window.

"Oh?" The room where they were being held in was in some respects quite nice, an airy bedroom with high ceilings and its own ancient but serviceable toilet, pedestal sink, and clawfoot bathtub in the attached bathroom, but as a whole it was rather dusty and Spartan. Pelham sat on a battered green velvet armchair, probably dragged up from the great old house's basement storage. The only other furniture in the room was a milk crate for a table, a set of wood-framed bunk beds, and a vinyl chaise longue, the kind where the back and foot portions could be folded up and down and locked in place, like you might find next to a swimming pool at a motel. There were rather more prisoners in the house right now than ever before, and the furnishings were becoming a bit haphazard as a result. "Do you have some plan to use our combined powers to escape?"

Rondeau stopped pacing and looked out the window. Pelham knew that vantage provided a view of grass and, in exciting moments, the occasional cow. The Blackwing Institute was in the middle of nowhere, and for good reason. Rondeau sighed. "No, it just sounded like a defiant thing to say. Get a little bravado going, you know."

"It's a shame you can't summon an oracle," Pelham said.

"Leaving aside how well that worked the *last* time, I do keep trying, but no dice. There's nothing *here*. I've never been someplace so absolutely neutral, magically speaking."

"I suppose that's considered a feature in a place like this," Pelham said.

"Keeping people like *me* locked up is the Blackwing Institute's whole reason for being. They managed to keep Elsie Jarrow confined until Dr. Husch went crazy and let her out, so preventing me from getting overly psychic is easy enough for them, I guess. I had some hope when they first locked us up here, knowing how Jarrow destroyed all the magical binding spells in the mansion, but that just left a clean slate when the new boss came in, so he could put his own security protocols in place."

"I thought Dr. Langford was a friend of yours?"

Rondeau flopped down on the chaise longue. "He never used to call himself 'doctor,' he was just Langford, the bio-mancer, mad-scientist-for-hire. I think the 'doctor' thing is an affectation, or maybe he figures since he's technically running a hospital for criminally insane sorcerers, the title comes with the job, the way all you gotta do to be a captain is own your own *boat*. And, sure, me and him were friendly, as friendly as you can be with a guy who looks at everybody in the world like they're something smeared on a slide and put under a microscope. But at the same time, I always kinda felt like he wanted to vivisect me to find out how I work. He used to talk about how I was unprecedented and one-of-a-kind and stuff, a rare psychic parasite, a mystery of science and magic. I think the only reason I've been spared a turn on his lab table is because Nicolette wants us alive for some reason."

"Mrs. Mason is awake by now," Pelham said.

Rondeau nodded. The two of them hadn't talked about Marla much. Rondeau seemed reluctant to talk about it now.

"She will come for us, don't you think?" Pelham said.

"Probably? Eventually? But there's that thing that escaped from Death Valley and killed all her cultists… she might be more concerned about dealing with that than dealing with Nicolette. You know how she is when it comes to priorities, and she's been a lot less… personable… since she became a goddess."

"She does have a great many responsibilities now," Pelham said loyally. "Perhaps she expects us to save ourselves."

"It's a good idea," Rondeau said. "Hey, I've got a brilliant idea, can't miss. How about the next time a homunculus orderly comes in to bring us our food, we hit him with something heavy and steal his keys and run away?"

Pelham suppressed a sigh. That had been his suggestion, two days previous. When they tried it, the homunculus had just looked at them, put down their dinner tray, and walked away. Artificial life forms were, apparently, impervious to being rendered unconscious by blows to the head. "There's no reason to be nasty, Rondeau."

"Yeah. Sorry. I'm just getting a little stir-crazy. Being locked up isn't really my thing. I'm more of the free and uninhibited type."

The door swung open, and Pelham and Rondeau exchanged a glance, because they'd already gotten their meal trays, and they weren't exactly getting visitors on a regular basis. Squat walked in first, dressed in layers of scarves and coats, looking like some kind of thrift-store-golem. Crapsey sauntered in after him, wearing an impeccable dark blue suit with a red tie and pocket square. Crapsey kicked the door shut behind him and beamed, hands shoved deep in his pocket, the copper inlays on his wooden prosthetic jaw gleaming in the light. "Hey, fellas. Just thought we'd drop by and see how you're holding up."

"We've got the Stockholm Syndrome real bad," Rondeau said. "I'm coming to identify way too much with my captors. Just looking at you, Crapsey, I swear, sometimes it's like looking in a mirror."

"You guys know I saw your girl, right?" Crapsey said. "Yesterday. I just flew into town this morning, actually—Marla's hell on a guy's travel plans. She was pretty foul, crawling out of the ground like that. I told her Nicolette had you guys all trussed up, that she probably torturing you and stuff, and Marla just said, 'Who cares, they're morons, fuck 'em.'"

"Yeah, that sounds like Marla," Rondeau said blandly. "What's up, Squat?"

The immense toadlike figure shrugged beneath his layers.

Pelham chose to ignore them both, though the breach of etiquette pained him. There was no point being polite, though. Crapsey was an unhinged lunatic, but Squat was worse. He had once been loyal to Mrs. Mason, and betrayed her, and disloyalty was one thing Pelham couldn't stand.

Squat looked at him and sighed. "Hey, Pelly. I'm sorry about… all this. You guys, you're okay. You're just on the wrong side this time."

"Yeah, Pelham's all right," Crapsey said. "Rondeau can eat dog shit and die for all I care, but I've got nothing against Pelham. Which is why he gets to leave the room for a while. You wanna take him, Squat?"

"Sure thing." Squat beckoned, and Pelham hesitated only a moment before nodding and following him toward the door. The man possessed inhuman strength and durability, had a tendency to sweat neurotoxins, and sometimes literally ate his enemies, but who knows? Perhaps Pelham would find an opportunity to escape.

"Where are we going?" Pelham said, as they walked down the hallway. He glanced at the closed doors they passed, wondering who was locked up behind them. The Blackwing Institute had once held only a few profoundly damaged souls, sorcerers who had gone mad and become a danger to themselves, and others, and the fabric of reality, but Pelham had the impression it was more of a prison for Nicolette's enemies and political prisoners, now.

"An old friend of yours heard you were locked up here and asked if you could sit down for a visit. Me and Crapsey said you could, if she'd do us a favor or two, and she agreed. She held up her end, so here we are."

Squat took an elaborate key ring from his pocket, opened up a door, and ushered Pelham inside.

This room was rather more lushly appointed than his own, with a four-poster bed, an elaborately carved wooden wardrobe, a vanity dresser, and other amenities of the antique furniture variety. A woman dressed in a shimmering gown of golden silk sat at the vanity, gazing into the mirror. She turned and smiled, and Pelham's insides wobbled. She was as beautiful as ever, her skin dark brown and perfectly smooth, her eyes large and compassionate, her lips touched with the barest suggestion of a smile. She inclined her head toward Squat. "Leave us, please."

"Ten minutes, yer majesty," Squat said, and shut the door behind him when he went.

"Chamberlain," Pelham said. "I did not realize you were here. Though I should have assumed you would be imprisoned, or else dead."

"I've never been a great believer in the efficacy of dying for a cause," she said. "Much better to live for it. Nicolette may have deposed me as chief sorcerer of Felport, but she is a chaos witch—her destruction and downfall are inevitable, built into the very nature of her power. She can't rule a city any more than someone could build a tower on quicksand."

"How did she manage to take over?" Pelham said. "And so quickly?"

"The element of surprise helped. As did her apparent invulnerability—she simply won't *die*. Her new lieutenant, Squat, seems to be similarly indestructible, and quite content to murder whomever Nicolette requires. By the time we realized what a threat she was, it was difficult to mount an effective defense, especially since many had sided with her." She sneered. "Sorcerers are too often pragmatists, concerned more with being on the winning side than the right one." She beckoned to Pelham. "We don't have much time—I need your help."

Pelham had grown up under the Chamberlain's tutelage, his family having served the founding families of Felport for generations, with the

Chamberlain as the steward of those powerful ghosts. Though Pelham served Marla Mason, now, the habit of obedience toward this woman was long ingrained. "What can I do for you? I fear I am as much a prisoner as you are."

"Magic is at a premium around here," the Chamberlain said. "Strictly controlled and hard to come by. I need some of your blood."

Pelham blinked at her. "Ah?"

The Chamberlain drew a long pin from her hair. "Just hold out your fingertip. Your childhood among the ghosts of Felport's founders, and the binding spells that joined your family line to theirs, imbued you with a certain amount of their magic. My connection with the ghosts has been severed, and with it most of my power, but I can use a bit of your blood, with its whisper of associations, to power a small spell or two. I need to see what my enemy is doing. If I can divine something of Nicolette's plans, perhaps I can take steps, even from here, to hasten her inevitable downfall."

Pelham obediently held out his finger, and the Chamberlain pricked it with the needle, then grasped his wrist and pulled him toward the vanity. She pressed his bleeding finger against the glass and dragged it down, drawing a ragged oval around the circumference of the mirror's surface. Once the circle was closed, Pelham felt a jolt, like he'd bitten down on tinfoil, and she released his hand. He sucked on the wound and watched as the glass inside the line of blood darkened, changed texture to something like velvet, and then revealed a scene:

Nicolette was there, no longer just a head in a cage, but attached to a woman's body, rather taller and more statuesque than her original form had been. Pelham wondered who'd died to provide her with new flesh. Hamil was there, too, looking exhausted, slumped over a table where a vast map of Felport was unrolled.

Nicolette spoke, but there was no sound from the mirror. "I wonder what she's saying?" Pelham said.

"Shh, I'm reading her lips," the Chamberlain said.

A moment later, in the most unladylike act Pelham had ever seen from his old employer, the Chamberlain shouted. "*Shit fuck no!*" and punched the mirror, shattering the image into shards.

"Oh dear." Pelham started picking up the bits of broken glass. "I assume she was saying something bothersome, then?"

Marzi in the Medicine Lands

THE STORAGE ROOM STILL SMELLED OF MOLD and dust, which wasn't pleasant, but at least it didn't smell of rattlesnake skin and burning sand. Marzi wore a broad-brimmed sunhat, a tank top, jeans, and hiking boots, and she'd slathered herself with sunscreen, because who knew what kind of carcinogenic rays an imaginary sun in an impossible desert pumped out? She also had her toy cap pistol tucked into her belt, feeling a bit silly about it, but The Stranger just nodded approvingly. "It's good to go armed."

"Sure, but you've got a magical dagger. I've got a plastic revolver."

"So maybe stand behind me, then," the Stranger said. She wore her long buffalo leather coat and a beat-up, soft brown cowboy hat Bradley had fetched from a thrift store. Her cowboy boots were elaborately patterned with skulls and crossbones and wings and scythes. The Stranger nodded her head toward Marzi's weapon. "Anyway, I hear that gun of yours is real enough when it needs to be. That's how magic is, sometimes. The metaphorical becomes literal. Just recently I heard about a woman who got shoved into an imaginary volcano that turned into a real one for a while."

Marzi blinked. "That's awful."

"Eh. She was a narcissistic mass murderer, so I don't mind. Shame she didn't die, though." The Stranger turned her head and spat onto the floorboards, and a look of utter shock flashed across her features. "I—whoa. I'm sorry. I don't usually go around spitting inside people's workplaces, at least, not unless I'm trying to prove a point. I don't know what came over me."

"Oh," Marzi said. "I think, ah… that's probably my fault."

The Stranger seemed to mull that over. "Explain."

"Well, see, I know your name is Marla Mason, but that's now how I'm *thinking* of you, if that makes sense. In my head, I keep thinking of you as the Stranger."

"That sounds... capitalized," the Stranger said.

"Oh, yeah. My brain is working in full-on archetype mode. You came in with that long coat and the shades and the blade and the boots, and Bradley was talking about how badass you are, and I got to thinking about who you'd be if I put you in my comic, *The Strange Adventures of Rangergirl*. You'd be the Stranger, the woman with no name, who rides into town to clean up the place, lays down a hellstorm of lead and thunder, and then rides out again."

Marla grunted. "I reckon that's a fair approximation of my modus operandi." She wrinkled her nose. "Did I just say 'reckon'?"

"Yup. It's like Bradley said, I guess. Reality gets a little bit soft around me, not all the time, but at times like *this*, when this door in the wall appears, and the lines between what's possible and impossible start to fuzz out. The last time my mind got all aggressive with the capitalization, I turned a formless spirit of earthquake and wildfire and mudslides into an Old West gunslinger, and we called him the Outlaw. Which worked out well, in a way, because it's hard to fight a formless primordial monster, but when it comes to fighting an Outlaw, you can stab him or shoot him or hogtie him and run him out of town on a rail."

"You turned the earthquake god into something more human," the Stranger said. "And now you're turning me into something *more* than human, the archetype of some kind of Old West avenger?"

Marzi spread her hands. "It's not like I do it on purpose, but yeah, at a guess. I'm pretty sure you're about two inches taller than you were when you came into the café, and you might say reckon occasionally, and spit more than you'd like, and generally be kind of laconic. But I bet you'll also be just about unkillable, and a dead shot with a pistol or long gun. I think the effect will wear off when you're not right next to me, if it's any consolation."

"Reweavers," the Stranger said. "We're just putty in your hands, ain't we? But if your minor transformation gives me an edge I need, I'll take it. All right, then. Let's saddle up and ride. Metaphorically. I don't do horses."

Marzi put her hand on the doorknob. "I've been to this place before. I can be the guide."

"Marzipan Psychopompos."

Marzi snorted. "I don't think it's exactly the land of the dead over there."

"Sure ain't," the Stranger said. "I mostly just wanted to prove I was still capable of making jokes in mangled Greek, even with this coating of trail dust you've laid on me."

"I think I just highlight what's already there, inside you. Maybe refract it through a different prism. Run it through a filter."

"Talk's cheap, partner." The Stranger almost seemed to be enjoying herself, but in an undemonstrative—and, yes, laconic—sort of way. "We deal in magic."

Marzi turned the brass knob, warm as a sun-drenched stone at noon, and opened the door into another place.

They stood for a moment, squinting into the impossible vastness beyond, where white sand dunes rolled endlessly, incongruously topped by cartoonish saguaro cactuses. "It's the desert that's all deserts," Marzi said.

"Should make a fair prison, then."

"You sure you don't want Bradley to come with us? He's a stronger psychic than I am—I'm still getting used to the idea that magic is partly something inside me, and not just something that *happens* to me."

"Bradley has a way of exciting supernatural creatures, sort of like you do, but without the touch of reweaving you have to shape them to fit your expectations. Taking him into a place like this? I worry he'd supercharge the horrors. Besides, he passed out last time he moseyed this way. Sometimes he's too sensitive for his own good. Reckon we'd best go on in."

Marzi stepped through the door, and the heat hit her like a falling boulder, dry and immense. The place felt absolutely *real*, the sand gritty under her feet, the breeze hot and arid, the sun—yellow as an egg yolk, seemingly smeared halfway across the crown of the sky—if anything brighter and more vibrant than the one in the real world.

The Stranger followed, looking around. "I thought Arizona in the summer was hot. So this is... what do you call this place, anyway?"

"I'm not really sure," Marzi said. "I knew a guy who called it the Medicine Lands, but now that I think about it, maybe that's kind of racist. It's not like he was a Native American. Isn't that some kind of magical cultural appropriation?"

"Sure," the Stranger said. "Lots of practitioners get pissed about people stomping in and laying claim to their traditions, and who can blame them? Back in Hawaii I met this haole dude who tried to use the native magic for his own ends, wanted to be the big white magician and show the locals how it was done. He ended up getting eaten by shark gods, and good riddance. That kind of rudeness isn't even necessary. You can make golems, or things that might as well be called golems, even if you're not a rabbinical scholar. You can summon animal spirits without being one of the First People, though I'm not convinced you get the same ones. I've discovered over the years that magic is sort of like… a soup in a great big pot. Some people dip into that pot with battered tin ladles, and some use silver spoons, and some use their bare hands, and some use teacups—but whatever tool you use, it's all the same soup. Those different traditions are just different ways of engaging with the same, what do you call 'em, fundamental central mysteries. That being the case, there's no reason to go and piss all over somebody's sacred rites, is there? Use your own—and if you don't have your own, make something new up. The guy who popularized modern Wicca was a real low-down scoundrel in a lot of ways, but he said one thing I like: 'Magic is the art of getting results.'"

She gestured around the desert. "So whether you call this the Medicine Lands, or the Dreamtime, or the Unformed Lands, or the Fields Beyond the Fields, or the crawlspace of the world, it's all the same place… just seen through different filters. And being the kind of place it is, shaped a bit by expectations, the thing you call it probably affects the way it appears." She shrugged. "Nobody never said magic was simple. The numinous don't give itself up easy."

The Stranger turned and looked at the door. "Like this thing, for instance." She walked around the free-standing door frame. Marzi's brain expected to see her appear on the other side of the open door, but of course, she didn't.

The Stranger reappeared. "Pitch black, on the other side, and when I say pitch, I mean it's *tarry*, like blackstrap molasses, something you could get stuck in. That sticky void makes me a mite uncomfortable. Any reason we shouldn't close this door?"

"Apart from the stark existential terror of being cut off from reality as we know it? I don't think so. Even if we can't get the door open for some reason, Bradley's on the other side to let us out. Assuming he doesn't faint again."

The Stranger pulled the door closed, then went back around to the far side. "Huh. Just wood now. Looks like just the other side of the door. Wonder what happens if I open it from *this* side? Wonder where it goes then? Back home—or elsewhere?"

"Let's save the metaphysical exploration for another day, maybe?" Marzi put her hand on the knob—on the *right* side of the door—and twisted, and was gratified when the door opened for her easily. She pulled it closed again. There were things wandering the desert, and while she was pretty sure they couldn't open the door as easily as she did, leaving a portal to her reality standing wide open was a whole different thing. No telling what might saunter through.

"Hmm," the Stranger said. "No big angry bug waiting just inside the door this time."

"We've come as penitents, seeking a boon, so we've got to walk a bit before we get anywhere, I guess," Marzi said.

"Suits me fine." The Stranger sauntered in the direction of the nearest dune.

Marzi hurried to keep up with her long-legged strides. "Do you know where you're going?"

"Don't imagine it matters much. Nothing 'round here has any true physical position anyway. This isn't a real geography, with tectonic plates and geological strata and glacier-scraped valleys. It's more like a mindscape. Whichever direction we pick will be the right one—or the wrong one, if whatever's in charge over here doesn't want to see us. But I imagine it's curious. I would be."

They crested a dune, and down below them stretched a sandy valley. Half-submerged pyramids dotted the valley floor, their pointed peaks rising from drifts of blowing sand. Black dots began to pour forth from the base of the largest pyramid, looking like ants, at first, until the sense of perspective shifted for Marzi and she realized they were human-sized.

"Those look like cynocephalics," the Stranger said. She spat into the sand. "Fellas with the heads of dogs, I mean."

"Your eyes are better than mine," Marzi said. "But if they look like they have dog heads… they're probably jackal-men. Like the Egyptian god of death. I've seen things like them before. They're not nice." Her hand went to the cap pistol at her belt. Even if the gun shot something like real bullets here, would it shoot *enough* of them, and was she quick enough on the draw?

"Ha. I'm'a have a parley." Before Marzi could object, the Stranger was skidding down the side of the dune on her heels, somehow not losing her balance. She slid to a stop at the bottom and walked toward the approaching jackal-men, waving her hat over her head to get their attention, as if they weren't already keenly aware of the intruders.

Half a dozen of the jackal-men dropped to all fours and began to lope toward the Stranger, snarling.

The Stranger shouted "Bad doggies!" and the jackals slowed, exchanging glances, before approaching more slowly, spreading out to flank her. Marzi raised her gun, prepared to pick off any who came for her or tried to take the Stranger from behind.

But the Stranger was talking, voice low, just murmurs reaching Marzi's ears, fragments of sound without substance. Was that something about "Hell?" And about "barks" and "bites" and "dog food?"

After a few moments, the jackal-men slunk away, tails literally between their legs, rejoining the others at the base of the pyramid. A few of them cast looks toward the Stranger, but eventually they all filed back into the pyramid buried in the sand.

The Stranger called, "Are you comin'? The place we want is the next valley over, supposedly."

Marzi made her way down the dune more slowly than the Stranger had, but even so she slipped halfway down and ended up sledding on her butt through soft sand the rest of the way. She stood up, brushing burning grains from her ass, and joined the Stranger. "What the hell did you *say* to them?"

"Jackals are pack animals. They respect hierarchies. I just let them understand I was at the top of *theirs*, and that you were under my protection. Once I made it clear they couldn't eat our flesh or harry our souls into the darkness, they were happy to give me directions. Or, if not happy, happier than they would have been if'n they'd refused me."

Marzi shook her head. "I thought they were going to tear you to pieces."

"Oh, they might've *tried*, but I've kicked hellhounds before. They don't scare me much. This way." She walked across the impossible valley toward another dune, which shifted as they watched and transformed into a rocky ridge, dotted with low brush. The Stranger didn't even blink. Was her unflappability a quality Marzi's presence was bestowing on her, or was the woman *always* this confident? From what Bradley had said about her, it might just be the latter.

They climbed up the rocks, scree shifting under their boots, but Marzi didn't lose her footing this time, and of course the Stranger might as well have been walking on a paved street. They topped the rise, and instead of another valley, they beheld a plateau: a high-desert steppe scattered with house-sized boulders. One of those boulders, in the distance, was more palace-sized, and appeared to have doors, windows, and pillars, all worn by the passage of time, but still recognizable. "Reckon that's the place," the Stranger said. "The high and mighty do like to put on airs."

"If we're going to see the scorpion oracle, that makes sense. When I talked to her before, in my dreams, she had a decaying palace for her lair. I think it's a 'look upon my works, ye mighty, and despair' sort of vibe—life continuing in a place that's been abandoned."

"I can't criticize. I've got a throne room, myself, back home. Sometimes it just goes with the job."

Why do you have a throne room? Marzi wanted to ask, but before she could, the Stranger pointed. "Shitfire. Look. A sphinx."

Something the size of an elephant, but with the contours of a lion, emerged from the shadow of a boulder halfway between them and the palace. The beast had a human head, bald and gleaming, its placid and unremarkable face nonetheless horrible because it was so huge, and because of the body it was attached to.

"Androsphinx," Marla said. "Shame. I like criosphinxes better. They don't *talk* as much."

"Doesn't *anything* surprise you?" Marzi asked.

"I reckon a few things might. Certain fools I know not acting like fools for once, maybe. But, no, not many things. Live long enough and you'll see most everything at least once. A sphinx is usually a guardian. Probably a trial we have to pass before we can talk to your big mama scorpion. Boring, but there it is."

"You can't just scare it off, like you did the jackals?" Marzi said.

"Never met a sphinx that scared easy. They're too sure they're the very tippy-top of the food chain to get scared. Overburdened with confidence, that's your average sphinx."

They walked toward the beast, Marzi happy to let the Stranger take the lead. As they approached, the air wafted the scent of the creature toward her, a bizarre mélange: part the cat-piss-and-blood smell of the lion pit at a cheap zoo, part the dust of ancient books.

"Welcome, visitors." The sphinx's voice was smooth and cultured, and Marzi thought automatically of a city-slicker dandy in a saloon, all impeccable black suit with silver buttons, an oiled mustache, and a gold watch chain across his vest. For an instant an oversized mustache flickered on the sphinx's face, but it disappeared and didn't return. Marzi was fighting someone *else's* conception of what this creature should be—probably the scorpion oracle who ruled this place.

"What business have you here?" The sphinx settled down on its immense front paws to look them level in their faces.

"We're here to speak to the creature denned up in yonder palace." The Stranger made a face. "Yonder? Really?"

"Sorry," Marzi said. "Blame my subconscious."

"Before you can have an audience with *her*," the sphinx said, "you must get past *me*."

"Move aside, then," the Stranger said. "Much obliged."

"Alas, it is not so simple. You have three choices. You may answer my riddle correctly, and be allowed to pass. You may answer it incorrectly, and be devoured. Or you may leave now."

"Reckon there's a third option. Dead sphinges don't ask riddles."

The sphinx purred, a sound a bit like a passing locomotive. "You got the plural right. No one ever gets the plural right anymore."

"What, they say sphinxes? Hell. It's just like 'phalanx' and 'phalanges,'" the Stranger said. "I hope my display of grammatical prowess didn't cause you to overlook the threat I was making, though."

"I heard it. I just wasn't threatened. Are you ready for the riddle?"

"Why not?" Marzi said. "Maybe we'll know the answer. And if we don't, there's always... the other way."

"I don't believe in letting cats set the terms of any situation, even if they do have the heads of giant babies, but fine, we'll try it."

"How marvelous." The sphinx smiled without opening its lips. "Here's the riddle: At night they come without being fetched, and by day they are lost without being stolen. What are they?"

"No clue," the Stranger said. "Stupidest damn question I've heard in all my born days."

"How delightful! You look delicious." The sphinx opened its mouth, and its teeth weren't human at all, or catlike, either: just row upon row of sharklike fangs.

The Stranger drew her dagger and flung it directly at the sphinx's face, and Marzi gasped. The throw looked unerringly true, aimed to take the monster right in the left eye, and the woman had made some big boasts about the power of her blade.

But the sphinx twitched aside at just the right moment, and swallowed the dagger whole instead. Then it smiled, open-mouthed, showing closed ranks of fangs. "What an unusual amuse bouche. Now for the first course."

Bradley in Trouble

BRADLEY DIDN'T HAVE A LOT OF FORMAL TRAINING in magic. He'd fumbled along, coping with his psychic powers as best he could, doing things by instinct, trying to help people, with results that ranged from mixed to disastrous. Later he'd worked for Sanford Cole, learning the arts of divination and some protective magic, and finally he'd served a brief (and lethal, in most timelines) apprenticeship under Marla Mason, where he'd mostly learned that stubbornness was practically a magical specialty on its own.

When Marla said he was supposed to figure out how the lure the Outsider into a trap, he couldn't bring himself to say, "I have no idea how to do that." He would have been more comfortable going into the land beyond the door, even though mere proximity to that soft spot in the skin of reality had knocked him unconscious not so long ago. Catching monsters was more Marla's sort of thing. There were versions of Bradley who'd been more attuned to violence and treachery and hunting things that howled in the night, but not this one, and he didn't have access to his whole panoply of memories from the multiverse just now.

So he did what he usually did when he couldn't figure out what the hell to do: he went looking for an oracle to summon. He'd called up a few oracles to try to locate the Outsider during his quest, without much luck—it seemed to frustrate divination spells somehow. Asking how to *lure* the thing was a different question, though, and might lead to a better answer.

Bradley didn't want to hunt oracles so close to the café, though, because who knew what kind of weird interference effects summoning magic could have in the vicinity of that impossible door, even if there was an oracle handy? What if he summoned the very creature Marla and Marzi had gone through the door to call up themselves? Better to wander a bit father afield.

As he walked along the banks of the San Lorenzo river where it cut through downtown, looking for that tingle that indicated the presence of the supernatural (or a place that boosted his latent psychic powers, or *whatever* happened when he called up an oracle), he thought about Rondeau's disastrous oracle mishap with the Pit Boss. He'd called up something weird and then let it *out*, allowed it to have real agency. How did that even work? What kept the Pit Boss alive? Was it feeding, to some extent, on Rondeau's psychic energy even now—a parasite on a parasite? Or had the Pit Boss attained full independence?

The demon wouldn't have gotten loose on Bradley's watch, but then, Rondeau didn't have Bradley's experience, or even his instinctive grasp of how the secret systems of the world worked. Rondeau was, in a way, crippled by his fundamental optimism: despite the bad stuff that had happened to him, Rondeau was still inclined to believe that, by and large, over a long enough timeline, stuff would work out for the best.

Bradley, on the other hand, despite being outwardly a cheerful guy, was more doubtful at his core. That probably came from screwing up a movie career, being an addict, losing his lover to an overdose, and being murdered and having his body stolen by a psychic parasite in a countable-but-large number of branches of the multiverse.

If an oracle had said to Bradley, "Hey, I'll do you a favor, and tell you what it costs you later," Bradley wouldn't have taken the deal—he would have just laughed, because everything *always* costs more than you thought it would. Some part of Bradley was always waiting for the next blow to fall. He didn't even feel comfortable in his fully-integrated self as watcher over the multiverse, despite being, in theory, immortal and unassailable. After all, he'd had a predecessor, the Possible Witch, and she wasn't around anymore. (In her case, the cause of her demise was something like suicide, but still.)

Bradley figured there was a decent chance the Outsider would kill him and eat him, if he managed to lure it at all. His death wouldn't be that big a blow to the over-Bradley—not much worse than getting a fingernail torn off, or maybe even a hair yanked out—but that didn't stop him from feeling a twinge about the potential loss of his own personal perspective. An oracle was his best shot to find out how to summon the Outsider without dying in the process.

Over the years he'd discerned *some* patterns in the placement of oracles. They tended to show up in wild places, and even more so in liminal places where the wild and the civilized met, mingled, and overlapped. Old things were more likely to house oracles than new things, but he'd summoned one from a brand new toaster once, so it wasn't a hard-and-fast rule. Strolling along the river wasn't finding him much, though, not a single naiad or kelpie, so when he found a path leading up from the bank back toward downtown, he took it.

Pacific Avenue that afternoon was bustling with tourists and locals and street performers, and Bradley took a few (slightly guilty) moments to just enjoy the feeling of being a human among other humans, walking past cute shops and cute boys, crusty punk panhandlers, a guy sitting on a plastic milk crate selling bespoke poetry, a man in heavy make-up and a shiny silver track suit shuffling along one mincing step at a time with a parasol over his head (performance artist or local eccentric?), a pretty girl with a tangle of tiny dogs straining at a bundle of leashes while she talked on her phone. Man, humans were great. He could forget that, overseeing the whole multiverse. Maybe he should bud off bits of himself and send them on field trips more often. Or maybe that was just the kind of addle-brained nonsense you got when bits of your godhead started thinking of themselves as individual humans again.

Bradley wasn't getting so much as a tingle of supernatural manifestation, and he thought maybe he should go into Bookshop Santa Cruz and ask if they had any copies of *Extradimensional Monsters and How to Attract Them*, since that could hardly be any *less* effective than what he was doing now.

An eerie warbling sound started up behind him, and he turned, looking for the source. There was a statue of an old man in a derby hat sitting on a bench and playing a musical saw, and if he'd been an *actual* man, that would be a plausible explanation for the sound, but statues of musicians didn't traditionally make a lot of noise. Bradley grabbed the arm of a bearded man walking by and said, "Hey, do you hear that statue playing music? Or, wait, do you even *see* a statue there?"

The man was wearing a t-shirt that said "KEEP SANTA CRUZ WEIRD" but apparently his personal tolerance for weirdness was lower because he widened his eyes, pulled free of Bradley's grip, and hurried away.

"Yeah, man, that's a statue of Tom Scribner." The speaker, seated on a low stone wall bordering an ornamental flowerbed beside the street, wore a sort of hemp poncho and was openly smoking a joint. "He used to play the musical saw around here back in the '70s, my mom used to see him around. He was, like, a street philosopher, you know?"

The man scratched his head. "You hear him playing the saw *right now*?"

Bradley listened, and it was still there, a mournful, every-shifting tonal drone. "I think so."

"Did you get whatever you're on locally? I've been looking for a new connect, it's hard to find psychedelics other than molly lately."

"I'm not on drugs," Bradley said apologetically.

"So this is more of a psychotic break sort of thing." The guy nodded, wet his fingers, pinched the end of the joint, tucked it away in a pocket, and stood up. "Take care of yourself." He walked away, only slightly less hurriedly than the bearded guy.

Bradley sat down next to the life-sized statue of Tom Scribner. He had the urge to put a companionable arm around old Tom's shoulders. This would be *two* oracles that had taken the form of ghosts since he'd arrived on Earth. He wondered if that meant something? He glanced around, wondering if the sight of a man talking to a statue would be strange enough to warrant a second glance from passers-by. Probably not, if he refrained from grabbing people as they went past.

"So... Mr. Scribner? Can you help me out?"

The voice that answered was not human, but made words out of the warbling of the saw. *I am not Tom Scribner... but the spirit of his saw....*

Bradley blinked. That was a new one. In Japanese mythology there were stories of objects attaining life and sentience, usually after they'd been around for a century or so, but if Scribner had played the saw here in the '70s, it probably wasn't *that* old. What were the odds that he'd only had one saw he played out here, anyway? And what did that matter when this was a *statue* of a saw anyway?

Like logic had anything to do with it. "Ah. Nice to meet you. I have a question."

I know.

Hearing words emerge from the constant warbling was strange, and it was frankly starting to give him a headache, but at least the oracle seemed friendly. "What will it cost me to get an answer from you?"

Sit here for an hour... talk to people... tell them stories... guide them....

Bradley winced. How time-sensitive was this monster-summoning assignment? There was no telling how long M and M would be in the land beyond the door, really. Or maybe they were back already. Then again, going looking for *another* oracle would be time-consuming and possibly fruitless—the few times he'd passed up an oracle, he'd often been unable to find another one anywhere in the vicinity. "All right. I don't know if anyone will want to talk to me, but sure, I'll do my best. So: how do I attract the Outsider?"

It is attracted to power. As your power is great, to call the beast you need only be yourself... but amplified. Draw a symbol of attraction on the floor.

Sit in its center. Light four candles, and place them at the cardinal points of the compass. Drone this note. And let yourself shine. The Outsider will be drawn to you. But it will arrive hungry.

The saw played a note, then, and though Bradley had never been much of a singer, he suddenly had perfect pitch, for a moment, and knew he could reproduce the tone at will. A symbol appeared in his mind, too, as if drawn in lines of fire: something like the veve of the loa Papa Legba, but with an angular symbol that looked sort of like an uppercase "P" incorporated into the center.

"Thanks," Bradley said. "So, that hour of service, it's going to have to start like right *now*. I'll have to go when the time's up, even if nobody—"

The saw's tone changed, and it was no longer headache-inducing: instead, it seemed a song of pure longing, and need, but with a hopeful intonation, too. A twenty-something girl dressed all in black, with her hair in an asymmetrical bob and a lot of sterling silver jewelry in her ears, nose, and lip, sat down beside him. "Okay, so, the thing is, I love my girlfriend, but she is *so* clingy..."

As Bradley listened to her lament and tried to think of something useful to say, he noticed people lining up behind her, drawn by the saw, waiting their turn to sit and listen to his wisdom, such as it was.

THE SAW STOPPED ITS DRONING of attraction promptly at the one-hour mark, and the people still waiting for Bradley's counsel looked around themselves, mildly confused, and drifted off. He got up, stretched, and started walking back the few blocks toward the coffee shop. Bradley felt wrung-out. To his surprise, he *had* been able to give pretty good advice to most of those people—his memories (however vague at this point) of being a multiverse-spanning consciousness gave him a sense of perspective that was probably tough to attain for those who'd only ever had one mind at a time to inhabit. He'd spent so long concerned with cosmic problems that it was refreshing to turn his attention to more personal, human-scale problems. Maybe if this whole overseer-of-the-multiverse gig didn't work out, he could come back to Earth, stage a dramatic return from the dead, and get a job doing a talk radio call-in show.

For now, though, he had a monster to attract.

He walked west along Pacific Avenue, then took a couple of turns until he hit Ash Street, just a few blocks east of the Genius Loci café.

Something made his flesh crawl: that cliché of scary stories, the hair on the back of his neck rising up. Horripilation. A remnant reaction from way back in the human experience, from the days when big cats crouched atop boulders waiting to leap out on you from the dark. (Up in the redwood-dotted hills by the university, people still occasionally got attacked by mountain lions dropping from tree branches; some days, no matter how hard you tried, you were still just an animal among animals.) That raising of the hackles was your body warning you about something your senses had picked up but your conscious mind hadn't processed, foregoing the higher-mind interventions, and just making you *look behind you.*

Bradley looked, and didn't see anything. Then, probably because he was more psychic than most, he looked *up,* and there was something after all: a ribbon of blackness, like a sheer scarf blowing on the wind, if scarves were twenty feet long and capable of hovering on the currents of the air while they undulated.

Shit shit shit. The Outsider. No need to summon the thing—there it was, and rather ahead of schedule. What had the oracle said? The Outsider was drawn to exhibitions of power. Well, Bradley had certainly exhibited some of that by summoning an oracle in the first place. He'd come to believe the creature had a mind, too, or something like one. The Outsider had at least rudimentary hunting skills, and had shown discretion and caution in its attacks, leaving very little in the way of survivors. The creature liked to wait until it could strike unobserved—it had probably stalked him from the crowded downtown to this street, which was entirely deserted except for a passing housecat. The creature's caution was heartening, in a way: why would it bother to be careful unless it could be *hurt?* Something had imprisoned it in a vault below Death Valley, after all. The memory of failure probably contributed to its caution now.

Then again, lions stalked antelope from the shadows, but not because they were particularly afraid of antelopes: they just didn't want to spook the prey, because then they'd have to go through the whole tedious process of acquiring a new target.

Bradley noticed the Outsider, and it noticed him noticing it, and the ribbon of blackness swam through the air toward him, undulating with the grace of a moray eel.

Marzi in the Oracle's Lair

"**WELL AREN'T YOU THE CAT** that got the cream," the Stranger said. Marzi thought the woman seemed remarkably calm for someone who was about to be swallowed. "Or the knife. My dagger's going to be rough on your digestion, and it'll hurt like hell coming out. Or are you one of those mythological monsters that doesn't have to shit?"

"Oh, don't worry." The sphinx stretched, extending its paws, and curved talons the length of butcher knives popped out and furrowed the sand. "Gobbling you up will settle my stomach. Do you have any other silverware you'd like to throw at me first? I don't wish to interfere with your prandial customs."

"Talks real fancy, don't he?" the Stranger said. "Me, I can't abide fancy talk. All wind and no rain, all thunder and no lightning."

"I have found that the coarse and unmannered are no different in flavor from the sophisticated and refined, though the latter tend to smell better." The sphinx yawned again. "This pre-dinner conversation is a delight, but I think I'll eat you now. Then we'll see if your friend can answer a riddle, or if she'll be my digestif."

Marzi put her hand on the butt of her gun. Could she shoot this thing? She had a sudden image of shooting off its nose, making it look like the Great Sphinx of Giza, and could barely suppress a giggle. Ah, there it was. Overwhelming terror messing up her brain, pushing her into irrational emotional reactions. Right on schedule.

"Talks real fancy," the Stranger repeated. "But I bet he can't whistle as good as me." She stuck two fingers in her mouth and shrilled a long, high, harsh note, loud enough to make Marzi wince and flinch away.

The sphinx licked its immense lips. "What was the point of that demonstration? Perhaps you'd like to do a bit of yodeling too—"

The creature's eyes widened as its throat ripped open, the Stranger's dagger tearing its way out of its own volition. The weapon didn't come out smoothly, but spun and whirled as it emerged, shredding the great beast's neck and throat so savagely that the sphinx was nearly decapitated in the process. Once the dagger was entirely free, it returned, hilt first, to the Stranger's hand. She wiped it absently on her sleeve and watched the sphinx gurgle and go cross-eyed.

Instead of blood, copious quantities of sand poured from the monster's wounds, and the sphinx's dangling head and body seemed to *deflate*, like a pool float punctured by a nail. Its tawny fur shimmered and became sand, and within seconds, its body had become just a small dune heaped on the plateau.

"What's the difference between my dagger and a housecat?" the Stranger drawled.

"What?" Marzi stared at the pile of sand.

"My dagger comes when it's called. If that was a test, I reckon we either passed it, or showed we don't want to take tests."

A flash of movement caught Marzi's eyes, and she looked up. "Crap, there's another sphinx. Three more." Marzi pointed toward the left-hand side of the plateau, where a trio of leonine figures had emerged from the heat haze. Had they climbed up onto the plateau? Emerged from burrows in the ground? Or just risen up from the sand? "Maybe more, maybe a whole herd." Her brain was still whirling wildly, and the gears were slipping a bit. "Or is it a pride, like lions?"

"In his treatise on supernatural collective nouns, David Malki asserts that it should be a 'finery of sphinxes,'" the Stranger said calmly. "I've never considered Malki to be definitive, though, and he doesn't use my preferred plural, either. I think it should be a 'riddle of sphinges.' Shouldn't matter, anyhow—they're solitary creatures, as a rule. Don't like the company of their own kind, or any other kind. They sure are making common cause today, though, and I fear that cause is you and me. We'd best get moving. I've only got one knife for them to swallow, and I'm not sure we can count on them to wait in line and take turns."

The Stranger set off running toward the palace, and Marzi went after her, casting glances back to the approaching shapes. The three sphinxes bounded toward them—one could have been the twin of the one they'd killed, another had long flowing hair and bare breasts, and a third seemed to have the head of a goat—but they stopped at the pile of sand the first sphinx had left in lieu of a corpse, pawing and sniffing at the ground. Maybe they were going to consume the power of their fallen comrade. Or maybe they were just going to use it as a litter box.

The air shimmered with heat and suddenly the palace was not hundreds of yards away but mere feet, and the Stranger and Marzi both slowed as they entered the shadows between the pillars. The temperature dropped so suddenly and significantly that pretty much Marzi's whole body jumped into gooseflesh as her sweat cooled.

"Should've brought a lantern," the Stranger said. "It's always the little things."

Flickering lights appeared, revealing a cavernous room dotted by pillars of rough-hewn stone, each holding a torch burning with greasy yellow flame. The vast room was filled halfway to the far-off ceiling with drifts of sand, a sort of indoor dune.

"Anybody home?" the Stranger called, and Marzi thought of people in snowy mountains shouting and setting off avalanches. That dune looked like it could bury them both if it shifted the wrong way. "Sorry we killed your housecat." She paused. "Hello? We're here to see the boss lady." She took off her hat, mopped the sweat from her forehead with the back of her hand, and put the hat back on. Then looked at Marzi and shrugged. "Oh well. Nobody's home. Let's go on back to the other side of the door and figure out a backup plan."

"You may not leave unless I allow it." The voice spoke inside Marzi's mind without bothering to go in through her ears. It was familiar, cold and emotionless. "None may open it from this side, without my leave."

"Thanks for taking our call," the Stranger said. "Are you the big scorpion I saw when I looked through the door earlier today?"

The dune shifted, as if something immense was burrowed beneath the sand. "Some see me as such a creature."

"She's a god," Marzi said, surprised at how calm she felt. The adrenaline spike of fleeing the sphinxes—or sphinges, whatever—had passed, and anyway she was on more familiar ground, now; if not necessarily safer. "She's the god of life in adversity. The god of small poisonous scuttling things. The god of surviving against all odds. I call her the scorpion oracle."

"Sounds like a practical, pragmatic sort of god." The Stranger hitched up her jeans and swaggered a couple of steps toward the dune. "I'm that kind of god myself, I think."

"You are... something," the scorpion oracle said, and was that a hint of perplexity? "Touched by divinity, but not divine. Yet you don't seem like one of the unfortunate offspring of a mortal and a god or monster, either."

"I'm just your average ordinary mortal, right now," the Stranger said. "Except not *mortal* mortal, since I can't die."

"You can't *die*?" Marzi said. How powerful a sorcerer *was* she?

"I cannot. And may I say, immortality is a considerable advantage when it comes to fighting monsters."

"Have you come to fight me, half a god?" the oracle whispered. "I am a *whole* god. You will not find me as easily defeated as a sphinx. Or as given to pointless conversation."

The Stranger displayed open hands. "No ma'am. I hope you'll forgive me the coarseness of my speech, as I realize it might seem a mite hostile. Some of that crudeness I come by honest, and some of it's a condition of my current circumstances." She didn't so much as a glance at Marzi. "Let me say clearly that I mean you no harm at all. In fact, I think we're a lot alike. I hear once upon a time you had a sort of opposite number, a fella devoted to scouring life from the Earth, who lived in here with you? The Outlaw, Marzi called him."

"I kept the god of earthquakes captive," the oracle said. "My old enemy was no more a *he* than I am a *she*, not really."

"Sure. How'd you like to play jailer again? We've got a prisoner you could watch over, or we will once my posse hunts him down. This particular miscreant is on a murder-spree that shows no sign of stopping, eating people whole, and I mean *whole*."

"Life is hard," the oracle said. "As it should be. Challenges refine us. The predator elevates the prey. Those who survive are stronger for it, and their descendants more likely to live on."

"I believe I may have read a book that espoused a similar theory once," Marzi said. "But this thing… it's *bad*."

"This *thing* is nothing to do with me. My relationship with the one you call the Outlaw was… personal. We were adversaries for a long time. I had reason to frustrate its plans. Why should I interfere with this other creature?"

"This beast is nastier than you know," the Stranger said. "It won't stop at killing people. It comes from *outside* our universe, and it wants to kill everything we've got here, from beetles to whales. Anything that has a soul, it'll eat that, too, and keep them from ever finding peace in whatever precinct of the afterlife might await them otherwise. This Outsider will use their life energy to make itself strong, so it can gobble up even bigger things. Won't stop until all life in the universe is extinguished, and to be honest, it'll probably keep on going until all the chemical processes are used up, too, and then it'll see if it can't break into the universe next door and eat that one, too. It's starting with people, but it'll end with the stars. What I'm saying is, if you're the god of some subset of things that are alive, you're not going to have anything *left* to be the god of, soon."

The sand shifted. "How can you hope to capture something so powerful?"

"It's just a baby right now," Marzi offered. "We want to trap it someplace where it can't get out, and can't do any harm, before it gets any bigger. It's drawn to this place, to the door that *leads* to this place, we think. It senses the magic, it's attracted to it, to the power, and we believe we can use that attraction to lure the Outsider through the door. If we do, can you keep it here?"

"I held the Outlaw," the oracle said. "This door does not open unless I permit it, not from this side. The Outlaw only escaped when it found *you*, Marzi—someone with the power to make the door manifest in the physical world, someone it could trick into opening the way. If I hold this Outsider of yours here, what will stop someone from opening it on the *other* side?"

"I will," Marzi said. "And my friend here has promised to pile on hexes and bindings and all manner of magic to keep that doorway sealed up."

The Stranger nodded. "We'll make it so the common folk can't even *see* that storage room, and if they start to drift close to it by mistake, they'll get a powerful hankering to move along right away."

"Mmm. Then I assent." The dune shifted around the oracle's immense body. One claw, the size of a bulldozer, broke through and gestured toward the entrance to the temple. "Go back. Lure this Outsider into my realm. I will never permit it to escape. But if someone opens the door on the other side and sets it free, it is *not* my problem anymore. I will not reach into dreams to guide you again, Marzi. If you cannot win on your own, this time, you do not deserve to win."

"Understood," Marzi said. Honestly, hearing the scorpion oracle wouldn't appear in her dreams again was some of the best news she'd had in a while. Those visitations hadn't made for restful nights.

The Stranger tipped the brim of her hat. "Much obliged, ma'am. I'd offer to shake your hand, but we've got a mild mismatch of scale between us."

"I will await the arrival of this prisoner," the oracle said.

"Uh, are those sphinx things going to try to kill us when we leave?" Marzi said.

The oracles cool voice seemed almost amused. "They prey on the weak, because the weak do not deserve to speak with me. I believe the two of you are safe. Leave now." The dune shifted again, an avalanche of sugary sand pouring down to reveal a flash of chitinous hide, shiny brown and segmented, and then that tail broke up through the sand, a lethal question mark tipped with a stinger the size of a medieval battering ram. Then that disappeared into the dune, too, either deeper into the temple or along some divine underground highway.

The Stranger whistled. "Damn," she said. "That is one hell of a mentor you got there, Marzi. All right. The arrangements are made. Let's see if B's figured out the right kind of honey to lure our nasty fly."

Bradley in the Streets

BRADLEY RAN, because when a monster is chasing you, your only choices are to run or to stand and fight, and he wasn't confident about his ability to fight the Outsider. He wasn't without his resources—anything with a working brain was vulnerable to his psychic assaults—but if this thing had a brain it wasn't made of anything Bradley knew how to mess around with. When it came to other methods of ass-kicking, he came up a bit short, and he knew it. Marla was the battle-mage in their duo, the one with the boots enchanted with inertial magic for nasty kicking, the one with charms of protection and deflection and displacement woven into her coat and her jewelry, the one with a knife that could cut through anything—

The knife! The chief sorcerer of Santa Cruz had given him that toy switchblade sparkling with either enchantments or inherent magic, and Bradley hadn't yet had an opportunity to determine the exact nature of its powers. As he ran along the sidewalk, he reached into his pocket and gripped the little plastic hilt, drawing it out. He glanced back over his shoulder, and the Outsider was *right there*, drifting at head level no more than three or four feet behind him. Bradley flung himself to one side, landing on his shoulder and rolling onto someone's drought-brown front lawn. The Outsider didn't overshoot him, or seem to suffer from the effects of inertia at all—just stopped instantly and then changed direction, angling down toward Bradley's supine form.

All Bradley's senses, psychic and otherwise, were strobing the reddest of all possible red alerts—this was death, dissolution, oblivion, the devouring of his soul, *again*—and he pushed the button on the switchblade and swung his arm in a desperate arc.

The blade that popped out of the toy hilt wasn't four inches of silvery plastic. It was more akin to a sword blade, three feet long and *burning*, like the sword of a cherub guarding a celestial gate, and it sliced through the shadow-substance body of the Outsider as easily as a razor through belly flesh. A foot or so of shadow fell to the sidewalk, where it turned to streamers of blackness and dissipated. The remainder of the creature's body *dropped*, fell from the air and landed on the sidewalk, where it writhed and twitched and gathered itself together in folds, like a dying serpent.

Bradley scrambled to his feet, blazing sword held out before him. Had he killed it, and was this thrashing its death throes? Maybe the thing *did* have an anatomy, despite looking like a uniform ribbon of shadow—and if so, Bradley might have cut off its foul head. He hoped so, because the fire in his sword was already fading, the blade shrinking, and the sparkle of enchantment he could perceive in the plastic hilt was growing duller, too. More like a taser than a machete, then, and he was rapidly running out of charge.

Bradley resisted the urge to prod the Outsider with the toe of his boot, as it had a history of devouring organic material and his boots were leather (and the toes inside flesh). He took a swipe at the creature with the sword, instead, before the fire could fade entirely, and the blade sank halfway into the middle of the writing ribbon before hitting resistance, causing the creature to redouble its writhing agonies. Then the fire winked out, and Bradley was just holding a toy switchblade again.

The Outsider went still, and a smile bloomed on Bradley's face. "You fucker," he said. "You messed with the wrong guy this time. I'm Bradley Bowman, you piece of shit—star of stage and screen, summoner of oracles, defender of the multiverse—"

The creature undulated and rose a foot off the ground, unkinking its length, and though its movement was more ungainly than before, especially with the deep cleft halfway down its body (if you could call it a body) where Bradley's last blow had fallen, it was clearly very much alive (if you could call it life).

His offensive options exhausted, Bradley fell back on running again. At least this time the thing wasn't quite as fast, and when Bradley looked behind himself occasionally the gap was holding steady, though he wasn't making up much extra ground. Plans, plans, plans—the problem was, there was no *time* make plans.

He could veer back downtown, and hope that the presence of other people would spook the thing back into hiding, and then summon it as planned later. But injured creatures weren't always rational, and what if the Outsider tried to kill *everybody* instead of running away? Causing the death of innocents was something he devoutly wished to avoid.

Better to go to Genius Loci and hope Marla was there, dagger in hand, ready to save his ass. There was the possibility of civilian casualties there, too, but fewer than he'd in downtown Santa Cruz. If Marla were even slightly psychic he would have tried to send her a mental message, but he might as well try to communicate with a brick wall. Marzi, though… if he could luck into the right psychic frequency….

Help! he shouted. *The Outsider is after me, and I'm coming in* hot!

He pointed himself at the café on the corner, now just two blocks away, and managed to put on a little more speed.

Marzi at Home

"So WHAT'S THE PLAN?" Marzi hesitated with her hand on the brass doorknob, the Stranger beside her scanning the unnatural desert horizon in case there were any last threats left for them here beyond the door.

"We hope Bradley figured out how to summon the Outsider. If he did, we lure the monster in here, slam shut the door, board it up with illusions and keep-away spells and eldritch bindings and maybe even actual boards made of wood, and hope that'll do the job." She shrugged. "Should be easy enough."

"I guess you do this sort of thing all the time."

The Stranger tipped her hat back. "Mostly I kill varmints like this instead of putting 'em in a box, but the principle's the same."

"I couldn't do it. Be a monster hunter on *purpose*. I'd never stop hyperventilating. Like, when do you have time to make comic books?"

"My proclivities are prob'ly indicative of some profound underlying psychological damage," the Stranger said. "But I reckon you play the hand the dealer gives you. Let's get."

Marzi opened the door and was instantly blasted with sound, so loud it made her drop to her knees, though a moment later she realized it wasn't *actual* sound, but more like the way the scorpion oracle talked to her: straight to her brain.

Bradley's voice, shouting "—*is after me, and I'm coming in* hot!"

The Stranger was helping her to her feet, through the door, and Marzi croaked, "Bradley's in trouble, I think he found the Outsider, I think they're coming *now*."

"Ain't that always the way." The Stranger pretty much just leaned Marzi against the wall, then reached down to take the pistol from Marzi's waistband and put it in her hand, closing Marzi's finger around the butt. "Cover me," the Stranger drawled. If this turn of events troubled her at all, she didn't show it. She reached into her pocket, took out a shiny piece of sea glass, then threw open the door to the storage room. "Everybody out!" she roared, vanishing from the room. "The café is closed!"

Marzi took deep breaths, the ringing in her head from Bradley's shout subsiding, and tried to think back at him: *We're ready.* Which was only half a lie. The Stranger sure seemed ready, and Marzi was keeping herself upright, gun in hand, pointed at the door. Ready to see what might come through.

The Stranger reappeared a moment later. "I tossed a stone enchanted with a compulsion to flee into the middle of your front room there. Everybody suddenly had an urgent yearning to be somewhere else. You might have some confused regulars and employees come in tomorrow, but at least they won't get et today." She wrinkled her nose. "Did you just make me say 'et' instead of 'eaten'?"

Marzi was feeling steadier on her feet now, and she even managed to smile. "Sorry. I can't help it. The door to the desert is still open, and reality is *really* flexible here."

"Then concentrate on making the Outsider dumb, and slow, and easily trapped, if you can. I peeked out the front door when I drove folks away and Bradley will be here in a few seconds. Hard not to go out there and pick a fight with that shadow snake coming after him, but we've got to lure it here. I hate being patient. At least I won't have to be for long."

Just then Bradley's voice howled "Incoming!"—not in her head, just normal yelling—and he burst through the door to the storage room. He reeled as soon as he came through the door, the portal to the desert inflicting some big psychic blow on him, and stumbled to one side, crashing against a stack of moldy old cardboard boxes that had been there since before Marzi bought the café.

"Cover me!" the Stranger shouted, and stood in the middle of the room before the door, legs spread wide, her glittering dagger in her right hand, a set of brass knuckles on her left. "You nasty sack of horse apples!" she bellowed. "You ain't getting past *me*! You won't get through that door so long as I'm drawin' breath!"

The Outsider slithered in, swaying, hovering about five feet off the floor. It looked thicker and more substantial than it had last time Marzi had seen it, though halfway down its length, its body drooped, seemingly damaged. Even wounded, it simply radiated power, and also *wrongness*—its very existence was as unsettling as seeing reverse lights on a freeway, as lifting up a spoonful of soup and finding a human tooth in the broth, as waking up to clumps of blood and hair on your pillow.

The Outsider started to dart at the Stranger but she slashed out with her knife and a piece of the creature came loose, turning to vapor, and the serpent *recoiled.*

"Cut it up!" Bradley cried, pushing himself upright. "I hurt it before, you can *kill* it!"

"I might at that," the Stranger said, and slashed again. "So long as it doesn't get through that door!"

Marzi had no idea if the Outsider could understand English, or if it was vulnerable to reverse psychology, but at that moment it zipped with unsettling speed around the Stranger and darted toward the open door to the desert.

"No!" the Stranger shouted. "Shoot it! Don't let it through!"

Marzi obligingly pivoted on her heel, brought up the gun, and squeezed off a couple of shots, the caps popping loudly. One of the spectral bullets hit the thing, knocking a chunk of shadow-stuff out of its tail, but then it disappeared into the land beyond the door.

The Stranger rushed over and pushed the door shut. Then she turned, looked at Marzi, and slapped her a ringing blow across the face with the hand wearing the brass knuckles.

Marzi stumbled backward, her head spinning, and sat down hard on the floor. She only faintly heard Bradley shout "Hey, what the hell!"

Marla knelt beside her and said, "Sorry about that. Had to take you by surprise, snap you out of it. But look—no more door. And I can say 'isn't' instead of 'ain't' again, and I'm not dropping my g's any more than usual, and I think I'm a couple of inches shorter than I was a minute ago."

Marzi groaned. "I'm thinking of you as 'Marla' again, too, instead of 'the Stranger.' Actually I'm thinking of you as 'you bitch.' Is that all it takes to get rid of my magic? Smacking me in the head?"

"With brass knuckles enchanted with spells that disrupt magic, yeah. I didn't get rid of your power, though, I just sort of… hit the reset button. The Outsider is out of our world, now, so his weird field of alien magic isn't heightening the local mystical background radiation anymore, making this thin place even thinner. I thought if I could get *you* to stop maintaining the portal, too, it might slam shut. Ta da." She gestured at the blank wall where the door had been. "I'm really sorry about the whole smacking-you-upside-the-head thing though. It wasn't concussion-force or anything, but still. I can make up a healing balm for you, but it'll take me a little while. Not really my specialty."

"You suck." Marzi got to her feet. "So… is that it? I mean…"

Marla shrugged. "The scorpion oracle said she wasn't going to open the door from *her* side, and if there's no door here for anybody to open on *this* side… I'll still cast some bindings and a keep-away spell on the storage room, to be safe, but I think the Outsider is imprisoned again."

"High fives all around," Bradley said, holding up a hand. "Huzzah for not dying." She smacked her palm against his while Marla rolled her eyes and turned toward the door to the kitchen, muttering about runes and lines of force.

Marzi felt… weird. Anticlimactic. If she'd written this in her comic, there would have been more derring-do, more hairsbreadth escapes, more dire injuries. Wow, how dumb was that? They'd gotten off easy. She should be glad. Still, killing the thing would have given her a more elemental sort of satisfaction. Just locking it up felt like simply postponing the problem. After all, it had been locked up before, under Death Valley, and it had gotten out eventually. Would it escape again in some later year, decade, century, to trouble someone else? Better if they'd killed it.

She wasn't going to offer to go through the door and try to kill it herself, though, so this would have to do.

THE THREE OF THEM SAT AROUND a table in the Teatime Room, sipping hot drinks. Jonathan hadn't gotten back from running his errands yet, which was just as well. Marzi wasn't sure how she was going to explain the events of the day to him. Probably she would downplay how close she'd come to death, and how often. "So what are you guys doing now?"

"Well, having neutralized the truly terrible cosmic threat facing us, I've got to go deal with more of a nuisance now," Marla said. "How about you, B? Are you returning to the collective overmind?"

"Whatever that means," Marzi said.

Bradley shrugged. "I haven't received a summons to return home, so I guess I'll tag along with you a while, if you'll have me."

"I can always use someone to carry heavy boxes," Marla said. She stood up, offering her hand to Marzi, shaking with a firm grip. "Listen, if you ever decide you'd like to learn more about magic… well, don't call me, I'm a shitty teacher—"

"This I can confirm," Bradley said.

"—and don't call *him*, because he's terrible about answering his phone and also he doesn't technically live on this planet. But take this number." She handed Marzi a slip of paper. "That's the direct line to a mage named Sanford

Cole who lives up in San Francisco. He owes me more favors than there are stars in the sky, and he'll help you out, answer any questions, stuff like that. That second number is mine. Call me if any weird supernatural shit starts to go down here again, but if you can't reach me—because sometimes I am way unreachable—try Cole instead, he'll mobilize the troops. All right?"

"Yeah, for sure. I hope nothing does happen, though. Maybe it's not adventurous of me, but I just want to do my art and eat eggs and bacon on the weekends and have good sex, you know? If I never have to face another horrible creature from beyond, that'll be okay with me."

"Ah, well," Marla said. "One woman's dream is another woman's nightmare, I guess. Take care of yourself, Marzipan. Stay sweet."

Bradley on the Road Again

THEY HITCHED MARLA'S MOTORCYCLE to the trailer in the back of the RV, then sat down inside, Marla in the passenger seat, Bradley behind the wheel. "It'll take, what, two days of driving straight through to get to Felport?" he said.

Marla snorted. "In this dinosaur? I don't see you hitting 80 on those nice middle-of-the-night empty freeway stretches, not in this bot. The trip will take longer than that."

"Mmm. Drive up to San Jose, then, and catch the next flight? I'm a little embarrassed in the ID department just now, but between the two of us I bet we could mindfuck our way onto a flight."

"Hmm. I am a goddess now, so first class seems reasonable. Are you sure you don't need to get back to the gazebo at the end of the universe?" She shifted in the seat, slumping down, hat half covering her eyes. "For that matter, did we make everything right here? Has our lonely little branch been reintegrated into the multiverse yet?"

"I think we have to wait for DNS propagation to fully complete." Marla lifted her chin and looked at him blankly, and he sighed. "Sorry. Computer science joke. I went to the bathroom before we left the café partly to see if I could reach myself in the mirror, but I didn't get an answer. I don't know what's up."

"Yeah, I'm kind of in the dark myself," Bradley's voice said from the radio.

"Is that you, super-Bradley?" Marla said. "Bradley Prime? Bradley Alpha-and-the-Omega?"

"Lord Bradley, King of the Multiverse will do," the radio said, followed by a staticky blare of polka music that quickly subsided.

"That is weird, man," Bradley said. "Taking over the radio? Our voice doesn't sound right through those speakers."

121

"Come on," the radio said. "You were an actor. You should be used to listening to yourself talk out of various electronic orifices. Anyway, I just wanted to say, you guys did good. I perceive no more existential threat to the integrity of the multiverse. The Outsider is still on my grid, still in your reality, but he's like a black fly buzzing inside a bottle. My hope is that, with no people to eat, he'll go dormant again soon, like he was all those centuries under Death Valley."

"So we're back online?" Marla said. "No danger of this branch of reality getting gangrene and falling off?"

"Well, see, there's my problem." The radio voice sounded apologetic, which couldn't be a good sign. "I can't actually see the future. I'm omniscient and omnicognizant, but not precognitive."

"Bullshit," Marla said. "I dealt with your predecessor the Possible Witch, and she absolutely told me what was going to happen in the future— or what was most likely to happen, anyway."

"Not exactly," Bradley said. "She told you what would happen if you didn't stop Mutex from raising a dark god—and she knew, because in a lot of other universes, Mutex had *already done it.* In those universes he got started days or weeks or months earlier, and he worked faster, and he didn't hit any snags—whatever. She wasn't seeing the future, she was just figuring percentages. I can look through all the adjacent branches of the multiverse, and see what happens most often, and consider the trends, you know? Like, I can say, 'In seventy percent of universes polled, your dumb plan actually works,' or, 'ninety-nine percent of the time, your ass does *not* look good in those pants.' Those little variations are just as good as seeing the future, for practical purposes. But since I froze your thread—there's another Internet joke for you, Little B, I've got your back—it's limited my predictive powers. There's only one branch where the Outsider got loose, only one branch where it got imprisoned behind the door in the desert world, so I can't really *tell* if your plan worked or not, because I don't have any similar realities to check against. My feeling is, you made a good plan, and it's probably all right, but what if this is the one crazy outlier reality where stuff goes way wrong and the Outsider escapes again? There's no way for me to know, so I'm going to keep you sequestered for a little longer."

"I thought we had a ticking time bomb situation here?" Marla said, voice dangerously calm. "Like, if we stay cut off too long, there's permanent damage to the structure of reality? *My* reality, where all my friends live, remember?"

"That's true," the radio conceded. "I'm not planning to cut it that close, though. You've got some time. I'm going to give it another week. If I see the

Outsider getting weak and fading out, I'll graft you back onto the tree of life. If something else happens… we'll figure out how to deal with it."

"That sucks," Marla said.

"If you were still running Felport, and a monster was eating everybody in an apartment building, and you locked the monster up in an empty apartment, would you tell everybody else to move back in, or wait a little bit to make sure the locks held?"

"Yeah, fine," Marla said. "I get it. That means I get to keep Little B here to help me out on this other thing?"

"I do not consent to being called Little B," Little B said.

"Sure. Enjoy your vacation on Earth, kid," the radio said. "We'll just keep doing the heavy lifting of making the universe run smoothly up here while you laze around."

"Fuck you, man," Little B said. "At least you get laid."

"I bet I can convince Henry to give you a travel pass, if you see somebody you're interested in," the radio said. "Maybe if you break Rondeau out of Nicolette's jail he'll be so grateful he'll sleep with you again. It was pretty fun, when we hooked up during that thing in San Francisco."

"Yeah, but he's inhabiting a copy of my own body now," Little B said. "I'm pretty sure sleeping with him would be some kind of deeply messed-up paraphilia."

"I read some fanfic about that kind of thing once," the radio said. "They called it 'incesturbation'—where you sleep with your clone or magical double or doppelganger or other self from another dimension."

"You spend way too much time on the Internet, Bradleys," Marla said. "Look, keep me posted, okay? I want to know when my universe is off double-secret-probation. Keep us cut off too long and psychics and sensitives and gurus and sibyls are going to start to sense something wrong with the nature of the universe and freak the fuck out. As the object of worship of a currently defunct death cult, I can tell you the last thing we need is a whole bunch of doomsday sects springing up. They're nothing but trouble."

"Roger that, over and out." The radio went quiet.

"Well, all right, then," Little B—damn it, he was thinking of himself that way now—said. "Off to the airport?"

"Stop by that beach first," Marla said. "I need to talk to the chief sorcerer of Santa Cruz."

MARLA TOLD BRADLEY TO WAIT in the car while she went down the hill to the beach to talk to the Bammer. Bradley sat and watched the sun sink toward the waves for a while, listening to the breeze blowing past the windows and the cries of seagulls and the susurrating crash of the surf. It was all very restful, and after the day he'd had, with the near-death experiences and all, it was nice to rest. He wondered what Marla was saying to the Bammer. He wondered if she was kicking his ass. She had strong feelings about how chief sorcerers should run things.

After about half an hour she came climbing up the hill and back into the RV. "We're all set."

"What did you do to him?"

"Threw him on the ground and sat on him and made him eat sand."

He stared at her. "Really?"

She rolled her eyes. "Gods, Little B, I'm not a *bully*. I beat *up* bullies. We sat down and had a reasonable discussion about his responsibilities, and about my views regarding the unfairness of his pressing Marzi into the role of champion without her consent, informed or otherwise. I discussed possible consequences of putting my girl into that kind of impossible situation again. I made it clear that he can tend to his city himself, or he can suffer the consequences of failure. I also told him that I would take a keen interest in Marzi's mental, physical, and financial well-being going forward, and that he should do his best to ensure she was healthy along all axes."

"Ah," Bradley said. "And he agreed?"

"He did," she said. "After I threw him on the ground and sat on him and made him eat sand. Come on, let's get to the airport. If I can kick Nicolette's ass as fast as we locked up the Outsider, maybe you and me can have a little fun before you have to go back to your magic space gazebo."

"You mean we aren't having fun *now*?"

"That's my Little B," she said fondly.

THEY LEFT THE RV and the motorcycle in a corner of the airport's long-term lot that was marked as a no-parking zone, but that was okay, because the vehicles were enchanted so no one but a sorcerer or psychic would notice them anyway, and if any such clued-in types tried to touch their rides, the busybodies would lose a limb or two.

The first available flight out of San Jose was a redeye with a connection through New York that would get them into Felport International Airport around 8 a.m. the next morning. That wasn't ideal, but while it was possible to expend enough magic to take over another flight and send it where they wanted, that was the sort of thing that would doubtless draw the attention of whatever magician ran the city of San Jose, and they could end up being shouted at by angry mages in a small room, which would waste even more time.

They bought tickets with cash and checked no bags without raising any particular alarm, breezed through security (Bradley used a dog-eared jack of hearts from a deck of cards as his ID, with his psychic powers making it look legit, and Marla didn't even have to take her cowboy boots off), and settled into a booth in the first class lounge. Marla spilled some salt on the table and drew a rune of privacy so they could talk without people overhearing and thinking they were insane.

"Is it too much to hope that you have a plan?" Bradley slumped on his side of the booth, half asleep, unshaven, sweaty, and generally not feeling his best.

"I was going to take advantage of the shower they've got in here, and I would urge you to do the same. I've got an Elmore Leonard paperback I got the take-a-book, leave-a-book shelf at Genius Loci. A Western, natch. I figured I'd read that. Then, sleep on the plane."

"Did you leave a book? When you took one?"

"No, but I saved the world, which I think entitles me to a free book."

"Figures. No such thing as a free lunch." The shower was very tempting, but he wanted to make his point first. "But when I asked about your plan, I meant, is there a plan for what to do in Felport?"

She shrugged. "Depends on what Nicolette's got going on. She seems to think she's got some clever shit going on, but then, she always does. I'll see to what extent and in what specific way she's fucked things up, and act accordingly."

"Any temptation to kick her off the throne and take it back yourself? Run Felport again?"

"Oh, the thought crossed. But I'm busy with my whole dread-queen-Persephone gig half the year, and my city deserves better than a part-time leader. I might find myself in a position to elevate a new chief sorcerer, though. Not sure who I'd put in the job. Someone other than the Chamberlain, though. Almost anyone would be better. Nicolette excepted."

"I didn't get to know the Chamberlain well, but she seemed to know her shit," Bradley said.

"Yeah, she's good at that bullshit ghost-magic she does, but I hate her, so she's obviously unfit for leadership. There's Hamil, I guess—he was my number two, so he's the obvious choice."

"Marla, he voted to kick you out of the job and exile you."

Marla nodded. "Sure. And he betrayed our friendship in the process, potentially making me a terrible enemy, etc. But he did that terrible because he thought getting rid of me was best for the city, see? The fact that he made that hard decision tells me he's qualified to run things. The problem is, he doesn't want the job. He's too smart to want to sit on the throne. Who else is even halfway qualified? Langford's a sociopath, which I'll grant you isn't necessarily a flaw in a leader in some situations, but he's happy running the Blackwing Institute and running experiments I'd rather not run about—he never even really wanted to sit on the council. The Bay Witch is strong enough to run a city, but she's only halfway in our reality most of the time, and it's hard to imagine she'd pay attention to anything beyond the waterfront." She sighed. "The other obvious choices are all dead. Maybe there's somebody on the council who has chops, I don't know. I could set up a ruling triumvirate or something. Or a rotating leadership thing like they had in San Francisco before most of their sorcerers got killed."

"So you don't have any doubt you'll be able to knock Nicolette off her perch?"

Marla actually laughed. "Bradley. My superpower is I *don't lose*. No matter what it costs me. I win, or I die. And just lately, I can't die." She shrugged. "That's nothing but math, Little B." She yawned behind her hand. "Besides. It's just Nicolette. She ain't shit. I'm taking a shower." She rose from her seat and ambled toward the restrooms.

Bradley sat and brooded. In this particular skin he hadn't known Nicolette well, but in some other realities, now only vaguely recalled, he'd known her better—in at least a couple they'd been lovers, despite his total lack of sexual interest in women, due to some love-spell shenanigans. In still others they'd been devoted allies. In most realities he was aware of, Nicolette was a bad person, selfish and violent and spiteful, and she had a tendency to fixate obsessively on people as mentors or enemies, contorting her life around theirs as acolyte or adversary. But in a few timelines, she'd fixated on someone more noble than her mentors in *this* world, and devoted herself to doing good, or at least not to doing *bad*.

In some realities, Nicolette had even been an ally of Marla Mason, both of them fighting in resistance forces against supernatural despots and interdimensional conquerors—enemies bad enough to make them join forces despite the inevitable clash of their wills. In those worlds, Nicolette often looked up to Marla with something that could only be called love, and she'd lived or died inside based on Marla's opinion of her.

Bradley wondered how much of that applied to the Nicolette *here*. In this world, Nicolette was Marla's implacable but inconsequential enemy, a gadfly who wanted to be a monster. How much of her villainy over the years was just down to her wanting Marla's respect? Crapsey had made the same argument, and while the murderous parasite wasn't famed for his understanding of psychology, Bradley thought he might be on to something in this case.

Not for the first time, Bradley really wished he trusted himself enough to order a double Scotch. He'd have to settle for a shower and a nap, which were just about the worst substitutes for getting drunk imaginable.

THE FLIGHT WAS UNEVENTFUL, and the seats reclined fully into beds, so Bradley even slept well. (He had experience sleeping in abandoned buildings full of addicts, and in alleys, and on freezing cold location shoots, and in more cars and fields than he could count during his pursuit of the Outsider, so anything resembling a bed was too glorious to be believed.) He didn't wake until a flight attendant nudged him to tell him they were about to begin their final descent, but Marla was already conscious beside him, looking out the window and sipping orange juice.

Bradley got his seat into its upright configuration, hurried to the bathroom before the pilot could demand they stay in their seats, and then dropped in beside Marla. He leaned across her and looked down at the sprawling city by the bay, split by the curve of the river. "That's Felport all right. Looks almost pretty from up here, the light shining on the water."

"Makes my heart ache in my chest. Damn. I didn't expect that." Marla sighed. "You ready to make some moves? Bust Rondeau and Pelly out of wherever they're held, assuming they didn't bust themselves out yet? Kick Nicolette out of office and put someone better in her place?"

"I'll do whatever you need me to… as long as I think it's a good idea."

"Apprentices are so disobedient nowadays."

"You know, your goddesshood, I think I outrank you in terms of mystical celestial might."

She snorted. "The Over-Bradley does, maybe, but you're just the middle toe on his right foot or something. A skin cell that got ideas above its station."

"I've always had aspirations beyond my abilities."

"Yeah. Don't we all."

They sat silently as the plane began to descend, until Bradley said, "Do you think they're expecting us?"

"Nicolette might have people watching the airports and roads, though I wouldn't count on it. She's never had to organize anything more complicated than a birthday party. Any surveillance she does try to put on us, we'll breeze right past. We'll jump out at her in our own time, in our own way, after I gather some intel."

The plane landed, and they were the first ones off, Marla carrying her shoulder bag, and Bradley a backpack slung over his shoulder holding a change of clothes. They stepped into the gate area... and a tall, slender black woman with a profusion of white dreads, wearing yoga pants and a flowing white shirt and lots of bead-and-crystal necklaces, approached them with a smile. She was followed by a small serious-looking middle-aged man in a derby hat. "Marla!" the woman said. "So glad you could make it."

Marla frowned. "Perren?"

The woman nodded, smiling, and turned to Bradley. "And this is Bradley Bowman? I'm Perren River, big fan of your work, both the films and the magic."

"Uh," Bradley said. "Nice to. Uh."

"You remember Mr. Beadle, Marla?"

The small man nodded at her. "Ma'am."

Marla frowned. "Wait. Nicolette sent you?"

"To meet you, yeah, and take you to you hotel. She figured you'd want to freshen up before she met with you."

"Mr. Beadle works for Nicolette now? I thought you two were mortal enemies."

"That's right," Bradley said. "You're an order mage, aren't you?"

"Yessir. Nicolette and I were more opposed philosophically than personally, but." He shrugged. "That's all worked out now. May I take your bags?"

Marla shook her head. "No. I have weapons in my bag, and I might need them in case Nicolette tries to mind-control me like she did *you* two."

Perren shook her head, long dreads shaking. "If she were controlling our minds, we would've had an easier time with the transition. Come on. We'll tell you about it. There's a limo waiting."

"Look, thanks for the offer, but we'll make our own way wherever we're going."

Perren shrugged. "Suit yourself. What should I tell Pelham and Rondeau?"

Marla shifted her weight, and Bradley wondered if she was preparing for a fight, or easing back from her readiness for one. "What do you mean?"

Mr. Beadle gestured vaguely back through the terminal. "They're waiting in the car."

"Are they prisoners?"

"I won't lie to you," Perren said. "They certainly were, for a while there, though they were treated well. But now they're free. They wanted to see you, so we gave them a ride."

"Why would Nicolette just let them go?" Bradley asked.

"They were taken as leverage to make you come to Felport," Perren said. "And… you came to Felport. As soon as Nicolette got word you were en route, she ordered their release."

"What's to stop me from grabbing them and getting on a plane and flying out of here without bothering to see Nicolette at all?" Marla asked.

Perren smiled. "Nothing, except everything everyone who's ever met you knows about how your mind works."

Marla didn't smile, but her lips twitched, and that was remarkably close—Bradley didn't think anyone who was less perceptive than he was would have noticed. "You know, that's almost enough to trigger my natural contrariness and make me leave *anyway*. But you're right. I do want to see Nicolette. And then hit her with things. And then send her back to Hell."

"It wouldn't be the first epic clash in the halls of power we've had in the past month, mum," Mr. Beadle said. "I've been quite content with my own moderate level of power, lately. It's safer not to be too big a target."

"Shall we?" Perren said.

"Fuck it," Marla said. "Let's shall."

Rondeau in a Limo

"SEE, THIS IS PROPER STYLE." Rondeau sorted through the little built-in liquor cabinet in the back of the limo, pulling out stoppers from plain glass bottles and sniffing to identify port, brandy, single-malt scotch, and some kind of blackberry-infused vodka.

"I can't help thinking it must be some kind of a trick," Pelham said. "Nicolette... the things she's capable of... Why would she just let us go?"

"She's a chaos witch, Pelly. If she were predictable, she'd be... some other kind of witch." Rondeau looked around for glasses but couldn't find them. Probably hidden in some secret compartment. Drinking straight from the scotch decanter seemed gauche, but then again, the alcohol content was sufficiently high to kill any germs he left on the rim, so why not? He took a swig. Mmm, what a wonderful burn. And it would quiet his psychic powers, which were pretty freaked out every time he looked at Pelham. There were ghostly chains wrapped around the man's head, translucent links visible only to Rondeau and presumably any other poor bastards who could perceive things on the magical spectrum. "Want a jolt?"

"No. My faculties are reduced enough by this spell Nicolette has cast on me."

"So you can't even give me a *hint* about what you saw in the Chamberlain's magic mirror?" Rondeau said. "Maybe act it out charades-style? Nothing?"

Pelham opened his mouth, winced, frowned, and then said, very slowly and deliberately, "I can say only that it does not pose an immediate threat to us, or to Mrs. Mason. And that it involves—" His teeth snapped shut, and he hissed, then fished a handkerchief from his pocket and put it to his mouth for a moment. When Pelham took the cloth away, Rondeau saw a speck of blood on his lip. "No, not even that much. Nicolette's spell makes me literally bite my tongue if I even come close to the secret. She told me she doesn't want me to spoil the *surprise.*"

Rondeau nodded. Pelham had been dragged back to their room after his visit to the Chamberlain by Squat and a couple of homunculus orderlies, under heavy sedation, not just asleep but practically comatose. When Rondeau begged to know what was going on, Squat would only say that Pelham gotten up to some unauthorized magic with the Chamberlain. "We heard glass break in her room, and when I rushed in, thinking they'd try to stab me with shards of mirror or something... I realized they were up to something else, and the doc handed me a couple of hypodermics to settle them down. We'll see what Nicolette wants to do with you." Squat shook his head. "You gotta give the little guy props for courage, though I don't know what they were trying to accomplish exactly. If Nicolette's too furious, I'll try to calm her down. I really would hate to have to eat you guys."

"Is Nicolette really a better boss than Marla?" Rondeau said. "I mean— do you still think you made the right choice, jumping ship on us?"

"Nicolette sucks," Squat replied. "But at least she doesn't pretend she gives a shit about me. Unlike Marla." He stumped away.

This morning, Rondeau was awakened by Nicolette herself, nudging him in gut with one meaty finger. He'd blinked at her for a few seconds and then said, "Your shoulders are broader than I remember."

"You like?" Nicolette struck a bodybuilder's pose, her white skin-tight t-shirt straining against bulging musculature. "I wasn't sure about using a dude's body, but this one's pretty strong, and it's got some other amusing qualities. I've got a couple of chick bodies put aside I can use, too, when I feel like going that way instead."

"The meathead thing doesn't really go with your bone structure." Rondeau sat up on the bunk. "You're too delicate. It's like, I don't know, a bird's head on a rhinoceros."

"You say the sweetest things. But tell me the truth. You kind of want to fuck me in this body, don't you?" She turned around, wiggling her ass at him.

"I like the slim-hipped pretty boys more, to be honest," he said.

"No accounting for taste. Come on, you're getting set free today. After I put a gag order on your boy there."

Rondeau slid off the top bunk to the floor and eyed Nicolette warily. What did she mean, a gag order? If she tried to cut out Pelham's tongue or something....

Pelham was still asleep on the bottom bunk, though at least he was snoring a little—his earlier drugged-out stillness had been unsettling. Nicolette leaned over him, a silver necklace in her hand, and did a little muttering incantation while twisting the chain between her fingers. That's when the ghostly links wrapped themselves around Pelham's head. He groaned and blinked his eyes.

"What'd you just do?" Rondeau said.

"I've got a surprise for Marla, and I think your boy Pelham stumbled onto it, looking at things he wasn't *supposed* to look at, peeking in on my private business. Can't have him spoiling the big reveal." She reached out and patted Pelham's head, making him blink and groan more.

"Wait," Rondeau said. "We're going to see Marla?"

"Her plane lands shortly. I'm sending you to meet her." Nicolette rose and turned to face Rondeau. He wasn't used to her looking down at him, but in her new body, she was about six-foot-four.

He fought the urge to take a step backward. "Then, uh, I guess we'll be facing you soon on the field of battle? Or whatever?"

Nicolette shook her head. "There won't be any battle. Which, in a way, is disappointing, except I know Marla will be *more* disappointed, because she doesn't know how to deal with anything unless she's beating on it with a lead pipe. Frustrating her… you know, it's funny. I used to think making her miserable was the most important thing in the world. And I still care about doing that, but it's more like… a tasty dessert after a meal that was already totally satisfying. You don't *need* dessert—it's just nice."

"So what's the main course?"

"Wouldn't you like to know? I'll leave you to get dressed alone. I don't need to see that bare bony ass of yours. Not when I've got this sweet one all to myself." She slapped her own ass with both hands, winked, and left the room, not even bothering to shut their cell door behind her.

"Rondeau?" Pelham said, sitting up and rubbing his face. "What's happening?"

"You got the whammy put on you," Rondeau said. "But now we're going to see Marla. Apparently."

And here they were, waiting in the back of the limo. Maybe it *was* all a trick, Nicolette just fucking with them one more time, but she usually wasn't that subtle. Her idea of a good joke was filling your bed with snakes or setting your car on fire, not pretending you were going to see your friend. Even so, he wasn't going to be entirely comfortable until—

The door opened, and Marla slid in. "Move over, Rondeau, I've been in an airplane seat all night, I need space."

Then *Bradley Bowman* got in too, sitting across from Rondeau and Marla, next to Pelham. "Ignore her, we flew first class. Our seats were bigger than this whole car."

"Commercial air travel takes an existential toll, regardless of where you're seated." Marla looked Rondeau up and down. "Stop gaping. Yes, that's B. Not exactly *our* B, obviously, but the closest possible equivalent."

Bradley gave him a little wave. "Yeah, I come from the universe next door, where you didn't steal my body—you took Danny Two-Saints's body instead."

"Couldn't have happened to a nicer guy," Rondeau mumbled, flushed with shame all over again at the way he'd stolen Bradley's body. He hadn't *meant* to, but that didn't change the reality. "Wow. Uh. Things must be a lot different over there, where you're from."

"Oh, yeah. Marla never got ousted from her job as chief sorcerer of Felport, for one thing. From one little change—"

"Right, sure, for want of a nail the kingdom was whatever," Marla interrupted.

Rondeau couldn't help but smile. "Good to see you again, boss. Thanks for coming to get us."

She reached out and patted him on the knee, a little too hard. "You are a couple of colossal fuck-ups, but you're *my* colossal fuck-ups." She looked at Pelham. "You couldn't keep a better eye on him?"

"I must admit that many of the mistakes were my own, Mrs. Mason."

"Damn. Can't leave you two alone for a month without the world almost ending."

Perren River got into the limo, sitting beside Marla, looking at Bradley with great interest. "Did you say you're from a parallel universe?"

"I did not," Bradley said. "Those words did not pass my lips."

"Shut up a minute, Perrin," Marla said. "Bradley, do a diagnostic on everybody, okay?"

Bradley squinted at Rondeau, shook his head, turned his gaze to Perren, shook it again, then looked at Pelham and whistled. "There's some kind of binding magic on Pelham."

"Yes," Pelly said glumly. "I regret that I am not able to fully serve you, Mrs. Mason. Nicolette has placed limitations upon me."

"Magical gag order," Rondeau said. "Pelham got a glimpse through a magic mirror and saw some big secret Nicolette has, and she doesn't want you to know about it."

"More precisely, she wants to reveal it to you *herself*," Pelham said. "I suppose so she can have the pleasure of seeing you become very upset in person."

"Well that's a burning bag of crap," Marla said. "I hate surprises, especially Nicolette's." The limo started up and pulled out. "Where's Mr. Beadle?" she said.

"Up front driving," Perren said. "With you in the car, Nicolette didn't trust sending a lackey to drive."

"A member of the council for my chauffeur. Looks like I'm a VIP." Marla leaned back, lacing her hands over her belly, and looked at Perren through half-closed eyes. "I had my eye on you back when you ran the Honeyed Knots. You were the only addition to the council I really approved of. Maybe that was a mistake. I thought you had spine, but you just rolled over for Nicolette, huh?"

Perren sighed. "The council changed a lot after the Mason's Massacre."

Marla winced. "You said that like it's a proper name. Everyone calls it that?"

"Some call it Marla's Massacre." Perren's voice was bland and entirely non-judgmental. "I never thought that was fair. The Mason was your double from another universe, but that doesn't make her *you*. Anyway, after she killed half the leading sorcerers in the city, and you were exiled, we had to rebuild things from the ground up, divide up the city again, all under the Chamberlain's direction."

Marla looked like she wanted to spit, and Rondeau thought only the fact that she was in a limousine stopped her from doing so. "I never liked her. Thought she'd be a terrible leader."

"Oh, she was," Perren said. "Diplomatic, always polite, but if someone disagreed with her, she just… ignored them. Her own powers were so substantial, she didn't feel the need to build coalitions, not even to the extent you did. Hamil tried to be a moderating influence on the council, but…" Perren shrugged. "Who did he have to work with? Mr. Beadle is good at infrastructure, he keeps the garbage collection and mail delivery and everything humming, but politics is too disorderly for his tastes. Langford doesn't care about anything but his experiments, and since he took over running the Blackwing Institute, that's kept him occupied—he doesn't even come to meetings anymore. The Bay Witch keeps things working in the water and around the ports, but again, she couldn't give less of a crap about the city as a whole. Hamil and I tried to do what we could, but…" She shrugged. "The Chamberlain doesn't pay attention to anything that happens south of the river, except maybe the financial district a little bit."

Rondeau whistled. North of the river was, basically, the rich part of town, the big houses, the old families, the golf courses and country clubs. South of the river was... everything *else*. The Chamberlain had always been the voice of the wealthy in Felport, and the keeper of the ghosts of the founding families, who provided Felport with a reservoir of magical power that could be used to protect the city. The fact that taking over the city as a whole hadn't made the Chamberlain care about the other 99% of the city's citizens was troubling but not shocking.

"That's exactly why she should never have been made chief sorcerer," Marla said. "Ignoring everything south of the river? Gods."

"To be fair, didn't you ignore everything north of the river when *you* ran things?" Bradley said.

Marla scowled. "Yeah, but those rich fucks can take care of themselves, and anyway, they had the Chamberlain looking out for them, chasing disobedient ghosts out of their attics and keeping succubi from seducing bi-curious debutantes. The rest of the city *needs* help."

"It's been bad since you left," Perren said. "But none of us had the power to oust the Chamberlain. You need a unanimous vote to kick out a sitting ruler, and she had Langford in her pocket completely, and the Bay Witch, too, for some reason—something about owing her a favor?"

"Do a solid for the Bay Witch, and she'll do one for you," Marla said. "Even if it's something like 'never vote against anything I want to do ever.' So the best you could hope for in *any* vote was a deadlock, and in a tie, the chief sorcerer gets her way. First among equals, right?"

Perren nodded. "That's when the Chamberlain even bothered to bring a vote before the council, instead of just doing what she wanted. Not good times."

"Ha. And then Nicolette showed up, and times got even worse. How the hell did a head in a birdcage take over the whole city?"

Perren made a face. "She came in with heavy muscle, this guy Squat? Magic just bounces off the guy, he's invulnerable. He's about as subtle as a chainsaw murder at a shopping mall, too, but he gets things done. Somehow Nicolette got to Langford, I don't know how—blackmail or black magic or simple persuasion. They flipped a few lieutenants to their side and kidnapped the Chamberlain, locked her up in the Blackwing Institute. Some of her people tried to stage a rescue, and Squat...."

"How many of them did he eat?" Marla said.

Perren's eyes widened. "Only one. The others got the message and backed off. Do you know Squat?"

"He used to work for me, but Nicolette recruited him. Seems like a not uncommon approach for Nicolette. I'm not sure how she does it. She's not exactly charming."

"She's not that, but she's brave and audacious. With the Chamberlain gone, Hamil stepped up as chief sorcerer, but Nicolette got to *him* somehow, too, I don't know how—only that it's not mind control."

"How the *hell*," Marla said. "Hamil is with *Nicolette*? Willingly?"

Perren nodded. "Maybe under duress—I don't know. He elevated Nicolette to his old position on the council, and then voted to let her take his place. We resisted, of course, but apparently Hamil had a favor to call in with the Bay Witch, too, so she voted. That was Hamil, the Bay Witch, and Langford on her side, so..." Perren shrugged. "Apparently that kind of voluntary transfer of power doesn't need to be unanimous? Or so the bylaws say. Procedural shit. What was I supposed to do then? Resign in protest? Nicolette can't be killed—we figured *that* out pretty quickly—and Squat can get to anybody. They are not people you want for enemies. Well, maybe you do, but *I* don't. I figured I'd go along to get along, look for a chance to take control of the council myself, and make things *sane* again."

"Yeah, how's that working out?" Marla said.

"Well, the thing is... It's only been a couple of weeks, but... Nicolette is doing a great job."

Rondeau couldn't help it: he groaned. Pelham looked as alert as a rabbit in the presence of a wolf, and Bradley seemed to be holding his breath.

Marla's voice was low and utterly uninflected. "What."

Perren shrugged. "She just... she's got it down. The changes are already obvious, and the plans she's set in motion are going to pay off in a big way. Look, my territory is the inner city, you know? The place my gang comes from, my people. Drug use has plummeted. There haven't been any murders. *None*, not drug-related, not personal grudge related, not even being-an-asshole related. Thieving is way down, burglary too, even vandalism. Services are being offered, and my people are actually taking advantage of them. Everyone's just *happier*. It's like a balance has shifted in the city. I'm hearing similar reports from elsewhere, the other at-risk neighborhoods. Government grants that have been held up for years are coming through. Ancient grievances are being sorted out. It's like... all the things that used to work against each other are just working *together* now. Stuff that used to clash is running smoothly now."

"Tyranny," Marla said. "Despotism. Fascism. Right? Everyone behaves well when there's an iron boot on their neck."

"I admit, Nicolette came in hard," Perren said. "She was all murder all the time and we figured we were in for nightmare times going forward. But once Nicolette took the big chair, I don't know, it's like something in her changed. She started making deals, giving people what they wanted, and even better, what they *needed*. She asked my advice, and she *took* it. She couldn't be more different from the Chamberlain."

"This is bullshit," Marla said, voice still flat. "She *can't* run things well. It's not possible. Chaos witches can't run cities any more than dogs can play piano. She's a fucking head in a cage!"

"She's got a body now," Rondeau said. "Actually several, I think."

Marla glared at him, and he shrugged and looked away.

Perren spread her hands. "I don't know how to explain it. I agree, from everything I know about Nicolette, she should be awful at this job, but she does it like she was born to and trained for leadership."

Marla sank back into her seat. "How long before we get where we're going? I want to see this amazing enlightened philosopher-queen for myself."

"Not long," Perren said. "We can—"

"Shut up then," Marla said. "I need to think."

Your thinking looks a whole lot like brooding, Rondeau thought, but sure as hell didn't say.

"Okay," Marla said after a while. "Pelly and Rondeau, you guys are going to get out of town."

"You don't want our help?" Rondeau said.

She shrugged. "I've got B, and no offense, Rondeau, but anything you can do, he can do better."

"He's had more time to learn how to use our powers," Rondeau said. "I'll get there."

"Given how little you practice, I don't think you're ever going to make it to Carnegie Hall. You guys could certainly be helpful, but Nicolette's demonstrated a willingness to use you as leverage, so let's take that tool out of her box, okay? Besides, you should get back to Vegas."

"Uh," Rondeau said. "There's this big demon, see, and—"

Marla shook her head. "That's all taken care of. The Pit Boss has agreed to pay you a fair rate for taking over your interest in the casino, and he's giving you back the rest of your shit."

Rondeau grinned. "Marla. Really? I'm rich again? I like being rich."

"It's occasionally useful for me to have a rich guy who owes me favors. You might not want to hang out in Las Vegas, though. Take your money from the Pit Boss and then go to San Francisco. Sanford Cole will set you up someplace. Try not to do anything apocalyptically stupid in his city, all right?"

"Yes ma'am."

"Mrs. Mason," Pelham said, "I would very much like to remain here to assist you. What Nicolette has done…" He winced, clearly skirting too close to the boundaries of his magical restrictions. "You might need all the help you can get."

"I need you to keep Rondeau out of trouble, Pelly. Do a better job this time, all right? Perren, tell Beadle to pull over and let them out—they can make their way from here."

"You're the boss." Perren's tone was only mildly ironic.

"Damn right," Marla said. "The once and future boss."

Marzi in Conversation

AFTER MARLA AND BRADLEY LEFT, Marzi did her best to get right back to real life, but somehow washing dishes or doing laundry or setting up the Kickstarter campaign for the next print collection of her webcomic seemed less necessary or compelling than usual, what with all the world-saving she'd just done.

"Damn it." She closed her laptop and went to the little round window, looking down at the street.

"What's up?" Jonathan said from the bed, where he was sitting surrounded by books festooned with bookmarks. He was working on an essay for an art studies journal—he hadn't entirely given up his academic side for the fast-paced world of café ownership.

"You remember after we defeated the Outlaw, how for a while afterward, everything seemed, I don't know..."

"Drab, washed out, grayscale, or maybe sepia at best?"

She nodded.

"Yup," he said. "Being flooded with adrenaline, having crazy focus, even magic I guess, it all makes for heightened reality, and after that goes away, everything seems a little bit flattened for a while. There's probably a name for the phenomenon, but if you want to know what it is, you should've shacked up with a psychologist instead." He rose and went to her, putting his arms around her waist and resting his head on her shoulder, so they were both looking out the little window at the dark street. "I'm sorry you had to go through all that alone today. If I'd had any idea, I would've stayed here. I wish I could've met this Marla character. She sounds like something else."

"She's that, all right," Marzi said. "Well, it's all over now."

"Do you miss it?" he said. "You want to get back into monster-fighting? You said Marla gave you a number you could call, if you want to find out about... all that stuff. Frankly it scares the shit out of me even thinking

141

about it, but you know I support you in whatever you want to do. If that means you want to become a wizard or something, well, okay. I've never made out with a wizard before. It'd be a new one for the life list."

"I don't know. It seems like making that call would be like dropping a bomb on my life, for maybe no good reason." But if learning about magic could make her as self-assured and effortlessly badass as Marla, wouldn't that be pretty amazing? Except she'd seen Marla as the Stranger, and the Stranger was not exactly a happy archetype. Being a brooding, damaged loner, at home nowhere in the world, always drifting—that went with the job, didn't it? Was it better to have a *big* life that was full of potentially awful things as well as awesome ones, or a little life that was mostly good?

Usually her life didn't feel too small for her. She had imaginary worlds in her head at all times, after all. But now the *real* world was starting to seem weirder than any fantasy realm, a sensation she hadn't experienced in years. "I think I shouldn't make any major decisions right after trapping an extradimensional monster in an imaginary desert behind a nonexistent door in the storage room of my café. Probably I'm not entirely in my right mind."

"So how's that different from any other day?" Jonathan said.

She elbowed him in the gut, and pretty soon, they went to bed, and a while after that, they went to sleep.

HER DREAMS, PREDICTABLY, WERE TERRIBLE.

That sky-spanning serpent of shadow was back, but now it rippled over a desert landscape, gliding above pyramids and towers of silence and temples carved out of cliff rock.

The perspective shifted and Marzi was looking down through the shadow creature's... not eyes, obviously, but some analogous sensory apparatus. She flew closer to the sand, where a scurrying rodent darted for safety, and then enveloped the animal, all the poor creature's organic material broken down and transformed into a sort of delicious-to-inhale vapor. Feeling stronger, she flew on, devouring a hare, a snake, and even a cactus next. Flying faster, she spiraled up to the heights, looking down for juicier targets. A pride—no, a riddle—of sphinges crouched together, belying their solitary reputations, gnawing on what looked like severed human legs, complete with gold ankle bracelets, except the legs were covered with black hair like a dog's. *The jackal-men*, Marzi thought distantly, but the tentative sort of body she was now inhabiting or riding-along with took no notice of her comment. At least she wasn't sharing the thing's *thoughts*, if it even had any.

She glided down to the sphinges, but they snarled and swiped and little whirlwinds of fire rose from the sand, making the shadow creature shy away. She moved on in search of easier prey, and eventually found a pack of jackal-men slouching toward one of their pyramids. She waited, watching, until one of them fell behind the others, distracted by a wounded foot—or paw, or whatever. Then the shadow dropped, and engulfed the jackal-man, the gold jewelry it wore tinkling to the sand when its tissues and bones and teeth were consumed. Then the shadow moved on, chasing after the others, feeling faster stronger better more *real*, adapted to this new place somehow now. The jackal-men raced into the pyramid and tried to roll a stone across the opening, but the shadow twisted and squeezed thread-thin and slithered through the gap, pursuing the howling jackal-men down torch-lit stone corridors. Hungering, satiated, hungering again, always chasing the next bite of reality—

Marzi sat up in bed, gasping, and Jonathan groaned and rolled over but didn't wake. She glanced at the clock. Just past midnight—she'd been asleep for less than an hour. She got out of bed, shivering—the nights were getting cool, and like most houses in this part of California, her place didn't have much in the way of insulation. That dream was just typical anxiety crap, right? It wasn't necessarily what Bradley called "one of *those* dreams"—

NOOOOOOO

An anguished syllable tore through her head, and she dropped, gasping, to her knees. It was a cold, alien, but familiar voice—the voice of the scorpion oracle.

Something was wrong. She had to get to the door, the door that had disappeared, but which she instinctively knew had returned. She got to her feet, glanced at Jonathan, and decided not to wake him. He was wonderful, he was her rock, but this was not his territory. Like it or not, this was her problem to solve, and bringing him into it would just give her something else to worry about. She was, apparently, the goddamned sheriff in this town.

Marzi grabbed her cap pistol and put it in the pocket of her robe, then went down the outside stairs in her slippers, letting herself into the café through the back door under the stairs. She stepped into the Teatime Room, trying to use her magical senses to get some idea of what exactly was happening—when her perfectly ordinary senses alerted her to the fact that someone was sitting in her closed and dark café.

She flipped on the light switch, one hand in the pocket of her robe.

A man sat at one of the tables, smiling at her. He looked exactly like the sphinx Marla had killed, except he had curly black hair, and one of those ridiculous hipster mustaches, with the ends waxed into curved points. He was dressed like an Old West dandy, in a fine gray suit, and there was a felt John Bull top hat on the table beside him. "Evening, ma'am," he said. "I hope you don't mind my making myself comfortable." He sounded like the sphinx, too. "Sit with me a while, would you?"

"We're closed." Marzi didn't move.

"Sit with me, or I'll eat you now," he—no, *it*—said matter-of-factly.

"How did you get *out*?" she said.

"I'll tell you, if you sit. I'm trying to learn to pass for human. Manners matter, don't they? Shouldn't *you* be more polite?"

Marzi moved toward it, though everything in her screamed that doing so was like walking toward a wild tiger. She pulled out a chair and lowered herself into the seat, never taking her eyes off the Outsider, or her hand out of the deep robe pocket that held her pistol. "Sure. I'll be as nice as you are."

"Isn't this better? I just wanted to thank you—before I eat you—for sending me to that wonderful place. It was like a buffet. And the main course! That immense scorpion! I have *never* felt so real as I do now, even in my home universe."

Marzi shook her head, not so much disbelief as *unwillingness* to believe. The scorpion oracle wasn't exactly a friend, but she had certainly saved Marla's life. "You... there's no way you ate her. She's a *god*."

"She was, yes. And all the more delicious for it. Oh, she was too much for me to take on immediately, I admit. My teeth, if you like, were too weak—my jaws could not open wide enough to accommodate her. But there are little spirits beyond that door, and I devoured those first, you see. Then I ate bigger things, like the jackal-headed men. When I was strong enough, I ate the sphinxes, too."

"Sphinges," Marzi said automatically.

"Quite so." The Outsider nodded as if she'd made a good point. "I learned a bit about manners from them, actually, even more than I did from the humans I ate before you showed me the way through the door. Sphinges are very sensitive to rudeness, did you know that? I have chosen to adopt that idiosyncrasy. Once I felt sufficiently strong, once I'd *grown* enough, I tracked that immense arachnid you call a god through her burrows and temples and tunnels. She altered reality in her attempts to escape me—the world over there is so much more *malleable* than this one. But I watched what she did, and I learned—I am always learning—and soon I could change things there as easily as she did. So I shrank her to something the size of a shrimp and picked her up and popped her into my mouth." The Outsider leaned across the table and smiled. It had rows of fangs, now, like the sphinx they'd faced beyond the door. "I'll eat you, of course—why wouldn't I? But I confess, I won't enjoy the taste as much as I would have a few days ago. I am a thing that eats gods, now. I have developed a taste for caviar, and you, my dear, are tuna salad at best. I want to eat *more* gods. I can feel them, out there in the world, like the magnet pulls to iron. I can smell their divinity, like roasting meat on the wind. I just wanted you to know, before I eat you, that you failed. I will eat all the gods of your world, until I become strong enough to eat the rest of you creatures in a single bite, every living thing on this planet. It's too tedious to think of eating you one at a time—really, it would take *years*. You should be honored I'm attending to you so personally." It opened its mouth, showing all those teeth, and its mouth seemed to *grow*, widening impossibly, and she knew it would soon be big enough to eat her in a gulp.

"My friends will stop you," Marzi said, because when all else fails, fall back on bravado. She felt her mind flexing, holding the thing in its human form, making it from a devourer of worlds into something more ordinary—a riverboat gambler, maybe. A dandy. Turning it from an *it* into a *him*. His rows of fangs shimmered and became a mouthful of ordinary white teeth.

Yes. She could do this.

He closed his mouth, blinking, then reached up and touched his own teeth, clearly baffled.

Marzi took the revolver from her pocket and pointed it at the Dandy's chest. "Actually, forget about my friends. Who needs them? I'll stop you myself. Right here."

"Oh, *please*—" he began, and she shot him in the heart, the cap gun snapping loud.

The Dandy looked down at himself, quizzical, and pressed his palm against the hole she'd blown in his perfect white shirt. Blood welled around the hand, dripping, and the Dandy hissed. His tongue flicked out, but it was the segmented tail of a scorpion instead of flesh. Her resolve wavered. This wasn't a riverboat gambler—this was a monster from somewhere else. This was an Outsider. She stood, leaned over the table, shoved the barrel of the revolver into its open mouth, and pulled the trigger again.

Another loud pop, but the back of his head didn't explode, which was what she'd been hoping for. The Outsider *did* fall backwards in his chair and scramble toward the door. It turned its head, and she was gratified to see one of its—no, one of *his*—eyes had turned to a puddle of blood.

She cocked the gun again to fire into his back—not very sporting, but he was a low-down dirty cheat, and this was less like murder and more like pest extermination. She could *feel* him trying to cast off his shape, to become an *it* again, nothing even remotely human, nothing that could bleed, and she clamped down as hard as she could to keep him in his place. He was *small*, a thug and a liar and a con artist, nothing majestic about him, nothing impressive, just another river rat preying on the ignorant and those of naive good will. A trickle of blood flowing started from her nose, and a spike of pain bloomed in the center of her forehead from the effort of making him stay human, but she ignored the pain. There was a job to do, and she was going to finish it.

The Dandy limped through the front door before she could get off a shot, and she followed him on unsteady legs. She might have to gun him down in the street. He might keep on looking like a man once she'd killed him, and if that happened, she might go to prison, though she'd like to see the prosecution make a case that she'd killed a man with an antique toy revolver for the murder weapon. She stepped through the door, lifting the gun and sighting between the shoulders of the Outsider—no, the *Dandy*—as he started to limp down the steps toward the street.

"Marzi, what happened, I thought I heard a gunshot—"

"Jonathan, run!" she shouted. He'd come down the exterior stairs from the apartment, and now he was on the deck, off to one side.

The Dandy moved with a speed that belied the grievous injuries she'd inflicted, and in a flash he was behind Jonathan, an arm around his throat. "Drop the gun, law dog," he grated. Half his face was curtained with blood.

Jonathan threw an elbow back into the Dandy's guts, but it didn't faze the monster at all. The Dandy tightened his grip and leaned backward, lifting Jonathan off his feet, making him gurgle as the tension on his throat increased. "Drop it now!" the Outsider said.

Marzi gritted her teeth and tossed the pistol behind her. "Let him go," she said. "Get out of here."

"Or maybe I'll just eat you *both*, and get my strength back," it said, and opened its fang-filled mouth.

You're dying, Marzi thought, as hard as she could. *Your heart isn't pumping blood anymore, and every organ you have is starved of oxygen. You've got a bullet in your head, and all this talking, all this moving, is just the last spasms of a dying brain. You will* fall *and you will* die *and you will* rot—

The Dandy cried out and stumbled back, releasing Jonathan and clutching his chest, then gave her a last murderous glare and hurled himself over the railing of the deck, to the sidewalk beyond, then ran into the street and off, away, into the darkness.

Marzi started after him. She couldn't let him get away, she had to keep him within her sphere of influence, imposing her worldview on him, keeping him *mortal* until he bled out and died.

She took a step, and a second step, tasting blood, and then the world went blurry and swimmy and then entirely away.

Nicolette in Control

NICOLETTE WAS USING HER HOTTEST BODY, because it wasn't enough to *be* better than Marla Mason—she wanted to look better than her, too. This body had belonged to a tattooed twenty-three-year-old bartender/grad student with big boobs and a hot ass and the combination of youth, a lucky metabolism, and an active lifestyle that kept everything else all taut and smooth. Nicolette wasn't especially into girls, but when she put her head on these shoulders, she spent a little longer than necessary admiring herself in the wall of mirrors in her room, touching herself all over and adjusting to the body's particular rhythms, calibrating all the senses and such. Nicolette's head didn't look exactly right on this body, being so pale, since the body had belonged to some kind of Latina, but fuck it, everyone would just be looking at her tits anyway.

Nicolette dressed for her audience in a black tank-top that showed off the ink on her arms and shoulders (mostly thorns, vines, and flowers, with a sort of Mexican art vibe), and a pair of tight black jeans, and black motorcycle boots. She had a throne of dark carved wood set up in the middle of the dance floor in Rondeau's old night club, which had become her de facto headquarters, with various thugs and loyal retainers loitering around ready to fetch and carry and generally attend to her every whim. Being in charge was even better than she'd ever imagined. Shit finally ran *right.*

She snapped her fingers, and one of the attendants scurried off and then scurried back with a glass of red wine that was supposed to be exquisite and tasted pretty great to Nicolette, who'd never cultivated much knowledge about the stuff. The attendant was eager to please and worried she was failing, so Nicolette gave her a smile after she took a sip, and felt the girl's rush of reassurance and delight flow through their connection.

Nicolette shifted around, trying to decide on the perfect pose, and settled on sitting almost sideways in the throne, one leg hooked over the arm, trying to look like a louche goblin king. She held her dagger of office in her other hand, tilting it back and forth, watching the blade shimmer in the house lights. As near as she could tell, this dagger was an exact duplicate of the knife Marla Mason still carried, which she figured meant Marla had pulled a switcheroo, and that *this* dagger was actually from another universe, and had probably belonged to the world-conquering supervillain known as the Mason. Nicolette didn't mind. The blade still had a hell of a pedigree, even if it wasn't Felport's real original dagger of office. Her silver hand-axe, sacred to some forgotten moon goddess and with a nasty magical edge of its own, hung in a sheath dangling on a belt hooked over the back of the throne, within easy reach. There was probably literally nothing on Earth Nicolette couldn't kill with this dagger in one hand and the hatchet in the other.

But she wasn't here for killing today. She was here for something *so* much better.

"They're here!" one of the underlings called from near the front door.

Nicolette gestured lazily, not letting her excitement show. A moment later, the woman herself appeared, Marla Mason, still wearing that stupid full-length buffalo leather duster. Pelham and Rondeau weren't with her. They'd probably been left somewhere safe. Good. That meant Marla was being cautious about her. Why let her lost puppies into Nicolette's clutches again? Maybe she wouldn't let them go next time.

Why did *I let them go?* she thought. Why hadn't she boiled them in lead or something? It just... hadn't seemed very important. Rondeau and Pelham were a way to get Marla to the city, and once Marla was on her way, there was no need to keep her allies locked up. They weren't a threat, and anything that was useful once might be useful again. Destroying them would be... silly.

Nicolette was not overly given to self-reflection, so she stopped, and focused her attention on Marla—and on the guy with her.

"Shit, is that Bradley Bowman?" she said. "What are you, a zombie, brought back from the dead like me? Marla needs to have some dead person following her around all the time?"

"He's very much alive." Marla stopped a few feet from the throne and looked at Nicolette. The throne was on a raised dais, so Marla had to tilt her head back, which did Nicolette's heart good. "He's just visiting from out of town. You, though, are out of your *cage*. I put you there for a reason, Nicolette. I wanted you to stay in it. But you had to get all flyaway and—is that Squat back there?"

Nicolette glanced over, and Squat stepped out of the shadows, all bundled in the heavy layers of coats and scarves that hid his grotesque physiognomy from casual view. Poor guy. She was working on treatment options for his condition, but there was still a lot of nasty stuck to him.

Crapsey came along with Squat, making every step a saunter. The two of them got along surprisingly well. Squat repulsed everyone—was *cursed* to repulse everyone, in fact—but Crapsey didn't find the guy off-putting at all. Probably because he was so self-absorbed. It had never occurred to Nicolette before, but Squat and Crapsey were sort of reflections of Pelham and Rondeau. Almost literally so for Crapsey—he was a much more psychopathic version of Rondeau from another branch of the multiverse. Squat had much of the same calm omnicompetence that Pelham displayed, though his talents were rather more crude. He wouldn't be as much good serving as a footman at a formal dinner, say, but they had other things in common.

Marla regarded Crapsey and Squat for a moment, then clucked her tongue. "So that's the brawn. Which means, unfortunately, that Nicolette is the brains, which means you guys brought some idiots to a genius fight." She pointed a finger at Nicolette. "What's to stop me from just letting death take you? The only reason you're not rotting is because I asked the god of the underworld for a favor. And keep that in mind, too, Nicolette—I'm the kind of person the *god of death* does favors for."

"Only because you let him fuck you, Mrs. Death," Nicolette said. "I can't imagine why anyone would *want* to get naked and wrestle with you, I'd rather put my dick in a food processor—well, when I have a dick—but whatever." She spun the dagger around in her fingers, and pointed the tip in Marla's direction. "This is hilarious. You're totally fucked, and you don't even know it." It was finally here, the moment of triumph, the unveiling of her grand design that would humble and humiliate and best of all *annoy* Marla Mason, Nicolette's unwilling but unambiguous nemesis. "Do you want to know why you're totally fucked?"

"Oh, yes, please, Nicolette, enlighten me. I'll give you two whole minutes before I wave my hand and send that raggedy remnant you call a soul plunging to a very unpleasant part of the underworld."

"No, you won't, because you're totally fucked. And the reason you're totally fucked is because I went full Fisher King up in this bitch."

Marla massaged her temples with both hands for a moment before looking back at Nicolette. "As usual, I have no idea what you're talking about."

"Felport, c'est moi," Nicolette said. "Didn't you say that once or twice? But I am the city in a way you *never* were." She turned and leaned forward in her throne, still reveling at having a body again and being able to make appropriately dramatic gestures. "I've established a sympathetic magical link connecting my personal health and well-being to that of every single person living in Felport. Just like the Fisher King, my health *is* the health of the people. When I prosper, the city prospers. And if I *don't* prosper...."

Marla cocked her head. "So if I let you die, everybody in Felport dies *too*?"

Nicolette nodded. "Elegant, huh? Almost like something *you* would do. The ultimate dead man's switch." She grinned. "Pelham saw me talking about it, spying on me through a magic mirror, just yesterday. I was afraid he'd spoil the reveal, so I stuffed a magical gag in the mouth of his brain. I have to say, though, I was expecting more stamping and screaming and hollering from you. You never fail to disappoint, do you?"

"B?" Marla said. "You have any insight into this bullshit?"

"It's true." Bradley stared fixedly at Nicolette, gazing into some metaphysical dimension. "She's got all these threads, little silvery lines, thousands and thousands of them, rising from her head and leading off into the air. A few of them are connected to people in this room, but most of them just disappear through the walls. I wasn't sure what the threads were before, but the kind of sympathetic link she's talking about... that fits."

"Don't go thinking about severing those threads with your magical knife, either," Nicolette said. "You could do it, but the shock would vibrate down every line and kill the people connected to them instantly, just as quickly as they'd die if *I* did."

"Pretty shitty governorship," Marla said. "If you slip and fall in the shower or choke on a chicken bone, everybody in the city dies? You're not impressing me with your leadership."

"Oh, I'm not too worried about mundane threats," Nicolette said. "For one thing, you gave me immortality—thanks, by the way. We did consider the possibility that I might get so crushed or vaporized that I might as *well* be dead, even if I technically kept living, so we addressed that, too. Turns out when you link yourself magically to all the people in a city, including its most potent magic-users, they get really heavily invested in making sure you stay safe. I've got so many anti-injury magics wrapped around me that a direct strike from a dinosaur-killer asteroid wouldn't bruise me. There's a whole lodge of order mages who do nothing all day but make sure my defenses are maintained. The only thing they can't guard against is *you*, the death goddess who gave me this eternal life, but that's okay—your conscience is all the defense I need against that."

"Mmm." Marla's face was perfectly neutral.

Nicolette had expected more—some rage, some *out*rage—but Marla liked defying expectations. Nicolette decided to twist the knife a little harder, to see if she could get Marla to wince. "At first, I tried to handle the sympathetic links on my own," Nicolette said. "I figured I could make a link with one person, and then make the connection contagious, right? Chaos magic has a pretty good handle on how pandemics work, spreading infections through random contact, and I figured I'd have the city pretty well blanketed within a couple of weeks. After that, I'd just have to track down the shut-ins and loners and hook them into the network. Good idea, right?"

"Mmm," Marla said again. "So why didn't it work?"

Nicolette managed not to grind her teeth. "I misjudged how powerful the sympathetic link was, basically. Seems like my magic got amped up after the whole touched-by-a-goddess treatment. There were some mishaps."

"There were, in fact, spontaneous decapitations." Hamil rode into the room on one of those little powered scooters like you see at a grocery store. The work Nicolette had—let's say encouraged—him to do had taken a lot out of him, and he'd lost a lot of weight, was still sleeping most of the day, and had trouble getting around. He smiled wanly at Marla, and Nicolette watched her old enemy for some sign that Marla was feeling a gut-punch of betrayal right then, but there was no reaction on her face at all. Hamil had betrayed her before, after all, when he'd voted to strip her of her title as protector of Felport and exile her from the city, but Nicolette was hoping this latest turn would hurt Marla more personally, seeing her old ally standing with her greatest enemy.

"Pretty lousy way to begin a reign, making people's heads fall off," Marla said.

"We were all quite baffled." Hamil steered his little scooter over beside Nicolette, almost running over Crapsey's foot until he scowled and stepped out of the way. Hamil parked beside the throne and regarded Marla for a moment before speaking. "People would simply walk along, minding their own business, and then…" He drew a shaky finger across his throat. "Their heads would fall off as if severed by an invisible sword. The condition seemed to be contagious, too. We lost half a dozen in a day."

"My magic was just too heavy," Nicolette said. "But Hamil here fixed the problem for me, and made the connection work right."

"Did he now." Marla's tone was flat, but flat in that barely contained, pissed-off way Nicolette had heard so many times before. Oh, how gratifying it was, to make her take that tone.

"I had no choice." Hamil's voice was calm, too, all "just the facts." "Nicolette's consolidation of power was swift and expert. Her friend Squat was a great help in her campaign. None of us were prepared to deal with… something like him."

On Nicolette's right, Squat preened, which pleased her. Poor guy didn't get much in the way of compliments, because of his magical medical condition.

Hamil went on. "When Nicolette came to me with her problem, I was outmatched, and helping her seemed better than the alternative. It *was* quite an interesting challenge, too. The force of the sympathetic connection was so immense that when cast on just one person it was overwhelming— they essentially *became* Nicolette, magically speaking, at least for the few moments before their heads fell off."

"The failed experiments became my spare bodies," Nicolette said. "I've got 'em, enchanted to stay fresh, in a walk-in closet with the rest of my wardrobe. This one's nice, huh? There's no issue with my brain running their bodies, no organ rejection or anything, because like Hamil said, they pretty much *are* me, now."

"A murderer who wears the corpses of her victims." Marla nodded. "Yeah, that sounds like you, Nicolette."

The witch queen of Felport gritted her teeth and kept smiling.

Hamil cleared his throat and went on with his explanation. "I had to come up with a way to blanket the whole city at once, to spread out the force of the spell so that it didn't land on anyone too harshly. The difference, essentially, between lying down on a bed of nails, as opposed to lying on a *single* nail—"

"You kicked me out because you said it was best for the city." Marla's voice wasn't trembling with rage or anything, but Nicolette was pretty attuned to the woman's moods, and she could smell the suppressed fury. "Then you turn around and help a chaos witch with a history of doing stupid, dangerous things take over that same city, and endanger every single person who lives here? I'm a little confused, Hamil. Maybe you could explain it to me. You were always good at explaining things. My consigliere."

"Mine, now," Nicolette said. "But sure, big man, go ahead and tell her."

"Letting Nicolette take control was best for the city," Hamil said. "Because if she couldn't control it, she was going to *destroy* it."

"I realized I could make the whole heads-popping-off thing into a feature, not a bug," Nicolette said. "Tweak the spell to give it a slightly longer incubation period so the infection had time to spread, right? Then, in a couple of weeks, instead of having a magical link with almost everybody in the city, everybody in the city would be *dead*."

"Then we'd just have to track down the shut-ins and loners, like she said before," Crapsey added from his spot behind Hamil. "And cut off their heads old-school. Nicolette's a completist."

"You see my position," Hamil said. "When presented with those options—to make Nicolette into a Fisher King, or see everyone in the city die—the choice was obvious."

Marla shook her head. "I see that you had a moment when Nicolette was in a room with you, making her pitch, and in that moment you could have stopped Nicolette, before she unleashed her contagious decapitation plague, and you *didn't*. You could have smashed her stupid melon head into pulp. She wouldn't have *died*, because I have to let her die, but she would have been in a lot of pain, and she would've had trouble casting spells or sweet-talking morons like Squat when she didn't have a *mouth* anymore. Why didn't you do that, Hamil?"

He just shook his head.

Marla nodded. "Yeah. Because you would have died in the process. Squat would have eaten you. But protecting a city is about putting the city's interests *above* your own, Hamil. Instead, you put *her* in charge, a woman who's just interested in annoying me. She killed how many people, wrecked how many lives, for what? To show me up? And you thought putting her in charge was better than sacrificing your life?"

"I did," Hamil said quietly. "Because I understood something Nicolette didn't."

Nicolette had been on the fence about letting Hamil mention this part. On the one hand, admitting what had happened to her after she went full Fisher King maybe smacked of weakness, or at least a blindness to unintended consequences, but hell, she was a chaos witch by training (even if she'd become something *else*, now), and dealing with unintended consequences was a big part of that specialty. Ultimately she'd decided hearing the truth would annoy Marla more, so she'd agreed.

"I bet we all understand about a million things each that Nicolette doesn't," Marla said, "but which one are you talking about now?"

"The sympathetic connection I created doesn't just work one way," Hamil said. "It's not *only* that Nicolette has a gun to the head of every person in Felport. It's… You're familiar with the Stockholm Syndrome, of course? When hostages begin to sympathize with their captors? There's another condition, usually called Lima Syndrome, which is the exact opposite: it happens when captors begin to sympathize with their *hostages*. The moment I connected Nicolette to the people of Felport, that happened to her. They ceased to be simply pawns in her power game. They became *real* to her. In a magical sense, the people of Felport are part of her, and Nicolette cares about their well-being as much as she cares about her own."

"I can feel them." Nicolette couldn't keep a certain dreamy tone out of her voice. The city and its people thrummed in the back of her head, and through her body, like a second nervous system, lit up with thousands of pleasures and pains. She could focus on individual connections or let the whole pulse through her. "I can feel the whole city. It's part of me."

"That's just the city sense." Marla's scorn was open, now. "It comes with being chief sorcerer. I had it, too. You can get a feel for the general health of the city, it's economy, it's environment, all that. It's diagnostic magic. Feeling it doesn't make Nicolette a better person."

Hamil coughed into his hand and shook his head. "No, Marla, what Nicolette has is a much more profound connection than the city sense. She can focus her attention on individual citizens. Indeed, she's taken steps to help the lives of some of those individuals with personal attention, in addition to instituting reforms—with my guidance—that can benefit the city as a whole."

"Me and Crapsey spent all day yesterday delivering hot meals to shut-ins," Squat said.

"We didn't even decapitate any of them," Crapsey said. "We're the good guys now. Feels weird, but the pay's good, and it's less strenuous than genocide, so whatever."

"I think it's bullshit." Marla crossed her arms and scowled. "It's just the city sense, and you're telling yourself it's something more to make yourself feel better, Hamil, about the shitty decision you made."

"I don't know, Marla." Bradley was looking around the room, presumably at the invisible silver threads he saw extending from Nicolette's head.

Marla glared at him. Nicolette wanted to clap her hands. "Even if it *is* true," Marla said, "and Nicolette cares as much about the city as herself, what good does *that* do? She's a chaos witch. The fundamental fact of dealing with chaos magicians is that they can never be counted on to do *anything*, not even to act in their own self-interest. They get their power from uncertainty and unpredictability. Sure, she's helping people now, but tomorrow she might decide to douse the city in napalm instead."

"I'm not a chaos witch anymore, Marla," Nicolette said. "I switched specialties. I'm a Fisher King now. A ruler connected to her people. I prosper, and they prosper, and vice-versa."

"It's true," Hamil said. "She *is* the city, in a way no other chief sorcerer has ever been. The methods that brought her here were... unorthodox... but she is not, precisely, the Nicolette you've known all these years. She's something more."

"I haven't changed *entirely*," Nicolette said. "I still hate your guts, for one thing, and I'm really happy I get to rub your face in my success. I'm going to run Felport *so* much better than you ever did."

"You've been in charge for all of five minutes," Marla said. "Wait until a *real* challenge—"

A phone rang, loud, one of the annoying default ringtones that came with cheapo pay-as-you-go phones.

Bradley coughed. "Ah, that's me. Do you mind if I answer it?"

"Oh, yeah, absolutely, go ahead, you're not interrupting anything important here." Nicolette thought the sarcasm was unmistakable, but Bradley just nodded and took out his phone. She opened her mouth to object but he held up a finger and put the phone to his ear.

"Sorry," he said, "This isn't a good—Ah. Wow. That's... wow." He frowned, listening intently, for a couple of *minutes*, how rude, then said, "Okay. We're on our way." He put the phone away, shot an apologetic look at Nicolette, then turned to Marla, who was still staring straight at Nicolette with that disconcertingly direct gaze. Trying to find a chink in her armor. Ha. Nicolette was all the way bulletproof this time.

Bradley said, "Marla. That was our friend, the one with the coffee shop? You know that thing she was holding for us? It kind of... got loose."

Now Marla turned her head and sighed. "Damn it. Never trust a giant scorpion. Is our friend okay?"

"She's all right. For now. Shaken up. But... you know."

"Yeah. I know. Well. Okay then." Marla shrugged. "Sorry, Nicolette. We'll have to postpone our ultimate reckoning thing for a little while."

"Are you *shitting* me?" Nicolette said.

Marla rolled her eyes. "Look, I know you're new to the whole chief-sorcerer gig, so I'll cut you some slack, but let me give you a little thought experiment. Let's say there's an upstanding businessperson downtown who's got a serious problem with vandals and general assholes breaking her windows, spray-painting her signs, things like that. It's a problem, right? You should probably do something about, make sure a cop gets assigned to patrol the area, maybe arrange for somebody to get punched. But let's say at the *same time* a giant rock from space is streaking through the air headed straight for your city, ready to turn the whole place into a crater full of extraterrestrial pathogens. Which one do you deal with first? City-destroying space rock, or broken windows?"

"City-destroying space rock, duh," Nicolette said.

"Right," Marla said. "That's what I'm going to deal now. You… you're just a broken window. B, let's get out of here."

"You aren't going *anywhere*," Nicolette said, but that was demonstrably untrue.

Bradley in the Park
with Marla

A GOON TRIED TO GRAB HER, but Marla kicked out his knee and ran for the door, Bradley following as fast as he could. Nicolette shouted "Stop them!", and Crapsey and Squat did their best to obey. Marla spun and tossed a handful of pebbles behind her, and the rocks exploded into stalagmites, sharp shards of stone bursting up to block off pursuit. They made it out the front door and Marla rushed down one side street, then another, muttering spells of illusion and concealment as she went.

They paused a few streets later, Bradley breathing hard because he didn't get as much exercise as he should in his position as defender of the multiverse.

"Oof. That was fun," Marla said. "So. What did Marzi say exactly?"

"That the Outsider busted out around midnight last night, after eating everything behind the door, including the scorpion oracle."

Marla sucked in air through her teeth. "Damn it. I didn't see that coming. Why the hell didn't Marzi reach out sooner?"

"She got hurt. Knocked out, or else she passed out from using her reality-messing-with powers too much. Her man took her to the hospital, and she's fine, they said she was really dehydrated, that's all, though they want to run a bunch of tests on her brain. She called as soon as she had a moment's privacy."

"I really wanted to spare her this kind of shit," Marla said. "Did she give you any more details?"

"She said the Outsider appeared in human form, sat Marzi down for a little chat, and said it was going to devour her, but she drove it off with her magical cap gun—wounded it badly, she thinks, but who knows how fast that thing heals?"

Marla grunted. "She's got steel in her spine, doesn't she? Marzi's a champion whether she likes it or not, I guess. Damn. That scorpion oracle

159

was a tough god. I liked her. Well, vengeance it is, then. Locking up the Outsider failed, so now we hunt it down and figure out a way to kill it."

"Now that's it's presumably a lot stronger, having eaten a god?"

"Exactly," Marla said. "Finally, a challenge worthy of my talents."

"So, what do we do? Take another plane trip? Nicolette's probably watching the airport. I don't think she was happy with us leaving."

"Fuck her, and fuck her gloating. Fuck the airport, too. We need to move faster than that. We can teleport, but... well. The things that dwell between branches of the universe don't like *any* living creature too much, but they're especially drawn to beings of power. You aren't technically a meta-god right now, and I'm not officially a death god at the moment, but we both know we've got some residual-energy-by-association that might make us light up brighter than most if we pass through those in-between places. Do we risk teleporting anyway, or do you have a better idea?"

"You don't know that folding-of-the-Earth trick Elsie Jarrow used to do?"

Marla shook her head. "She studied—or ate the brains of—some weird deep desert witches to get that skill. Spinning the globe under your feet is a nice trick if you can do it, but it's beyond me. I can call on my husband and take a shortcut through the underworld, but I hate asking him for favors—it upsets the whole balance of power in the relationship."

Bradley laughed. "Giving your husband some power is more distasteful to you than potentially being ripped to pieces by many-angled monsters who dwell between realities?"

"Obviously. I'm surprised you don't understand that. I thought you and Henry were married." She sighed. "I mean, yes, I'll call up Death and ask him to make a door for us, if that's the only way, I'm not crazy."

Bradley scrubbed a hand through his hair. "There might be another way, though. Let's go to Fludd Park."

BRADLEY HADN'T SPENT MUCH TIME in the park since he did his apprentice training with the nature magician Granger, a wizard of slow wit but immense power. Bradley had been awfully fond of the big man. He stood for a while looking at the mound of lush grass that marked the place where Granger had died during the Mason's Massacre, in this reality at least. Marla seemed to sense his need to take now a moment, because she didn't cajole or rush him, and after a couple of minutes of contemplation, he linked arms with her and began walking toward the white-painted gazebo. It didn't look like much, just a white wooden construction, but there were no beer cans, no graffiti, no cigarette butts, no used condoms. On some level, people could sense that this was a sacred place, and treated it accordingly. "Ready to see wonders beyond human understanding?"

"Just like I do every Tuesday?" Marla said. "Sure."

They went up the steps into the gazebo, and stood in the center.

Nothing happened. Bradley cleared his throat. "Sorry, I'm not in full possession of my powers, gotta get the collective overmind's attention."

"Sure, that's fine. No hurry or anything."

Bradley concentrated on opening a conduit, then had the strangest feeling he was being stared at. He tipped his head back, looking up at the gazebo's ceiling.

An immense eye, the blue of tropical waters, gazed down at them.

Marla looked up, too, and barked a laugh. "Behold the Eye of Bowman, huh?"

The eye blinked, and everything went black and bodiless. Sparkles, fireflies, and golden glitter spun through the darkness, whirling and then stopping, an incomprehensible constellation. Other colors appeared, green and red and blue and white and yellow, and gradually an image resolved, built up one pixel at a time as the blackness was filled by dots of illumination. They stood—except they had no bodies, so they more simply floated—before a painting of a garden, with a farmhouse just beyond, and the railing of a white gazebo before them.

Weight returned all at once, and the painting became a three-dimensional reality: they stood in a double of the gazebo from Fludd Park, in the place at the still center of the multiverse that Bradley called home. Henry was in the garden, trimming rose bushes with a pair of clippers, and he raised one hand in a wave. Bradley felt a surging tug of longing in his chest so powerful it almost made him gasp out loud. Henry had died in his branch of the multiverse, too.

"Huh," Marla said. "Very homey." She leaned on the railing and waved at Henry, who smiled and then went back to pruning bushes. "The old Possible Witch, we just had to climb a ladder, walk down some hallways, like that. What's with the pixelated fade-in?"

A voice behind them said, "Turns out, when the entry to your realm involves ladders and hallways, motherfuckers can just *walk in*. It's a little harder to get to me."

They turned, and the over-Bradley was there, sitting on one of the benches built into the gazebo, behind a small round wrought-iron table that held a full French press and two coffee cups. There was one empty chair, also wrought iron, with a cushion. He frowned, and another chair and cup appeared. "Sorry, damn, it's hard to think of you as a separate person, Little B."

"Don't you start with that 'Little B' shit."

Marla kicked one of the chairs, making it wobble. "I'd love to sit and sip and chat with you, oh overseer of all reality, but we've got a monster to chase."

"I slowed down subjective time here, we've got a few minutes. Sit."

They took their seats, and Little B poured them coffee, since in this company he was pretty obviously the low man.

"Good coffee," Marla said. "Kona?"

"Nah, from one of the coffee plantations on the moon," Bradley said. "In one of the weirder realities."

"I'll have to take a tour of those realities sometime. I'd be nice to feel less weird by comparison."

They drank coffee in silence for a moment. "It was a good idea," the over-Bradley said. "Trying to lock the Outsider up. It worked once before, after all—somebody stuffed it in a hole and covered up the hole, centuries ago. I wish I could see into the past, let me tell you. I'd love to know what they did. It's pretty clear our mistake was locking it up in a place full of stuff it could *eat*."

"Well, you live and learn. Any idea where the Outsider is now?" Marla said.

"I don't want to look at it too closely, because it's powerful enough now to look *back*," Bradley said. "After eating a god, it seems to have developed a sense for them—and for meta-gods like me, too, probably. If it saw me, and figured out a way to get here, it could get *everywhere*, especially if it ate me first and took on some of my power. But I can figure out where it is anyway, even without direct observation. It wants to eat more gods, so I think it's going to head for the nearest one it can find."

"Which is?"

"You remember Reva?"

Marla nodded. "He's a meddling busybody, like most gods, but not a bad guy."

"This is the god of exiles, right?" Bradley said.

"Exiles, the displaced, refugees, expatriates, anyone who can't go home again, yeah," Marla said. "You think the Outsider is going to try to eat him, Big B?"

"It's a working hypothesis. Reva's in San Francisco right now, ministering to all the homesick newcomers who moved in during the latest tech boom, I guess. It just so happens you've got a friend in the city who can give you aid and comfort in your search for the Outsider, too."

"So open up a portal or whatever," Marla said. "Don't get me wrong, the coffee's great, but I'm a *little* bit anxious to take care of this monster before my branch of the multiverse rots off."

"Can I give you a little advice about how to kill it first?" he said.

"Because you know more about killing stuff than a goddess of death? Absolutely. Let's hear it."

"As the Outsider takes on additional ontological weight, it adapts itself to the structure of our reality. It's taking on more power by eating people and monsters and gods, but it's also taking on some of the *weaknesses* of people and monsters and gods."

"Marzi made it bleed," Little B—damn it, he was thinking of himself that way now, in this context at least—said.

"Exactly. As it becomes less alien, it gets better at manipulating things in our reality—but it also becomes more vulnerable to damage in our reality."

"So kill it just like you'd kill any *other* god," Marla said. "Got it."

"Yeah, there's that. I'm honestly not sure it can die, exactly, not as we understand the term. Being trapped under Death Valley for centuries might have weakened it, but it sure didn't kill it."

"So we have no idea what we're going to do when we find it, but we're going looking for it anyway," Little B said.

"Godspeed," the over-Bradley said.

"What other speed could I possibly go?" Marla said, and then reality changed around them.

Little B in the Big City

"How have you been, Marla?"

"Oh, fine," she said. "The toads that rained down are eating a lot of the locusts, and with this plague of darkness, you can't really see all the blood."

"Ah. That well. How can I help you?"

"We're looking for a monster," Marla said. "Except at this point we're pretty sure it just looks like a person."

The small, white-whiskered old man sitting in the velvet armchair across from them nodded thoughtfully. "Ah," he said. "A person. That narrows it down. There are only about eight hundred and twenty-five thousand of those in San Francisco. Closer to seven million if you consider the Bay Area as a whole. Can you be any more specific than 'a person'?"

Marla shrugged. "We heard it was in a body that appears male, so that cuts the options in half, except it's probably a shapeshifter, so never mind. It's not very nice. It seems to literally gain power from killing people and eating them, or consuming them in some way that might as well be eating them."

"It's eaten at least one god," Bradley offered. "So far."

"That's… alarming," Cole said. "Why not summon an oracle and ask it for the whereabouts of your target?"

"Oh, we've been there," Marla said. "Without success. Something about this thing resists divination. Which didn't stop us trying again when we got to the city, just in case. We went to an alley in the Tenderloin and Bradley talked to something that looked like the ghost of a three-legged dog. You ever play with a Magic 8-ball? 'Reply hazy, try again later.'"

"This thing, we call it the Outsider, is too strong already, and trying to get stronger. Since my usual skillset failed, we're falling back on other lines of inquiry. Have you heard anything that might point us in the right direction? Any mysterious deaths or disappearances last night or this morning?"

Cole stroked his neat little beard. "I had a report earlier today about a shapeshifter. I've had trouble narrowing down its location through divination—and as you know, that's one of my strengths. I assumed my failure was because its form is so malleable, but it could be your monster. The city is woefully short of battle magicians since Susan Wellstone's tragic demise and the defection of many of her people to neighboring organizations, so I haven't tasked anyone to track the creature down yet."

Marla nodded. "Good thing I'm here, then."

"I will give you what information I have." Cole sighed. "I do wish you had more time to talk. Especially Bradley here. I never thought to see him again."

"Well, he's not *exactly* the Bradley who was your apprentice," Marla said.

"I know," Cole said. "But he's close enough to stir the pain of his loss."

"I worked with your counterpart in my universe," Bradley said. "I miss you too."

"You're a couple of sappy sons of bitches," Marla said. "We've got a monster to hunt. Give us some leads."

Cole examined a piece of paper. "There have been four deaths in the past twelve hours or so, all by drowning—two in bathtubs, one in a pool, and one in a toilet, of all things. All the victims were new to the city. Our population is booming now, with many new jobs in the technological sector opening up, and our population is swelling. "

"Huh," Marla said. "So young brogrammers move here, get good jobs, pay three grand a month for shitty studio apartments, drive up rents, price out longtime residents, the usual churn. Right?" Marla shook her head. "Running a city is rough even when things are going well, isn't it?"

"Indeed. I assumed the shapeshifter was a local sorcerer, angry about the changing face of the city, trying to make a point or warn people away... but perhaps it's your monster instead?"

"The Outsider is more about eating people than drowning them," Bradley said.

"Yeah, but our theory is that the Outsider is trying to track down the god of exiles and eat *him*," Marla said. "If he's killing people new to the city, he's killing *Reva's* people, right? That's the sort of murder spree that might get a god's attention."

"I knew this Reva was in the city," Cole said. "Though he hasn't visited me personally."

"Of course not," Marla said. "San Francisco's the home of your heart. You're not one of his constituents."

"Why not try to find Reva directly?" Cole said.

Bradley shook his head. "Same thing—the oracle was no help there, either. Gods are tricky to find. Usually *they* find *you*. Though if Marla prayed to him, maybe…"

"I *am* a god," Marla said. "I can't go around praying to other ones. That sets a terrible precedent. Give us the details on your drownings, Cole, and we'll look into this thing. It's a start, anyway."

They said their farewells and went out into the hallway. Marla's brow was furrowed, her brain working something over. Bradley flipped through the thin dossier Cole had given him, all those death, and—"There's a survivor."

"Huh," Marla said. "This I gotta see."

THE VICTIM SAT IN HIS TINY ONE-ROOM apartment in the Mission, jittering in a high-end office chair and intermittently gulping at an energy drink. He was bug-eyed and wild-haired and his shirt was turned inside out, but Bradley couldn't tell if that was typical of his nature or an expression of his recent trauma. He *did* know he was sitting on a dirty futon and there were piles of dirty clothes and take-out boxes everywhere, and it was pretty gross. Marla looked right at home, of course. "Look, Mr.—Lin?"

"Uh, yeah. Andrew. Call me Drew. Everybody calls me…" He looked around, seeming to notice the mess for he first time. "Sorry to make you come here, I know it's, uh, but it's just, I'm kind of jumpy about going outside…"

"You met a girl last night and she tried to drown you?" Marla interrupted.

Drew blinked at her, then looked at Bradley, who shrugged affably. "That's right, yeah." Drew spoke slowly, frowning, and he was probably trying to remember why he'd let these people into his place, why he was talking to them at all, but before he could go too far down that road, Bradley gave him another little psychic nudge, and he snapped back into focus. "Right. So, look, I went to MIT, I'd never been on the West Coast at all, not even to visit, but I'd heard about San Francisco, how cool it was, how hip, how everything was happening here, you know? Also how it never snows, which after all those years in Boston, that's pretty great by itself."

Marla nodded, not very patiently. Bradley could have probably just ripped the knowledge they needed out of the guy's brain without forcing them to endure a conversation, but he preferred a more delicate approach. This poor guy had been through enough.

"So I got here," Drew went on, "and mostly I just worked a lot, you know, sixty-hour weeks, sometimes eighty-hour weeks during crunch time, the start-up standard. Occasionally I'd go out to clubs and bars and I'd see those San Francisco girls, with the piercings and the straight black bangs and the cool tattoos and the motorcycle boots and the heavy eyeliner, and I tried to make time with a few of them, but mostly they seemed to be laughing at me or bored by me, you know? They'd let me buy them drinks all night but then they'd leave with some hipster wearing tiny pants and giant glasses, or else with another girl. The only real date I had was with another programmer, who also went to MIT, and I mean, I could've stayed in Boston, right?" He took a breath. "But then last night, I was sitting in this little hole-in-the-wall burrito joint after another bad night at the bars, it was maybe two in the morning, and I met her. Llyn." He spelled the name, and Marla grunted.

Would the Outsider call himself by a name like that? Bradley wondered. What kind of name was it, anyway? Welsh, or just pretentious?

Drew went on. "She was… she was just this hurricane of a girl, you know? Tiny, maybe five-foot-one, barefoot, wearing a short skirt and a shiny top and about eighteen hundred scarves in all different colors, bangles on her wrists, ankle bracelets, red and green streaks in her hair, ukulele hanging on a strap on her back, purse made out of a plush toy squid. She ordered a big bowl of jalapenos and then just sat down across from me, looking at me with these huge blue eyes, popping peppers into her mouth and grinning. We ended up walking around and talking all night. She told me she was an art-school drop-out who was into doing sculptures with found objects, and that she spent a lot of time busking on her ukulele for the tourists, and that she liked meeting people who were new to the city because they still had a sense of wonder, and did I want to go back to my place, so, ah…" He blushed, and Marla rolled her eyes. Bradley gave Drew's sense of propriety a little nudge, and he said, all in a rush, "So we could do some molly and she could suck my cock and then make me pancakes."

"And you said yes," Marla said. "Hell, who can blame you? A manic pixie dream girl straight out of a stupid indie film offers you a totally San Francisco experience, who wouldn't say yes? So what happened?"

Drew looked down. "This place is tiny, but one of its good qualities is the bathroom." He rose and went to a door with a crystal knob and opened it up, beckoning them to look inside. The bathroom was almost as big as the rest of the apartment—clearly it had been the master bath, and his "apartment" had been the master bedroom, before this house was chopped up into tiny units. The floor was tiled in honeycombs of white and blue, and there was a pedestal sink and a toilet in a fetching shade of teal porcelain, but the space was dominated by was a huge claw-foot bathtub with a showerhead suspended above it.

"She came in, and we made out for a while, and then she wanted the tour, which was kind a joke, but whatever. She looked at the bathtub and her eyes got real big and she said we *had* to take a bath together. At that point I still had no idea what she looked like naked, every time I managed to get a scarf off her there were ten more underneath it, so I jumped at the chance. She took my clothes off and put me in the tub and sat on the edge while it filled up, and I mean, she had her hand in the water, and it was pretty nice...." He trailed off. "The tub filled up, and I asked her when she was going to get in with me, and that's when she pushed me under."

Bradley nodded. His first thought was: serial killer dresses up like cliché quirky girl to exploit the fantasies of young brogrammers, preying on the tech elite as a symbolic protest against the inevitable horrors of gentrification. But Cole said it was weirder than that, and it got that way fast.

"She was strong. Crazy strong. Couldn't have weighed more than a hundred pounds, but she pushed me under like it was nothing, one hand on my forehead, one on my chest. I looked up at her through the water, and I guess it was just the drugs, but... her face changed. Her body, too. Rippled like water, became translucent, it was like, she *became* water, but her hands were still solid. After a couple of minutes she stopped holding me down and left." He shrugged.

Bradley frowned. "Wait, so how did you survive? Did someone resuscitate you?"

He shook his head. "I'm good at holding my breath. Have been since I was a kid, when I went swimming a lot with my dad, and I just kept at it. I used to win breath-holding contests, it was my party trick in college. I mean, I'm not like those free divers who can stop breathing for twenty minutes, but two or three minutes? Sure. Once I realized she was trying to drown me I thought I'd better just play dead, and it worked. I think I would have freaked out a lot harder if I hadn't been on drugs, honestly. Molly saved my life."

"No sign of her when you got out of the tub?" Marla said.

He shook his head. "No, she was just gone. There were lots of puddles, though, all over the hardwood in the main room, like she'd dripped tons of water around. I called the cops, they took her description and told me not to pick up strange women in burrito shops anymore, and that was it. I don't get the feeling they're assigning a task force or anything."

"What time did she leave?"

"I mean, the whole thing from meeting her to her leaving, it only took maybe two hours."

Bradley could see Marla doing mental math. The Outsider flees Santa Cruz a bit after midnight, and appears as a cliché dreamgirl in San Francisco two hours later? It was an hour and a half drive at least, but the Outsider was capable of alternative modes of locomotion, so *maybe* it could work, if Drew was its first attempted victim. The other drownings had come later, throughout the remainder of the night and on through the day, the last one a death in a swimming pool just an hour before they'd sat down with Cole. But why death by water? The Outsider *had* been trapped in the caverns below Death Valley for centuries. Maybe it was feeling retroactively dehydrated? Something just didn't make sense.

Marla nodded. "Well, thanks for your—"

"Wait," Bradley said. "There's something you're not telling us."

Drew frowned, and Bradley pushed, and Drew moaned. "Okay, fine, she left one of her scarves, it's under my pillow. I know it's stupid, it's sick, but it still *smells* a little like her, she was so hot, I can't help it—"

"Show us," Marla said.

Drew went to his futon, lifted up a pillow, and picked up a long piece of ragged seaweed. He rubbed it against his cheek, sighed, and handed it to Marla, who took the slimy thing in her hands. "A… scarf," she said.

He nodded. "Smells like, I don't know, vanilla and baby powder and the cherry soda I liked when I was a kid…"

She handed it wordlessly to Bradley, and it smelled like salt and rotting fish to him.

"We'll have to take this," Marla said, "but on the plus side, we won't tell the cops you withheld evidence, okay?"

ONCE THEY WERE OUTSIDE, Marla took the seaweed again. "Well?" she said. "Does this look like a scarf to you?"

"Seaweed. But I looked into Drew's mind and I could see the psychic tampering. I fixed it while I was in there. But I left his caution about picking up ukulele girls in bars."

"You're such a humanitarian, B. Can you use this scrap of slime to track down our mystery woman?"

"Pretty sure she's not actually a woman," Bradley said, "but I'll do the psychic bloodhound thing, sure."

"It's not the Outsider, is it?"

Bradley shook his head. "I don't think so. We don't know what forms this nixie or kelpie or whatever has taken in other attacks, but in this one, it showed a pretty sophisticated understanding of human psychology and expectations—more than that, it seems to have a sense of *humor*. I mean, the ukulele? Infinite scarves? That's comedy, right? Like, it's a *reference*. I don't think the Outsider saw too many indie films in the impossible desert."

"Manic nixie dream girl," Marla said. "That is pretty funny, except for the death by drowning."

"So, I mean… do we go tell Cole we're sorry, this isn't our monster, good luck killing it?"

"Eh. We're here anyway, and this still might lead us to Reva—he's got to be looking for the thing that's killing his people, right? So let's track down little miss death by water."

THEY WOUND UP ON THE WESTERN EDGE of the city, down by the ruins of the Sutro Baths, the once-vast swimming pool complex on the beach that had been reduced by demolition and fire to concrete foundations and a few vestigial fragments of the old buildings. The place was usually popular with tourists who came to hike, take in the shattered grandeur, and look out at the ocean and the nearby Seal Rocks, but today it reeked of rotting fish, and the wind from the sea was salty and stingy, and it was just generally vile and unpleasant. "This place is awful, let's go somewhere else," Marla said, but Bradley grabbed her arm.

"Somebody cast a keep-away spell over here," Bradley said. "A strong one. Of course, I'm immune, but your puny mortal mind is no match for the magic."

"Who're you calling mortal," Marla muttered, shaking his hand off.

"Well, you're mortal at the moment. Here, let me clear your head."

"No thanks." She ducked her head and stomped down the path toward the ruins. Bradley probed into her mind, gently, just tapping into her senses because he was wondering how the spell felt to her, and it was awful: the stink making her eyes water, the wind battering her, the fear that she would slip and fall and be swept away and die (even though lately she couldn't die) growing ever stronger until—

—she broke through the bubble of the spell and blinked at the calm sea, breathed in the brisk salt air, and didn't worry about death a bit, as usual. Bradley stepped up beside her. He pressed the rag of seaweed to his face, sniffed, then pointed. "Down there, by the waterline, there's a cave. I'm pretty sure there's not *supposed* to be a cave, but somebody made one."

"Cave invasion time, then."

They picked their way down the rocks to the beach, and Bradley saw the shadow in the cliff wall where the cave must be. Marla drew her dagger and stepped forward carefully, boots sinking into the soft sand, toward the darkness. "Fiat lux," she muttered.

Bradley knew she was activating her enhanced night vision, but she didn't need it: the blackness of the cave mouth was an illusion, and once they stepped inside, the space was lit by battery-powered camping lanterns resting on rocks and hanging from pitons hammered into the cave walls.

An old man wearing a pair of black swim trunks and nothing else was snoring in a brightly-colored hammock swaying in a metal stand, next to an iron cauldron that would have done the witches from *Macbeth* proud.

Marla glanced at Bradley. He shrugged and leaned against the damp wall of the cave. This was more her kind of thing than his.

Marla walked over, put her boot on the hammock, and dumped the old guy out.

He sprang up, sputtering. "What the shit?" His eyes—they were red-rimmed, matching the burst veins in his nose—went wide and he shouted "Llyn!"

The contents of the cauldron bubbled up into a fountain, which turned into the watery semblance of a girl, translucent except for a few scraps of seaweed that sort of looked like hair, and teeth made of shards of shell. The nixie hissed, the water around her mouth boiling in the process, and started to climb out of the cauldron.

Marla lashed out with her dagger, right at the thing's face. It screamed and fell back when the blade cut across the indentations it had for eyes. Marla slashed down in a looping s-curve through the nixie's body, and water splashed everywhere, seaweed and shells splattering back down into the cauldron. The old man gaped. "What—what did you do?"

"This knife was made for me by the god of Death," Marla said. "Forged in an *awfully* hot Hell, a lake of fire conjured by the imagination of a dead guy with a lot of guilt but not much imagination. This blade can cut through anything I want it to. Stone, steel, astral tethers. Water molecules. Don't worry, your nixie will get her shit back together eventually, but right now a large portion of her anatomy has been reduced to hydrogen and oxygen atoms, and it takes a girl a little time to recover from that." She held up the knife. "Now, what should I cut *you* into?"

"I won't fight." He held up his hands. "Did Sanford Cole send you? I—I don't recognize his authority, you know. I'm a sea witch, Alexander Thelonious Shaw, my people have been here since the Egg Wars, and—"

"Hush. The hierarchy of the city's magical community could not interest me less. You were murdering innocent people with your little water goblin there. Why?"

He hugged his arms around his pale pigeon chest. "These new people. They're destroying the whole culture of the city. Altering the city's personality. Driving out the artists, the creative people, the ones who make it a world-class place to live. Soon it's going to be nothing but young technocrats, consuming without creating."

Marla snorted. "This new wave of people moving in isn't any different from the *old* waves of people moving in. The hippies pouring in here in the Sixties changed the whole nature of the city, too. The Beats changed things before that, in the Fifties. The people who came for the gold rush in the 1850s—I assume those were *your* people, Mr. Egg War—changed the hell out of the city too. Unless you're Ohlone, bitching about the arrival of Spanish missionaries in the Eighteenth century, I don't really want to hear it. Some of these new tech people are assholes, I'm sure, but some of them are perfectly nice people who heard San Francisco was a great place to live, and wanted to move here, so they did. Didn't you just *have* a tech boom like ten years ago? Gods. You should be used to this. Stop bitching and move to Oakland until the next inevitable bust in the economy drives the programmers out of San Francisco again if you hate it so much. Seriously, there's gotta be more to it than that. What made you start murdering people? Did you get kicked out of your apartment so some douche-bros could move in?"

Shaw lifted his chin. "I am a sorcerer. I can live wherever I choose." He sighed. "But my favorite bar, where I went every day for decades, was closed and replaced by an artisanal toast restaurant."

Bradley whistled. "Damn, dude," he said. "That is rough. I mean, murder's still wrong and everything, but… damn."

"Call Sanford Cole and tell him we caught his murderer," Marla said. "Tell him if he wants to reward us with riches and resources they'd be welcome." She sighed. "And then I guess we get back to work."

MARLA AND BRADLEY SAT ON THE STEPS leading down to the beach at Aquatic Park in North Beach, watching the sailboats cruise around the bay, and looking at the fog-shrouded towers of the Golden Gate Bridge.

They were eating double-doubles, animal style, that they'd picked up from the In-N-Out Burger a few blocks away.

"Wow, I missed cheeseburgers," Bradley said. "Being an omnicognizant super-god living in a pocket watchtower dimension overseeing the complexity of the multiverse is great, but there's a real dearth of local restaurants. I should do something about that."

"Just visit us mortals, and part-time mortals, more often," Marla said.

"Should've gotten sodas," Bradley said. He reached toward her bag. "Let me get a drink of—"

She slapped his hand away. "That's not water for drinking." He raised an eyebrow, so she picked up the plastic liter water bottle and shook it up, stirring the sand, flecks of seaweed, and jagged shards of seashell at the bottom around. "While you were talking to Cole's people about securing Mr. Sea Witch, I was having a chat in the cave with Llyn, who'd mostly reconstituted herself, and she's agreed to go traveling with us."

Bradley laughed. "You've got a nixie in a *bottle*?"

"Well, I'll have to dump her in a pond, or at least a full bathtub, if I want her to appear in human-sized body again—she needs more volume for that kind of thing—but, yeah."

"You haven't had the best luck in the past, taking on murderers as allies. Squat, Nicolette, your brother..."

"Oh, Llyn's not a murderer—she was a murder *weapon*. She was under a compulsion to serve old what's-his-egg, Shaw. I broke the chains of his spell with my dagger, and she's promised to repay me with a month of service, and then she'll go jump in a lake somewhere."

"Mmm. Don't nixies historically drown people just for fun?"

Marla stashed the bottle back in her bag. "She assures me she's entirely harmless. You know I've got a trusting nature. Besides, some creatures *need* to be drowned. We need all the allies we can get if we're going to face the Outsider and deal with my *other* problems. Me, you, and a magical knife are great, but more options don't hurt."

"Ain't that the truth."

Marla's phone rang. Cole. She handed it to her former apprentice. "You talk to him. I've been thanked enough."

Bradley spoke, listened, grinned, and then handed the phone back to Marla. "Cole gave us a line of credit, so we can afford to sleep in the kind of motels that don't have bedbugs without having to steal or mind-control people first."

"Good. Being a wealthy patron is more fun than having one, but I'll take what I can get."

"Better news," Bradley said. "Cole tasked his whole psychic corps over to me, the ones he uses to detect threats to the city, impending earthquakes, stuff like that. I'll get their brains networked together and make them look for dead spots—places they *can't* see."

Marla whistled. "The Outsider blocks divination, but if you can find those blank spaces on the psychic landscape…"

"Yep. The Outsider is hiding in the places we *can't* see. So this approach should give us some—"

"Hello, Marla." A dreadlocked shirtless white boy hippie in a rainbow knit cap and frayed corduroys and hemp shoes sat down on the steps beside them. He reeked of patchouli sufficiently to make Bradley's eyes water. "I just wanted to thank you for tracking down the man killing my people."

Marla gave him her most epic side-eye. "Reva? You're uglier than you were last time I saw you. Smellier, too."

"My bodies are constructed randomly to match local norms," he said. "This isn't my idea—it's just the nature of my corporeal manifestation." He looked Bradley up and down. "Dude. You are *way* far from home."

"He's from the universe next door. Don't worry about it." Marla put her arm around Reva's shoulder. "You're just the god I wanted to see. How do you feel about being bait?"

Reva frowned. "I feel… not good?"

"See, there's this thing, we call it the Outsider, and—"

"Whoa." Reva shook off Marla's arm and rose abruptly to his feet. He extended a long arm, pointing a finger at a figure in gray walking toward them along the waterline. "I thought your friend was a stranger here, but *that* guy is from *way* out of town."

Marla jumped to her feet, and Bradley wasn't far behind her. "Reva, you need to take off. Discorporate, turn into a flock of starlings, whatever you do, just *go*."

"Marla, there are *people* around, I can't just go around disappearing…" He trailed off. The approaching figure's body appeared to be smoking, now, black tendrils drifting up from its shoulders and head, surrounding it in a cloud of shadow.

"That's a thing that *eats gods*, Reva. Discretion is a privilege of those who aren't about to be devoured."

"I'll, uh, see you around." Reva took two steps backward and vanished, leaving nothing but the smell of patchouli behind.

The thing down the beach *howled*, a noise like an air raid siren, making the tourists and joggers and beachcombers and wave-watchers and sunset hunters all turn and stare.

Marla went to the packed sand at the edge of the surf and scuffed something in the dirt with her heel: a nasty keep-away sign, probably, based on how quickly everyone on the beach scattered, all of them practically running inland.

Marla drew her dagger. "Get your psychic arsenal ready, B. If this thing's got a body, maybe it's got a brain you can fuck with."

"On it." He followed Marla as she walked toward the Outsider, closing the gap from fifty yards to forty to thirty to twenty to ten. The thing had pulled its shadows back in by then, and it appeared much as Marzi had described it: waxed mustache, Old West suit, low-crowned top hat, face of a sphinx. It approached them, just a bit warily, which Bradley appreciated. The Outsider stopped, then turned and stared out at the bay and the islands and the sailboats. It took a deep breath, closing its eyes. "Ah," it said. "That's nice."

"Hey, Dapper Cthulhu," Marla said. "Eyes on me."

The thing in the suit turned its head, just a degree or two farther than should have been anatomically possible, and regarded her. It closed its eyes and inhaled again, like a gourmand presented with a bowl of exquisite consommé. "Mmm. Hello, old friends. I can see you so much better than I could before. You're touched by what passes for divinity in this abominable universe." Its head turned toward Bradley, twisting even more unnaturally, though it still didn't open its eyes. "And you... A psychic, yes, but mmm, there's something else, what is it? A hint of an echo of something more... do I see a gazebo? In a park, far away? Where does *that* lead? I can taste the residue of its power all over both of you."

Bradley did his best not to let the alarm show on his face. If this thing could sense his connection to the center of the multiverse, if it could somehow follow that thread *back* to Fludd Park, fight through the defenses and reach the realm where the over-Bradley dwelled....

"If you're done hallucinating, we can get started," Marla said.

The thing shook its head. "These flavors are *exquisite*. I didn't get everything emulated properly in this body, I don't think—I can taste sounds, hear scents, and everything bleeds into everything else. The two of you are so *rich*. Too delicious for this filthy world."

"Our world wasn't so filthy until you showed up," Marla said. "You're the cockroach in the candy bowl around here. We came to squish you."

Less bantering, more murdering, Bradley thought. He reached out for the thing's brain, to see if he could squeeze a few pathways shut, maybe cause it to pass out, but the Outsider wasn't really human, it was just disguised as one. Maybe if Marzi were here, imposing her worldview on the monster, his powers would have worked, but not in the current circumstances.

"I see." The Outsider opened its eyes and nodded at them, almost beatifically. "I should say, in the interests of common courtesy, that you have no *idea* what you're dealing with."

"Oh, I've dealt with things from beyond this universe before," Marla said. "They're not around anymore. I am."

"Oh, yes. I've reviewed the footage."

Bradley frowned. What the hell did *that* mean? This thing had capabilities they hadn't even considered.

The Outsider went on. "You refer to the thing you thought was a cloak. It came from the same place I do, yes. My people keep those creatures as pets. Your cloak couldn't even survive in this universe without latching on to a living host. As you can see, I am rather more adaptable."

"We'll see how you adapt to being cut into little pieces. You know, you should have stayed locked up. Putting you away in that desert was me trying to be merciful. It's something I've been working on lately. But screw it. Vindictive it is." She shrugged out of her coat and handed it to Bradley.

The Outsider didn't look particularly worried. "Can't we talk a little while first? I haven't had many opportunities for conversation. Something about inhabiting this body, taking on a semi-divine form, makes me chatty. Besides, there are some things you should know, before I eat you."

"Last words are acceptable," Marla said. "Just don't ramble on too long. I react badly to boredom."

It sketched a little bow. "Regarding your threats, I would normally say, 'Do your worst.' Perhaps you are capable of killing me. It seems improbable, but I found it improbable that Neolithic tribesmen could imprison me in a void embedded in the earth, and *that* happened. Perhaps you could even slay me. But this universe is a *multiverse*—that's part of what attracted me here in the first place. This is a place where anything that can happen, *does* happen. You might kill me, but the moment of my death would split, creating branches where I escape, and other branches where I kill you instead, and so on. This multiverse truly does have remarkable properties. I don't wish the end of my present continuity of consciousness, but I would die somewhat more peacefully in the knowledge that another version of me moved on to continue my work, and that in some branch of this universe, I *will* succeed. I *must* succeed, if there is even the slightest chance of success." It sniffed. "The place I come from is less… forgiving. Not a multiverse. Failure there has greater consequences."

"I don't concern myself with every facet of the glittering sphere of the multiverse." Marla shifted her stance, dagger in hand. "Let the worlds behind the looking glass take care of themselves. I'm concerned with the present moment and the present place, what we like to call the here-and-now. Though I admit, I do take comfort in knowing that, if it's possible for me to kill you, I'll kill you in *some* universe. I think there's a good chance I'll kill you in *all* of them."

The Outsider chuckled. "That's the thing I wanted to tell you. Your sensitive friend must realize. Surely he *feels* it, even if he doesn't understand *what* he feels. This particular branch of the multiverse has been rendered acarpous."

Marla frowned. "What does that mean? 'Without fish'?"

"Sterile," Bradley said. "It's a botany term. A plant that can't produce fruit anymore." The Outsider wasn't supposed to know this branch of the multiverse had been cut off from the rest. What kind of senses did this thing *have*?

"Yes." The Outsider bowed its head a fraction in acknowledgment. "The tree itself continues to thrive, I suspect, but *this* branch has been sterilized. What happens here, now, is the *only* thing that can happen. No more branches. No more possibilities. I wonder if it's a natural defense mechanism of the multiverse, when faced with a creature like me, to freeze the infected portion to protect the whole from my depredations? I don't think so. I suspect there is… an agency… guiding this phenomenon. An intelligence. Something as high above your gods as the gods are above mortals." It rolled its head on his neck, like a wrestler limbering up before a bout. "If so, I will continue to gain ontological mass until I become sufficiently powerful to perceive that agency. To *threaten* that agency, and force it to open this universe to me." The Outsider grinned, and though they weren't shark fangs this time, they *were* all canines. "Wait. That's what the gazebo is, isn't it? A physical portal to a metaphysical place. Oh, my."

Fuck fuck fuck, Bradley thought. And then, for good measure: *Fuck.*

"Oh, how wonderful." The Outsider shivered all over, face transported with ecstasy. Seeing that made Bradley's guts clench. It was like watching a genocidal madman achieve orgasm. "Devouring you, my sensitive boy, and you, my demi-god, will be a good start toward making me strong enough to eat whatever lives beyond the gazebo. I could content myself with consuming this tiny branch of the universe, I suppose, but why limit myself? In a multiverse, the energy available is functionally, if not technically, *infinite*. I can suck this entire cosmos dry, and then tear my way through the tissue-thin membrane separating it from the dimension next door, and drain that one, too. My universe is a husk, sucked dry. This one... well. I've always been something of a glutton, when left unchecked, and I see no need to check myself." It opened its arms wide, and black smoke trickled out of its pores, its nostrils, its eyes, its ears. "And so, you see, I cannot simply let you do your worst. I can't risk the chance, however infinitesimal, that you might succeed. I—"

"Boredom threshold exceeded." Marla lashed out with her blade, and the dagger parted the cloud of shadow forming around the Outsider like it was gauze, leaving a ragged tear. The thing hissed—and then surged forward, lightning quick, reaching out with both hands. Marla dodged out of the way, actually *laughing*, and cut up more of the shadows, sending tatters to the sand, where they turned to acrid vapor. She'd always been graceful in battle, but she was in rare form now, moving more fluidly than Bradley had ever seen her move without her purple battle cloak.

The Outsider kept trying to close on her, and she simply drove it back with slashes, landing a cut on its chest that made its howl and dodge away. She moved in close herself, then, and simply *flurried* stabs at the Outsider, thrusting the knife into its guts and chest faster than Bradley's eye could follow. She'd told Bradley about knife fighting before, how it was all well and good to be fancy, but the best way to kill someone with a blade was "The Folsom City Rush": just hitting them fast and hard and filling them full of holes before they knew what was going on.

The Outsider howled and backhanded her across the face. Bradley heard her neck snap, and she flopped onto the sand, unmoving. The Outsider knelt to pick up the dagger, but it twisted in the monster's hand, severing most of its fingers. The Outsider hissed, its form losing cohesion, part of its face sloughing away to reveal the shadows underneath, the eyes empty holes full of darkness. "I will *eat* her, and then you—"

The door of the low stone building on the beach opened, and a long-haired handsome man in a dark suit of elegant cut emerged. "No, you won't." He reached out one hand, rings glittering on every finger, and eight-foot high pillars of flames burst from the sand all around the Outsider.

Holy shit. Bradley wrapped Marla's coat around himself, its protective magics keeping him safe from the furious heat as he stumbled away. He couldn't see what was happening, but there were roaring sounds, and howls of pain, and then silence.

Bradley turned to find the newcomer kneeling on the sand, vomiting. He straightened, and looked at Bradley, and Bradley's focus *shifted*. That wasn't a man at all. It was the god of death, Marla's husband. Death shouldn't be that pale and trembling, but he was.

"I drove it away." Death rose unsteadily to his feet. "Things like that… they're abhorrent to me. Utterly outside the natural order. *My* natural order. I thought Marla's cloak was bad, but *this*, it makes the cloak look like… a butterfly. A fluffy bunny. If it hadn't already been hurt, I don't know if it would have fled even under my assault."

"Where did it go?" Bradley asked.

"Turned to shadow and flew off to the east." Death shrugged. "I assume you and Marla were hunting it?"

"Yeah. It's an end-of-the-world deal."

"Isn't it always?" He extended a hand. "I'm Death."

"Uh, yeah. Bradley. Bowman." He shook. The hand felt perfectly normal.

"Of course. I'm going to resurrect Marla now."

"Oh. Yeah? Okay. Good. That's good." Bradley wondered if he'd ever reach a point where *nothing* struck him as weird anymore. He clearly hadn't gotten there yet.

"Normally she just heals, even if her body is entirely destroyed, my presence isn't necessary—I try to give her space during her months on Earth. But that thing… it was going to do something drastic to her, something we don't even have words for—'devouring' doesn't begin to cover it. I wasn't sure what would happen, if it consumed her, so I thought it best to intervene, though it annoys her when I do."

"Well, that's married life." Bradley knew he was being inane but he couldn't help it. Seeing Marla get her neck snapped had messed with him a little bit.

Death knelt, touched Marla's cheek, and she shouted and leapt to her feet, brandishing her dagger. Then she noticed her husband. "Oh. Hell. Dapper Cthulhu got in a lucky shot, huh?"

"Apparently. The creature has run off."

"Then we've got to do some running of our own."

"Marla," Bradley said. "If the Outsider knows about the gazebo, if it can figure out where it *is*, trace our scents or 'review our footage' or whatever the hell it does—

"Yeah," Marla said. "I know. We've got to go back to Felport."

"Is all this necessary, darling?" Death said. "I hate to see you in pain."

"The best cure for my pain is causing pain to someone *else*. Thanks for the intervention, but we've got it from here." She sighed. "I even have an idea about how to solve this problem. And maybe how to solve my *other* problem, too."

"I'll see you in a few weeks, then," Death said. "Try not to let that thing consume your essence."

"Turn your back, Bradley," she said.

He frowned. "Why?"

"Because I disapprove of public displays of affection, but I need to kiss my husband now. I also need to ask him for a favor, which is even more embarrassing. So turn your ass around and make this public beach private for a minute."

"Hetero make-outs? Ew. You don't have to tell me twice to avert my eyes." Bradley turned, looking at the Ghirardelli chocolate factory for a few moments, until Marla said, "Okay, all clear."

He turned, then frowned at the little stone building on the beach, the one Death had emerged from. "Wait. That's not real. Or, I mean, it's not supposed to be there? That building, I mean. It *looks* real, but it wasn't there before."

"That's my husband's thing. He opens a door from the throne room in the underworld and steps out of it into wherever he needs to go. He comes through existing doors if they're handy, and if not…" She shrugged. "He makes a new door, and a wall for it to open from, if it comes to that."

"But he's gone. Don't his doors usually disappear when he goes back through them?"

She sighed. "Yeah. That's the favor I asked. I'm gonna have to *owe* him one, now, but there's nothing to be done, this Outsider thing has gotten out of hand." She held up her hand, revealing a black iron key as long as her middle finger. "This key will help us get where we're going, fast. Which is good, because I have a couple of stops to make before we hit Felport. But now… ugh. I have to make a call."

"Who are you calling?"

"The Outsider is on its way to Felport, almost certainly, to try to get through the gazebo and kill the *real* you, no offense. I figure stopping that is our priority."

"I would agree that protecting the multiverse from complete destruction is a priority, yes."

"Yeah. Except so far a demi-god, a whole scorpion god, a psychic reweaver coffee shop owner, and a fragment of the overseer of the multiverse, have all failed to keep a bad monster down. Which means I have no choice. I have to ask for help. You know I hate asking for anything, but this is fate-of-the-world shit."

"Who are we calling? Genevieve?"

"She's the nuclear option, and by that I mean, using her is so catastrophically destructive that it's pretty much a war crime. She could probably weave the Outsider out of existence, but she might turn the entire east coast into an eighty-trillion-pound pumpkin in the process. No, I have to...." She shuddered. "Just give me the phone, would you, before I lose my nerve?"

Crapsey in Felport

CRAPSEY AND SQUAT WERE SHOOTING POOL while the grown-ups talked about whatever they were talking about. Crapsey lined up a shot and sank the two ball, but scratched in the process.

"You're terrible at this," Squat said.

"We don't play this game in the universe where I come from. We have a different game, one you play with rat heads and rocks and buckets."

"Sounds delightful."

Crapsey shrugged. "The winner gets to eat all the rat heads, so it had its fans."

Squat wasn't wearing his usual hobo-blanket of overlapping coats, but just a white t-shirt (stained yellow by the fluid oozing from the sores on his back, each sore full of tiny lamprey fangs) and oversized cargo pants. He was short and wide, like a deep-chested bulldog, his hands monstrous talons that nevertheless handled a pool cue with dexterity. His eyes had creepy hourglass-shaped pupils, he was entirely noseless, and his mouth was vertical instead of horizontal, which didn't stop him from talking. He'd been cursed by the great chaos witch Elsie Jarrow—a former employer of Crapsey's—to never be loved or liked or even tolerated by anyone, and as a result, he physically mutated to become repulsive to anyone who spent time with him. Some of his mutations had granted him power—poisonous sweat, nasty fangs, the aforementioned talons—and he had the kind of physical strength that led him to occasionally tear car doors off by accident. He'd also been granted immortality and invulnerability by the curse, presumably so he could suffer indefinitely. In all, he was a terrifying variety of muscle—and the closest thing Crapsey had found in Felport to a friend.

Becoming friends should have made the curse kick in and turned Squat repulsive enough to overcome even Crapsey's liberal standards for the company he kept, but it didn't, because Nicolette had found a way to arrest the progress of his malady—and even reverse the parts that made him smell bad. She'd just cast some kind of olfactory neutralizing spell, really: Squat still stunk, it was just that nobody could smell it. Apparently Elsie Jarrow's death (or at least discorporation) had weakened her curse enough to let Nicolette pick at some of the threads, so, as horrible as Squat was, he at least wouldn't get any *worse*. Such things would have been beyond Nicolette's abilities not so long ago, but since taking over Felport, Nicolette had grown exponentially in power... and even seemed like a marginally less terrible person than before.

While Squat merrily sank one odd-numbered ball after another, Crapsey looked toward Nicolette and Perren, talking at a table in the corner. They were in the office in the back of a dive bar, Perren's base of operations, and the boss and the proprietor were discussing some boring-ass urban renewal shit. Nicolette was still wearing her tattooed-hottie body, and she was even more attractive than she had been in her original body, which was annoying. She used to tease him relentlessly, and nastily, about the fact that he wanted (against what passed for his better judgment) to fuck her... but she'd cut back on that kind of behavior since taking over the city, too.

The old-fashioned touchtone phone on the desk rang, and Perren startled, then stared at it. "That's weird."

"Yeah, who the hell has a landline anymore?" Nicolette said.

Perren shook her head. "I just keep the phone around because it makes a handy blunt object if I need to give someone head trauma. It's not even plugged in." She demonstrated by lifting the trailing, unconnected cord and holding it up. The phone rang again.

"Somebody's being a show-off." Nicolette inclined her head. "You going to pick that up?"

Perren shrugged, lifted the phone, and said, "Sorry, wrong number." Then her face went stony. "It's Marla Mason. She wants to talk to you."

Crapsey glanced at Squat, who rolled his eyes—probably, it was hard to tell, his eyes were so fucked up—and started racking the balls for another game. Oh. He'd won while Crapsey was ogling Nicolette's new ass.

"The stones on her, calling after she ran out on me," Nicolette said. "She must've cast a divination spell and made her phone call the phone nearest me—pretty cute."

"Do you want to talk to her?"

"No. Never. Hearing her voice is like shoving live wasps into my brain. But I will." Nicolette took the phone. "What the fuck do you—Wait. What do you mean coming *here*?" She went silent, scowling, then held out a hand, snapped her fingers, and made a scribbling motion. Crapsey reached into his jacket and took out a little spiral-bound notebook and a pen and put them on the desk in front of his boss. Nicolette said, "Marla, shut up. Where did the thing escape from? No, not the coffee shop, stupid, I mean *originally*. Could you for just once not ask why and answer the question? Okay. Don't suppose you have exact coordinates? Of course not." She wrote something down. "Hold on a second." She turned her head toward him. "Crapsey, call Mr. Beadle, and Langford, too, tell them I need a meet ASAP." Back to the phone. "You still there, Marla? You have a more precise ETA on this thing? Uh huh. Uh huh. I'm on it. I can reach you at this number? All right. Just out of curiosity, how many times are you going to be directly responsible for unleashing gods or extradimensional monsters that threaten to destroy this city? Because by my count this is four—yeah, *four*, you mean you can't count to four, Marla? There was Death, and the Mason, and this Outsider thing, and those weirdos that called themselves elves. Yes, those were *too* your fault—What do you mean I caused two? I'll grant you the nightmare king, you can trace that back to me, but you can't seriously say that stupid mushroom magician actually threatened the city, he just threatened *you*. Ha, yeah, sure, you saved the city too, saved it from shit *you* caused, but this time I'm going to save it, *also* from something you caused. All right, Marla, not that I don't enjoy hearing you yell, but I've got a city to run, you remember what that's like, don't you?" She switched off the phone and glared at Crapsey. "Did you forget how to follow orders?"

Crapsey pulled out his phone and dialed Beadle's number. While it rang, he said, "What's going on?"

"Marla fucked something up," Nicolette said, "and she called to ask me to save the city." She grinned. Crapsey couldn't remember ever seeing her look so happy.

Bradley on the Beach and Beyond

MARLA DID SOMETHING TO THE PHONE, punching in a long multi-digit code and murmuring an incantation. Bradley didn't recognize the exact spell, but part of it was familiar from some of Sanford Cole's more hardcore divination spells.

After a moment Marla spoke. "Perren, let me talk to Nicolette. I know she's with you."

Bradley widened his eyes. "Why are we calling—"

She flapped her hand at him, and he went quiet. "Nicolette, be quiet, there's a multiverse-destroying monster called the Outsider on its way to Felport right now." She paused, then sighed. "If you shut up, I'll *tell* you. This is the big problem I had to deal with, the planet-destroying space rock. My stupid death cultists accidentally released this creature from another universe, and it's been merrily murdering people and eating gods and getting stronger. I had it locked up in a magical pocket universe in the back of a coffee shop in Santa Cruz—never mind, it's a long story. Anyway, it got loose, and I took another run at it, but I couldn't kill it, and now it's on its way to Felport, looking for a locus of magic in Fludd Park. I think you're the worst person for the job, but you *are* the chief sorcerer there, and you've got some resources, if you don't fuck them up. The Outsider is maybe not killable, but it *can* be trapped, obviously, some ancient-ass humans did it centuries ago—what?" She shook her head, as if flies were buzzing around her. "I *told* you, I trapped it in a pocket universe in a coffee shop—oh. Why do you care? It was in California, in a cave under Death Valley. No, of course I don't, you think I walk around looking at a GPS all day? I—what do you mean hold on a second?"

She looked at Bradley. "I tell her a monster is coming to destroy her and she asks me dumb questions and puts me on *hold*?" She scowled and returned her attention to the phone. "Yeah, I'm here. I don't know, it just left San Francisco. It's been appearing in human form, mostly, but it can turn into a flying shadow, too. Maybe a day or two? Best assume it'll be there *soon*. Yeah, this number's good. Anyway, I'm coming, and I'm bringing Bradley and maybe another hired gun or two—Sure you're on it, you'd *better* be."

"Which hired guns?" Bradley said, but Marla hissed in an angry breath.

"Where do you get off? How the hell do you come up with *four*? Those stupid elf things were *not* my fault, that was Tom O'Bedbug, how was that *my* responsibility? Anyway, what about *you*, miss two-time-destroyer, you're the one who caused Genevieve to get out of Blackwing, and *that* brought Reave, and then you sicced that crazy mushroom magician on us." She kicked sand toward the ocean, hard. "Anyway I *saved* the city, those times and more, what have *you* ever—oh, I almost hope you fuck this up, Nicolette, you are the ultimate Dunning-Kruger case, you have no godsdamn idea how much you don't know—Did you just hang *up* on me?" She hurled the phone to the sand.

Bradley sighed, bent down, and picked it up. "Seems like that went well."

"Nicolette is so far out of her depth she's never even *heard* about the bottom, but she's the boss now, so I had to let her know what was coming. If she scrambles Hamil and Perren and the other heavy hitters, such as they are, maybe they can at least hold the Outsider at bay long enough for me to get there and take care of business."

Bradley nodded. He wondered, though. Nicolette had seemed... well... damn near *queenly* in Felport. Her usual jittering twitchy energy was gone, replaced by serenity and confidence. Oh, she was still deeply unpleasant, and her enmity for Marla was way into obsessive territory, but she was more capable than Marla gave her credit for, and she had the resources of a whole city at her disposal, too. Not that he was going to sit back and say, "Let Nicolette handle it." The whole reason he was on Earth was to stop the Outsider, after all. "So what do we do? You said something about hired guns?"

"First we're going to Santa Cruz, to see if Marzi wants to saddle up and ride."

Bradley whistled. "I thought you wanted to spare her from dealing with crap like this?"

Marla nodded. "I do, but, like we keep saying: fate of the world shit. If I had to ask Nicolette for help, you better believe I'll ask Marzi too—she hurt the Outsider worse than either of us managed to, it sounds like. I won't insist, though. Then… Well, I had a thought, and now we have to stop by Las Vegas."

Bradley nodded. "Pelham and Rondeau could be helpful, now that we're all on the same team and Nicolette isn't going to kidnap them anymore. I'll call and tell them not to leave Vegas before we get there."

"Yeah," Marla said. "We can take them along, sure. But we're mainly going to Vegas for something else."

"Dare I ask?"

"What," Marla said, "and spoil the surprise?" She jerked her head toward the door. "Come on."

"How's it work? You put in the key, click your heels three times, open the door, and we're in Santa Cruz?"

"Nah. It's more like… taking a shortcut. Through this door, into someplace else, out another door to our destination."

"Someplace else, huh?"

Marla grinned. "What, are you afraid to go through Hell?"

"Um, yeah, actually. I've been there before. I showed you the train to the underworld, remember? But there's a little rule about not going to Hell more than once while you're alive, or you forfeit your soul, right? If it's a choice between a road trip and losing my soul, I'll buy a bus ticket."

"The old god of death had all kinds of rules," Marla said. "Me and my Death are reformers, though. We've streamlined things. You'll be fine, trust me. You have Dread Queen Marla's promise. Come on. Let's see what's behind door number impossible." She stepped to the door, then paused. "But, uh, just so you know, when I go through this door, I might get… a little weird. Just roll with it, okay?"

"When you say a little weird, you mean…"

"I'm not myself when I'm in the underworld. I'm more Dread Queen Marla, Lady of Hell."

"Ah. So you're not as warm and cuddly as you are now?"

"You tread on dangerous ground, Bowman."

IF BRADLEY HADN'T BEEN PSYCHIC, he might not have noticed anything was wrong at all. They opened the door, and stepped into what looked for all the world like a foyer in a gloomy Gothic mansion: hardwood floors, dark wood paneling, flickering sconces on the walls, and a chill that settled immediately into his bones. But his psychic senses kept screaming at him that this place was *not for him*, that it was inimical to life, and from the corner of his eye he saw looming shadows, and firelight, and immense creatures moving with slow deliberation in his direction.

Then he made the terrible mistake of looking at Marla. She was taller than before, dressed all in white silks, her skin pale as a sheet of paper, her hair dark—as if she'd been rendered in black-and-white and then the contrast got pushed way up. The being before him was not exactly Marla, but she *contained* Marla. The goddess of death was a great tree, and the mortal Marla Mason was merely the seed. He could barely stand to look at her: it was like looking directly at the sun. A terrible, cold sun.

The dread queen turned her head toward him, her deep black eyes shining, and smiled, showing off teeth that were more fanglike even than the Outsider's. She raised a hand toward him, and her fingers were dripping blood: somehow he knew it wasn't *her* blood. "Living man," she said. "You should not be here."

He swallowed. "You brought me here. We… we're on our way to save the world."

She chuckled, a sound like skulls rolling down the stone steps of a crypt. "Ah yes. I see now. You are Bradley. You just look so much… smaller than I remembered. Mmm. Yes. This Outsider is beyond any death I can wield here. But there is another life, an irritant, the one called Nicolette. She has been given too much liberty. She belongs here in the underworld. I can take her, before we leave this place again, and I relinquish my true power."

"But—everyone in Felport will die if she does!"

The goddess shrugged. "They will die soon anyway. Death is inevitable. New ones will be born. This will take but a moment." Her gaze became abstract, faraway.

"We need Nicolette to stop the Outsider!" Bradley shouted, even though shouting at her felt like shouting at an uncaged lion. "We can't do this alone, there's a *plan*, don't you remember?"

The goddess focused on him again—it felt a bit like having his skin peeled away in layers, one millimeter at a time—and then sighed. "Ah. Yes. The plan. How petty. But it will serve, I suppose. Very well." She flashed across the foyer, her movement a flicker of speed impossible to follow, and opened the door on the other side. "Please. I will follow."

The thought of stepping through first, and turning his back on her, made his skin crawl, even though he knew it wasn't particularly dangerous. After all, she could kill him just as easily to his face.

Bradley went through the door, and the sense of terrible wrongness receded, though he sank against the wall of the desert-painted storage room in Genius Loci and gasped, his eyes closed.

A moment later, he heard the click of a closing door. "You all right, B?" Marla said, her voice perfectly mortal again.

"You are awesome and terrifying, Marla."

"On my good days. I can't remember anything that happens to me when I'm… her. The goddess. The whole experience just gets wiped out of my brain, like I signed a cosmic non-disclosure-agreement. Was I nasty?"

"A little bit scary, yeah."

"Cool. Come on, open your eyes, we have to talk to Marzi."

Bradley was afraid to look, but when he did, she was just Marla again, no sign of the supernatural vastness she'd just contained. There was no magical door in the room, either, which was comforting: apparently they'd just emerged through the door that, in the normal world, led into the kitchen.

"I just looked death in the face," Bradley said.

Marla patted him on the cheek. "I know. Won't be the last time you do that today, either, kid."

MARZI GROANED. "Jonathan will *kill* me. If I go off monster-fighting and die he'll never forgive me."

"You'll just be backup, riding drogue," Marla said. She sat in the office chair by Marzi's drawing table, swiveling gently back and forth. She drawled, she was taller than usual, and her hat cast unnatural shadows across her face—all alterations caused by Marzi's presence—but they were such minor differences compared to the way she'd changed as the goddess of death that Bradley hardly noticed.

He and Marzi were sitting on the edge of the bed, though, giving her lots of space anyway. Marla didn't look like someone you wanted to crowd right now. She said, "The main posse will have the big guns trained on the Outsider, don't you worry. You'll just be exerting your psychic pressure, and Bradley can help you boost *that*, too, so you won't get brain damage or nosebleeds."

Marzi nodded. "Sure, but I might still die, right?"

"Might could," Marla said. "If'n we don't stop the Outsider, though, *everybody* dies."

Marzi sighed. "All right then. I'd better leave Jonathan a note."

"I'm serious," Bradley said. "Close your eyes. I can spare you that much." He held out his hand.

Marzi shrugged, took his hand, and closed her eyes. Bradley gave it a reassuring squeeze. "Okay. Let's go."

Marla put the key in the door of Marzi's room—the key shouldn't have fit, but reality didn't seem to mind—and opened it onto that grim foyer again. Bradley stepped inside, leading Marzi, and Marla followed.

Then Marla walked past him, and she was the dread queen again... except she was still wearing a cowboy hat. The goddess took off the hat, frowned at it, and the hat turned to ash without bothering to burn first, gray dust sifting through her fingers. "Hmm. This Marzipan has great power... by human standards. Come. The longer I stay here, the harder it is for me to remember why I should ever leave, when I have the business of life and death to attend to. If this Outsider didn't threaten everything in the multiverse, I would leave you two here and get on with more meaningful work."

"Damn." Marzi kept her eyes closed as she spoke. "I thought you were bitchy in the real world."

"What she means is, we're ready when you are," Bradley said.

The goddess flickered her tongue—black and pointed, of course—at him, then opened the door.

They stepped out of the wall of a hotel onto the Las Vegas strip at dusk, and Bradley said, "You can open your eyes now."

"Dang," Marzi said. "That's a nice way to travel. Beats the hell out of driving to Vegas."

"You gotta go through a pretty bad neighborhood on the way, though," Marla said. "Y'all go fetch Pelham and Rondeau from the hotel."

"Where are you going?" Bradley said.

Marla hitched up her pants, turned her head, and spat onto the sidewalk. "Gotta go see a demon about a woman."

Rondeau, Here and There and In Between

RONDEAU LOUNGED IN HIS SILK ROBE and watched Pelham fuss over Marzi, offering her tea and sparkling water and whatever else. The girl had a definite sparkle of magic, a bit like his own, but subtly different—like two different strains of weed, Sativa versus Indica, maybe.

Bradley sat beside him on the couch, and he elbowed Rondeau in the ribs. "So the Pit Boss is cool with you staying here?"

"Hmm?" Rondeau stuck a finger in his ear and twiddled it around. "Oh. I dunno what Marla said, but she put the fear of… something… into my demon-tulpa-kid-whatever. He had a couple of goons—humans too, not trash golems—here to meet me, and they gave me a warm welcome. Gave me a big old briefcase full of cash in exchange for my share of the casino, and returned access to my bank accounts, so I'm actually better off than I was before, in terms of straight-up liquid assets. They even offered me use of my old suite, for life, whenever I want it. I get the feeling the Pit Boss doesn't much want me around, though—he's just afraid to be inhospitable."

"Well, sure," Bradley said. "No wonder he doesn't want you around. You made him, so you could unmake him."

Rondeau frowned. "I could?"

"He came out of your *brain*, man. You literally conjured him, or at least gave this particular shape to some lurking primal force, endowed it with sentience and consciousness. So it follows that you've got the power to dispel him, too."

"How the hell do I do *that*?"

Bradley shrugged. "I dunno. Do some research, find the right spell. Or just summon up an oracle and *ask* it how."

Rondeau groaned. "Just thinking about doing all that makes me tired. Having your power is too much for me, B. I liked it better when I was just a simple psychic parasite with a knack for causing bursts of magical chaos. That was a *manageable* kind of magic. This shit… nah, fuck it. The Pit Boss did me a solid, got rid of Regina Queen, held up his end of our deal. He's not screwing with me anymore, so I'm not screwing with him, either."

"Seems silly to worry about it, since the whole multiverse might get destroyed in a day or two anyway," Bradley said.

"Yeah, about that. When do we leave for Felport? I could've just *stayed*. Though it is nice to be back in my suite for a minute."

The door to the hallway swung open, and Marla walked in.

Regina Queen came in behind her, as regal and ice-faced as ever, dressed in her long fur-lined cloak.

Rondeau whimpered and jumped over the back of the couch, crouching behind it.

After a long moment of silence, Marla said, "Rondeau, come out from behind there."

He stuck his head up. Regina looked at him with infinite amusement. "What the fuck is she doing here?"

Marla shrugged. "I asked her along to help us deal with our little problem in Felport, that's all." Something about Marla was strange—she looked a little taller, and her voice was slow, laconic.

"Marla. She's…" He shook his head.

"She *is* an unrepentant mass murderer, Mrs. Mason." Pelham said, as if pointing out that she had a bit of spinach in her teeth.

"She wants to redeem herself," Marla said. "Ain't that right, Regina?"

"Oh, my, yes."

The temperature in the room dropped noticeably—and Marla reached over and smacked Regina on the arm. "None of that. Behave, or its back to the pit with you."

The cold snap abruptly stopped.

"Am I missing something?" Marzi said.

Regina looked the woman up and down and smiled frostily. "Oh, my, yes, dear. You probably miss almost *everything*."

"Wow." Marzi whistled. "That's some fancy new kind of a bitch you've got there, Marla."

Regina hissed, and icy fog puffed out with her breath. Marla smacked her again, and Regina flinched, then looked ashamed. "I will wait in the hallway." She turned and swept out of the room.

"Marla." Bradley cleared his throat. "Asking for Regina Queen's help… isn't that a little bit like asking for a rattlesnake's help to kill a spider?"

"Strange bedfellows and shit, B." Marla dropped onto the couch where Rondeau had been. "I went to the Pit Boss and told him I needed Regina, and after a little chat, he agreed to hand her over."

Something clicked in Rondeau's head. "Son of a bitch," he said. "You threatened the Pit Boss with *me*, didn't you? Told him you'd teach me how to un-summon him? Right? Send him back to my id or the spectral ether or wherever he came from?"

Marla shrugged. "You use the carrots and sticks you've got on hand. I figure making a monster of molten rock who runs Las Vegas a little bit scared of me is good, even if I have to use *you* to scare him."

"Yeah, great, but what if he decides to *murder* me? Remove the threat?"

Marla waved a hand. "Oh, I told him his life might be tied to yours, that if you die he might cease to exist. He's gonna be looking out for you, actually. Though I did have to dissuade him from putting you in a medically-induced coma with round-the-clock medical care, keeping you alive and out of danger forever, which is what he *wanted* to do."

"Oh, good. Now I just have to worry about Regina killing me for throwing her in a volcano."

"She's harmless. We did a circle of binding. I'm not an amateur here, Rondeau. Promises were made, the unbreakable kind, and she was willing to make a lot of concessions in exchange for me letting her out of the hellish pocket dimension where she was trapped. Regina won't hurt you, or any of my people. She'll help us with the Outsider, and then she'll fuck off back to the frozen north. She's got some crystal palace up there full of ice golems or something, who knows. Having her up there's actually good for the whole climate change thing—she's keeping at least some bits of the polar ice cap from melting. I'm being a responsible steward of the Earth, here."

"You people are into some heavy shit," Marzi said. "There are more magical motherfuckers in this room than I knew existed in the whole world."

"Ha," Marla said. "You ain't seen nothin' yet, darlin'. We're gonna grab some food and some shut-eye, and in the morning, we're attending a gen-yoo-wine council of sorcerous war."

RONDEAU SAT OUT ON THE BALCONY late that night, smoking and brooding, looking at the never-darkening lights of Las Vegas. Regina Queen was *down the hall*, booked into another room, sleeping by herself, assuming she even slept. Marla insisted the bindings on her were sufficient to keep her from turning fugitive, but it didn't make him feel too restful, having her so close.

Marzi came through the sliding glass door and sat down beside him. "Can I bum one of those?"

Rondeau nodded and handed a cigarette over, then gave her a light. "I didn't think anyone from California still smoked. Apart from weed."

"There are still a few terrible disappointments out there." She drew in a lungful, then slowly blew it out. "I don't smoke, usually, but I'm a little stressed. Just got off the phone with my boyfriend. He's not real happy about me taking off without warning, going on a magical misadventure. He's pretty supportive about things, but he says I should have talked it over with him first. He's big on talking. Does have a point, though. I feel bad."

Rondeau nodded. "That's why I never make meaningful human connections."

Marzi snorted. "So, you do this kind of stuff all the time? Magic, I mean?"

Rondeau hesitated. Explaining that he wasn't human, but a psychic parasite of unknown provenance currently residing in his second stolen body, might be a little on the overwhelming side, so he just said, "Since I was a kid, pretty much. I met Marla when I was living on the street. She gave me a hand up, taught me some stuff. It's a better life than I would have had otherwise, that's for sure, but there are definitely periods of unrelenting terror."

"Damn." Marzi put her feet up on the railing. "Part of me is really curious. There's a whole secret world out there, I know that—I helped kill a god, once, it's not like I didn't realize there must be *more*. But I've spent the last years trying not to think about it, to have a normal life, one focused on love and art. But am I living in a tiny room, when there's a whole big mansion out there, if I just have the courage to step through the door?"

Rondeau nodded. "I should warn you, I'm pretty famous for making terrible decisions and giving terrible advice, but I will say this: if you get into sorcery and all, it doesn't replace regular life. Regular life is still there. You drive places, you get drunk, you talk shit with your friends, you make out with people, you do your job—regular stuff. Like, you own a café—before I sold out, I used to run a night club. Sure, I'm a wizard, or whatever. But I still had to call in the liquor order. Still had to check IDs at the door. Still had to pay taxes, at least a little bit. Joining the magical community, it's not trading one life for another life. It's *adding* more to your life. It's like if you had a really hardcore hobby, one that ate up every bit of your free time. Sure, it might piss off your loved ones a little, but it also gives you something to fill your hours."

She grunted. "Man, I already draw comics. I need *another* hobby? One that's more dangerous? I might as well take up alligator wrestling."

He shrugged. "You gotta decide what to do on your own. Some of us, magic fills a part of our lives that would be empty otherwise. If she hadn't found magic, I don't know *what* Marla would be—except she'd probably be dead. She sure as hell wouldn't be a part-time goddess of death. But if you don't have that kind of hole in your life, or if you've got love and art to fill it, shit. I can't promise magic would make things *better*."

Marzi flicked her cigarette butt over the railing. "I don't know. Your advice doesn't seem so terrible."

He nodded. "You know, sometimes I even surprise myself."

Mazi in the War Room

THEY ALL LINED UP IN A LINE before the suite's door, Bradley holding Marzi's hand, her holding Pelham's hand, Pelham holding Rondeau's. Regina Queen refused to hold anyone's hands, and scoffed at the suggestion that she close her eyes. "I fear nothing in this world or any other."

"Hell can get a little warm, in places," the Stranger said. "But suit yourself."

"Are there not realms of terrible ice in the underworld as well?"

The Stranger chortled. "You're talking about Dante, now? Regina, that's just infernal fanfic. Sure, there are probably icy parts of the underworld, but then, anything anyone finds unpleasant is probably down there *somewhere*. Let's go."

Marzi closed her eyes, the door clicked open, and she followed the tug of Bradley's hand, pulling Pelham along after her. As before, she was hit with a rush of heat, and a profound sense of disorientation: the psychic GPS in her head basically glitching-out, informing her that she was *nowhere* and *no place* and *in danger*, and she gritted her teeth and rode it out. Pelham murmured, "Are we there? Is something happening?"

"Damn, you non-psychics are lucky," Rondeau said.

"Slime mold," a cold voice said. Cold, but not Regina's. The Stranger's? Sort of, but also *something else*. There was magic here *way* bigger than Marzi's. "Cockroaches. Too much life. Out. Out. Get out."

Bradley pulled at Marzi, and the disorientation lessened and then vanished, and when she opened her eyes, she was standing in what looked like a night club, with a dance floor and a DJ booth and a bar along one wall. The house lights were on, and half a dozen people were sitting or standing around a big table set up in the center of the dance floor. One of them, a youngish, sharp-featured woman with a bleached-white duck fuzz of hair, whistled. "Damn, Marla. Did you bring the entire rhythm section of the Polyphonic Spree with you? What a fuckin' menagerie."

The Stranger pointed people out. "Nicolette. You know Rondeau and Pelham and Bradley. That's Marzi McCarty—she's a low-level reweaver with experience fighting the Outsider, and some success with limiting his powers. I also brought Regina Queen, the ice witch."

"Damn. I've heard of you, Regina. You're Viscarro's mom, right?"

Regina just sniffed, drifting around the club, peering at everything with obvious distaste.

"All right, she at least might halfway useful," Nicolette said. "Ha. We three queens." She snorted. "The Ice Queen, the Queen of the Dead, and the Witch Queen of Felport."

"You're more like the Lady of Misrule," the Stranger said. "But you'll have to do. What's the plan?"

"The plan is, shut the fuck up, we're getting a transmission here." Nicolette walked across the dance floor, and the big screen over the bar flickered to life. At first, Marzi couldn't make sense of the image, and then it resolved into something like a found-footage horror movie, a handheld camera jiggling around in a dark cavern of some kind. The camera spun around and focused on the dust-streaked features of a middle-aged man.

"Is that Mr. Beadle?" the Stranger said. "Where the hell is he?"

"Shush it," Nicolette said. Marzi glanced at the Stranger, who scowled, her hand drifting toward the dagger in her coat. There were all kinds of politics here Marzi didn't understand, but it was obvious these two women didn't have much use for each other. This was clearly a "united against a common enemy" type of thing. Which was actually one of Marzi's favorite kind of stories to write: the best arc of *The Strange Adventures of Rangergirl* was probably the one where Rangergirl and the tyrannical Aaron Burr joined forces to fight the Outlaw. There was a little more tension when you were living *inside* that kind of story, though.

"I found the fragments of the seal," the man on the screen was saying. "I have reconstructed the symbols, and have transmitted them to Hamil's team. They predate human language, though there are traces of a kind of proto-Aklo—"

"Save the etymological stuff for a scholarly paper, Beadle," Nicolette interrupted. "Can those seals hold this thing, or what?"

"Hold it, yes. There's no evidence to suggest how the ancients lured the Outsider *into* the vault in the first place, but if you can find a way to get the creature inside—yes, those symbols will hold it."

"Whoa." The Stranger stepped forward. "Beadle, are you in Death Valley?"

"Yes, Marla. Nicolette dispatched me straight away when she got your call." He made a sour face. "I had to *teleport*—it was harrowing. Once I arrived I used forensic magic to piece together the magical prison your cultists destroyed when they released the Outsider. If we seek to hold the beast, after all, why not see how it was held before?"

"I… shit. I never thought to do that."

"Of course you didn't." Nicolette shook her head. "You're all about breaking shit, Marla. You're crap when it comes to putting stuff back together."

The Stranger took off her hat, wiped her brow, and put it back. "That's… Hellfire. That's a fair cop, Nicolette. This time anyway. So we can build a box to keep the Outsider in? So the only problem's putting it *in* the box."

"Shouldn't be hard to set a trap," Nicolette said. "We know where it's going: the gazebo in Fludd Park. I had it looked at, Bowman. You gonna start paying me rent for keeping an entry to your realm in my city?"

"No more than I charge you rent for living in my multiverse," Bradley said. "I'd advise your wizards to avoid trying to use the gazebo to get to my realm. The journey would be… unpleasant. Though, fortunately, quite brief."

"Focus, people," Marzi said. "We still have to get the Outsider into the box. We managed to trick it into a prison before. Of course, if the monster is smart, we might not be able to trick it the same way again."

"Oh, don't worry about that," Nicolette said. "Anything you can do, Marla, I can do better."

Bradley in, and Just
Outside, Felport

THE PSYCHIC CORPS OF FELPORT—the seers, sibyls, and oracles pledged to serve the chief sorcerer, guided by Bradley, because he knew what he was doing—got their first ping on the approaching monster in the morning two days after they arrived in Felport. Bradley had explained Cole's idea to the psychic corps, getting them to blanket the area in constant surveillance and look for spots they *couldn't* see, and it had finally worked: there was an impenetrable dead zone, moving toward them at the speed of a walking man.

Marla leapt to her feet from the futon when she got the word. "Thank the *gods*, even the ones I'm not fucking." She and Bradley were staying in her dusty old apartment, in an abandoned building Marla technically still owned, though Nicolette was talking about having the whole structure demolished as soon as she had a spare moment.

Bradley rose from the armchair where he'd spent the past six-hour shift, hooked into the mental grid of Nicolette's psychic monsters. "The Outsider's a few miles outside of town, approaching from the West. Doesn't seem to be in a big hurry."

"Even so, I don't know what took it so long." Marla put on her coat and filled the pockets with pebbles. She'd spent the past few days enchanting the stones with who-knows-what nasty magics, because Nicolette wouldn't let her take part in any of the planning. Nicolette had happily dragooned Regina, Marzi, Rondeau, and even Pelham, who had a surprising amount of tactical acumen, into the cause. Making Marla remain idle while her onetime home city was under threat was a really elegant way to fuck with her, Bradley had to admit. "Should've been here a couple days ago."

"Maybe it took a detour to eat a river god in Mississippi or a slaughterhouse god in Chicago," Bradley said. "You know, picking up a canapé or two on its way to the main buffet. We should be prepared for it to be stronger than before."

"Road trip food. Right. I hope it didn't get Reva. Who knows how well this thing can track gods? It got a whiff of the gazebo off of us easily enough." She sighed. "If I could put the Outsider in a bottle, like I did with that nixie from San Franciso, it would make a handy monster-detector. Guess it's too dangerous. I need another one, though. I don't have Nicolette for a psychic bloodhound anymore."

"How are you, ah, doing with all that? With her? The situation?"

Marla shook her head, then sat down to slip on her cowboy boots. "Nicolette… Damn it. She seems to have a handle on things. She's got Felport running like a beautiful machine. As much as she's tried to shut me out, to discourage people from talking to me, still, I can tell. The place is humming, and the sorcerous community has never been so coordinated. For me, getting them to do *anything* was always like herding cats, and also, the cats were on fire."

"This Fisher King thing she did gave her a connection deeper than any you ever had here," Bradley said. "The sorcerers are all connected to her, too, and her to them. It's big magic."

"Imagine if someone who didn't *suck* had cast that kind of spell. If I'd done it, for instance. I would've been the greatest ruler this city had ever seen."

Bradley smiled. "Yeah, but you wouldn't have risked the spontaneous decapitations. I think this process needed to start with a terrible person who didn't care about human lives. It's kind of satisfying, in a way, don't you think? Nicolette, the most selfish, small-minded, petty chaos witch I've ever met, turned into a supernaturally dedicated civil servant. She was trying to screw with you, but she got trapped in a new role in the process. Honestly, apart from how much she hates you, she hardly even seems all that warped and dysfunctional anymore."

"Ha. I'm supposed to take comfort in that? She wanted to prove she could rule the city better than I could, and she *is*. At least, assuming she doesn't fuck up this thing with the Outsider, she is. Gods. Anyway. Where are we needed?"

Bradley consulted the orders dropped into his brain by the psychic network. "You and me and Marzi get to be the welcoming committee. Nicolette says, quote, 'Put up a good fight, and if Marla gets eaten in the process, that's fine with me.'"

"She wishes. I wouldn't give her the satisfaction. Come on."

A CAR WAITED FOR THEM on the curb, a sleek black low-slung sedan of no identifiable make or model, its windows *and* windshield tinted a disturbingly opaque black, its engine idling.

I'm Sierra, a voice said in Bradley's head. *I'll be your ride today.* It sounded like the soothing voice of a good GPS system.

"What the fuck," Bradley said. "Marla, this car is *talking.*"

The passenger door opened, and Marzi got out. "Hey, guys. Sierra says hop in."

"Sierra." Marla walked around the car. "What is this thing?"

"Nicolette found her in some junkyard." Marzi said. "Just sitting up on cinderblocks. She put new tires on, and the car just... woke up. Sierra says she doesn't remember where she came from." Marzi shrugged. "Magical car. Drives herself. Heals damage like she's alive. We've been hanging out. I am very cool and jaded about magic now."

Marzi keeps trying to turn me into a stagecoach, the voice in Bradley's head said, and he laughed. Marla frowned at him.

"Is it haunted or something?" Marla said. "You got a read on it, Bradley?"

"It is a car," he said. "Not, like, a monster that looks like a car. Magical car, for sure. Beyond that... Not something I've ever encountered before."

"Why is your name Sierra?" Marla said.

Why is your name Marla? the car replied, and Bradley and Marzi both laughed.

Marla rolled her eyes. "I don't even want to know what she said. Psychics. Everywhere I look, psychics. Even the *car* is psychic. Fine. Sierra, take us to the edge of town."

They climbed in—Marla and Bradley in back, Marzi up front, everyone avoiding the driver's seat. There was no steering wheel anyway. The interior of the car was dark, the seats made of something soft and plush that wasn't exactly leather. The engine didn't roar, but the car leapt forward like it had some major power under the hood. Bradley wondered if there was even an engine in there, or something else.

"What's the plan?" Marzi said.

"We set up on the road where the Outsider's approaching, and we try to kill it. Bradley will boost your power, you'll try to squeeze the Outsider down into something human, and I'll stab it in the face over and over while you shoot it with your pistol."

"Ah. I thought we were just a distraction detail, to lull it into a false sense of security or whatever."

Bradley nodded. "We are—the main body of the assault is happening in the park—but the more we weaken it, the better chance the rest of the sorcerers will have to knock it on the ground long enough to get it sealed up in Beadle's box. When we fight it, go all out."

"I want to kill it." Marla cracked her knuckles. "It would be pretty sweet to rob Nicolette of her big moment."

"Glad to see we're all working together in harmony," Marzi said.

"Teamwork for the win," Bradley agreed.

THEY PARKED UNDER THE TREES outside of town, on a two-lane blacktop road lined with keep-away spells to keep the ordinaries off the route. The sun filtered down through the trees. Bradley and Marzi sat on Sierra's hood while Marla paced around and did knife katas and muttered darkly to herself.

Marzi nodded in her direction. "That is one high-strung chick."

"She comes by it honest. She feels responsible for the Outsider, because her cultists are the ones who set it free."

"You have weird friends, dude."

"Ain't that the truth." Something in the psychic network hooked up in his head tingled, an opacity where there'd been transparency before, and he slid off the car and stared down the road. Marzi joined him. "Someone's coming."

Marzi stepped out into the middle of the road, knife in her hand.

"We'd best make sure he's someone manageable, then." Marzi held out her hand, and Bradley took it. The link between them, prepared in a ritual earlier, activated, and his brain lit up like a crystal chandelier. Marzi's mind was a great engine, and he was helping to take some of the load so it wouldn't overheat. Or something. Metaphors weren't his strong point.

The figure walking down the road toward them stumbled, shook its head, then continued, moving faster now. Marzi had locked onto it, made it more human, and thus more manageable. Maybe even killable.

"Sierra," Marla called. "You want to go run that fucker down?"

Marzi and Bradley moved out of the way as Sierra's engine purred. Marla stepped aside too, making an "after you" gesture.

The car accelerated faster than seemed possible given the physical laws of the universe, covering the few hundred yards between itself and the approaching Outsider seconds.

The Outsider didn't dive out of the way, didn't even *flinch*, and Bradley heard Marla mutter, "Oh, crap."

The car hit the Outsider and then *flipped*, flying through the air and landing on its roof half in the ditch by the side of the road. The Outsider rose from a crouch, one of its arms dangling at an angle that suggested broken bones, but it seemed otherwise unharmed.

Sierra, are you okay? Bradley thought.

I'm upside down in a ditch, *so I've been better,* the car said. *Kill that thing for me. It scratched up my paint.*

"He shouldn't be able to do that," Marzi muttered. "I am squeezing him down *so hard.*"

"He must have eaten another god or two on the trip. He's gotten stronger." Bradley raised his voice. "Marla, be careful! He's tougher now!"

The Outsider closed the distance, coming at a run now, and Marla stepped back into the middle of the road. "He ain't shit!" she called.

The Outsider was close enough to see, now, still in a form caught somewhere between seedy and suave, dressed in an old-fashioned suit and a low-crowned top hat, with ostentatious rings twinkling on its fingers. "You again!" it called. "Come to escort me to the gazebo? It's not necessary, really. I'll find my own way."

This time, Marla didn't banter. She flung a handful of stones at the monster, and cacophony reigned.

Some of the pebbles burst into flame. Others exploded into shrapnel. A few landed on the ground and spun out tendrils of slime and spider silk and vines, crawling up the Outsider's body and entangling it. The creature ducked, snarled, and lashed out with its fists. Black fire burst from the ground around it, destroying the entangling elements, and if any of the concussive stones had harmed the Outsider, it wasn't letting on. While it was distracted, though, Marla moved in with the knife, slashing at the creature, making it dance back.

"Can't get a clear shot." Marzi was trying to flank the Outsider, pistol in her hand, but Marla was dancing around too much to give her an opening.

"Concentrate on making it more human." Bradley felt the strain of Marzi's psychic pressure, and suspected that, if she'd been doing this on her own, she would have popped a blood vessel in her brain by now.

Even so, the Outsider was easily evading Marla's attacks, and its wounded arm seemed entirely healed. Marzi was pressing her vision of reality on the Outsider as hard as she possibly could, and boosting Marla into an avenging badass at the same time, and they *still* weren't making a dent. The Outsider had leveled up. If Nicolette's plan didn't work, this world—and possibly all *other* worlds in the universe—was doomed.

The Outsider got in a lucky shot and knocked Marla's legs out from under her, sending her sprawling to the ground. It walked over her, literally stepping in the middle of her back, and came toward Marzi and Bradley.

Marzi lifted her pistol, her mind *surged* so hard that both hers and Bradley's noses began to bleed, and she shot the Outsider in the eye.

The monster clapped one heavily ringed hand to its face, howled, and raced down the street, moving with inhuman speed and grace—but at least it wasn't eating them, and if they were lucky it would reach Fludd Park bloodied, in pain, and disoriented.

Marla pushed herself to her feet. "Gods *damn* it!" she shouted.

Bradley handed Marzi a couple of tissues—he'd come prepared—and put one to his nose, too. Marla staggered toward Sierra, and they joined her. Bradley said, "I guess we could flip her over. I think I remember a temporary strength spell."

"Nah, fuck that. A door's a door." She shoved the big iron key into Sierra—the car squawked in Bradley's head, but only in surprise—and tore yanked open the upside-down door, climbing inside.

Marzi leaned down and looked through the door. "Should I keep my eyes closed this time?"

"It's kind of unpleasant in there, but it's your call. We should hurry, though—I don't know if she'll wait."

"In we go."

Bradley crawled inside first, Marzi on his heels. The foyer was different, this time. The floors were uneven, bulging in places and sunken in others, and the paneling on the walls was cracked. Half the flickering wall sconces were dim or extinguished entirely, and there were great blooms of mold on the ceiling. Marla was already disappearing through the door at the far end, so they ran to keep up with her, Bradley terrified of being stranded in this place. Why was it so ugly now? Did its physical nature respond to Marla's mood or something? If so, she was in an even fouler temper than he'd supposed.

They emerged from the door to the women's bathroom in Fludd Park. The broad expanse of green meadows, stands of trees, lichen-covered boulders, and the duck pond—the green natural heart of rusty soot-stained Felport—was filled with easily four-score people, including every remotely offensive sorcerer the city had to offer: Perren, the Bay Witch, Hamil (not in a scooter anymore, but leaning heavily on a cane), Mr. Beadle, Langford, and all their lieutenants and retainers and enforcers and button-men, along with the mad dog types kept locked in cages in basements and only brought out when bodies needed to be dropped, the poltergeisters and other wild, unreliable talents. Perren's old gang the Honeyed Knots was there, along with their rivals the Four Tree Gang, eyeing one another with open disdain, but kept in check by the treaties and rules that made everyone in the city bind together for mutual protection in times of bad outside trouble.

The only obvious missing piece was the Chamberlain and her crowd of ghosts... but now that Bradley looked, there *were* ghosts, back by the amphitheater, milling around under the eye of a Latina woman in a gentleman's morning coat, shouting something incomprehensible through a megaphone.

"Who's that?" Bradley said.

Marla shaded her eyes and squinted. "Oh. Evelyn Park. One of the Chamberlain's lieutenants. Looks like she's taken over the ghost-herding. If Nicolette's letting her walk around loose, I guess that means she betrayed the Chamberlain, which doesn't say much for her loyalty."

"At least she knows how to pick a winner," Bradley said, and Marla made a disgusted noise.

Evelyn waved her arms, and the ghosts shuffled forward. They seemed nervous, which was understandable. They were the founding families of Felport, bound to the city, and if the city fell, they'd be claimed by whatever inimical afterlives awaited them. The ghosts moved reluctantly along at Evelyn's shouted directions, forming a defensive perimeter around the white gazebo—the structure itself was barely visible beneath a dome of coruscating violet light, protected from some kind of hyped-up forcefield. They didn't want the Outsider slipping through it while they were trying to wrestle him into Beadle's box. Which... Ah, there it was, resting on a patch of green some distance from the gazebo: the box for the Outsider, like a coffin for a giant, made of exotic wood, carved all over with eye-watering runes, surrounded by Beadle's order-mage apprentices.

Nicolette stomped over to them, and Bradley blinked at her. She was wearing the 'roided out body of a male bodybuilder, and she was even more wreathed with protective magics than usual. She was so protected that a nuclear bomb dropped on Felport would have left a glass-bottomed crater with Nicolette standing unharmed in the middle.

"Huh. The Outsider's coming and you didn't even die trying to stop it." Nicolette clucked her tongue. "Nobody's got any *resolve* nowadays."

"Where do you want us?" Marla said.

Nicolette stared at her, flexing her pecs and making them bounce under the tight white tank-top she wore. "What, no smart mouth, no talking shit, no excuses?"

"This is a war, and you're the general. Today, right at this moment? I'm a soldier, and I'll take orders."

Nicolette seemed genuinely taken aback. "Uh—I—Hell. Join the second rank." She pointed. The sorcerers were lining up behind the ghosts, forming semicircular rows to defend the gazebo, each row spaced about ten yards apart. After the ghosts in the front lines, it was all apprentices and mad dogs—the expendable and the cannon fodder. The gangs, battle-hardened but independent and formidable, were next, and then the lieutenants and enforcers to the city's leading sorcerers, and then the council members themselves in the back rank.

Marla nodded and started to walk over. Nicolette ground her teeth. "Wait, wait—fuck it. Marla, the rest of you, get in the back with the Bay Witch and Perren and them."

Marla looked at her levelly. "Are you sure? Wherever you need me. I'm here for Felport."

Nicolette waved her hand, irritated, and Bradley almost smiled. "Yes, in the back, shit. If you were up front, the kiddies would get distracted, standing with legendary-ass Marla Mason. I need them focused. Get in position." She stomped off, shouting orders.

"You guys have a serious frenemy vibe going," Marzi said.

"You're half right." Marla headed across the park, and they followed, joining the loose knot of heavy hitters closest to the gazebo. Bradley greeted the Bay Witch, who'd once hit on him pretty regularly, but she just looked past him to the east, and the Bay. She didn't like being on dry land at the best of times. Hamil limped over, leaning on his cane. "Bradley. Ms. McCarty. Marla."

"It's stronger now, Hamil." Marla did a few stretches, limbering up. "I couldn't even make a dent. The Outsider has been eating its Wheaties or its spinach or whatever. More gods, probably."

Pelham and Rondeau were in the back row, too—whether they'd been assigned here or just drifted to the back, Bradley couldn't say. Pelham was good at following orders, but Rondeau followed whims instead. They both came to stand with Marla, silently nodding at her. Pelham had his walking stick. Rondeau was holding a bicycle chain, which was kind of funny: a straight-up street gang weapon, nothing that would even put a dent in the Outsider, no matter how it was enchanted, but he was here, and he was ready to swing.

Perren joined them too, her face unreadable behind her sunglasses. "This is it, huh? We stop this thing, or it eats us, and then the world?"

"The multiverse." Bradley shrugged. "The world, I mean, shit. At this point, I'd give up the world if it spared the rest of creation." Did anyone besides himself, Marla, and their closest allies know the stakes here? If the Outsider reached the gazebo, that was it: the over-Bradley would have no choice but to cut them off. This world would be severed from the tree of the multiverse before the Outsider could reach the place at the center of the multiverse. Their universe would be sacrificed to spare the greater tree of the multiverse. Anyone the Outsider didn't devour would soon die anyway, as the rules of reality broke down and metaphysical gangrene set in.

"It's here!" Nicolette's voice boomed, godlike, and Marla winced and drew her dagger. Everyone settled into place, the great crowd murmuring.

The Outsider walked into the park, hands in its pockets, looking the same as it had before, except it had a piratical black eye patch now. Bradley felt a little surge of pride come from Marzi through the residue of their link.

"Why, hello. What a nice welcoming committee." The Outsider spoke in a low, even voice, which was somehow as audible as if it were standing right beside Bradley's ear. From the way the crowd shifted, it was the same for all of them. "I see Marla made it back up on her feet, and is lurking in the back. I—"

Evelyn Park shouted through her megaphone, and the ghosts charged forward, bellowing as they half-ran, half-floated. The Outsider suddenly burst into a cloud of shadow, and the grey insubstantiality of the roaring ghosts disappeared into that inky, roiling darkness. After a long moment, the shadows vanished, drawing inward, like footage of a smoke bomb going off, played in reverse. The Outsider stood there, still in its suit, its hat not even askew. "Mmm. That was impolite. I was in mid-sentence. They tasted disgusting, too. Like eating a bowl of dust and cobwebs. Some of you seem juicier—but this is ridiculous. Those who run away now, I promise, I will not pursue. I have no interest in you. Only interest in *that.*" It pointed at the gazebo—and the force field around it popped like a soap bubble, vanishing.

"Forward!" Nicolette yelled, and the cannon fodder moved, apprentices throwing bullshit cantrips, wild men transforming into animals or scaly monsters, poltergeisters causing the ground to erupt or stones to fall from the sky. The Outsider walked through all that mayhem, strolling as if no one was attacking at all. It didn't deflect, and it didn't dodge: it just didn't get *hit*, by anything. The wild men stumbled into one another, and some of them even fell into the paths of destruction wrought by the poltergeisters, and got torn apart in the process. Some of them regrouped and ran for the Outsider's back, but without even looking back, the monster gestured with its hand, and the attackers flew through the air, crashing into the dirt or breaking against trees or landing in the duck pond.

The Outsider paused and looked at the box Beadle had made to contain it. "Oh, no, that won't do at all." It extended one hand, then closed it into a fist. The order-mage apprentices jumped as the box they surrounded shattered, cracked, and fell into sawdust and splinters.

"Fuck this!" one of the gang members shouted, and the Honeyed Knots and the Four Tree Gang both broke ranks and fled. The lieutenants and retainers wavered, looking over their shoulders at their leaders, but as the Outsider implacably walked toward the gazebo, most of them fled, too, and the others shrank back out of its way.

"Very smart, very wise, save yourselves, scuttle away. I am the eater of all things, swallower of souls. I am the unmaking. I am death in a stylish hat." That insinuating voice, in everyone's ear at once, was enough to make Bradley's legs tremble.

The rulers of Felport stood together, Nicolette at their head, and Marla's crew around them. Marzi lifted her pistol, and Bradley could tell she was ice-water calm, even knowing they were doomed. Marla had her knife. Pelham and Rondeau brandished their weapons. Okay then. It was a "die valiantly" situation. Well, if you had to go, go standing tall.

Then Regina queen stepped out of the gazebo, yawned, and flicked her fingers toward the Outsider.

Marla and the others gasped as all the moisture was sucked out of their mouths, and the duck pond emptied itself, too, as Regina's magic pulled moisture from the area. The Outsider was instantly encased in a crystalline shell, a globe of magical ice several feet thick.

"Beadle!" Nicolette shouted. "You're up!" Marla looked at her in confusion, but Bradley smiled. Damn. Nicolette had a plan *under* her plan. That was like something Marla would do.

Beadle gestured, and several of his lieutenants ran forward, carrying ice picks and chisels and knives toward the globe of ice. Beadle set them to scribbling symbols on the icy shell, shouting orders, sometimes stepping in himself to correct or refine their work.

"Whoa." Marla walked over with Bradley and Marzi and the others to join the knot of sorcerers congratulating Nicolette. Marla shouldered them all aside and stood before the new chief sorcerer. "*That* was the plan? You never intended the box to hold it at all?"

"If that had worked, it would've been great, but yeah, there was a backup. Plans within plans, Marla. I know my shit."

Marla crossed her arms. "Sure. I'm the one who brought Regina, though. Your backup wouldn't have worked without me."

Nicolette threw back her head and laughed. "Oh, yes, because I'd never be able to find anybody else who could do containment magic, Regina's the only one in the whole wide—"

The shell of ice exploded, raining fragments down on them, and Regina Queen screamed, a terrible keening sound, and fell to her knees, as if the breaking ice hurt her physically—and maybe it did. The Outsider strode out of the icy remnant, shaking frost off its limbs, and stormed toward the gazebo. The monster was sweating shadows, growing taller with every step, and Bradley's heart sank. They were doomed. This world was going to be cast adrift to rot and die.

Marla drew her blade and started toward the Outsider. Bradley glanced at Nicolette—and she was *smiling*. He couldn't read her mind, not without some effort and getting a headache in the process, but he had a sudden flash of intuition. He looked at the gazebo, really closely, and this time, he saw it. He rushed forward and grabbed Marla's elbow. "No," he said, voice low. "*Watch.*"

She looked at him like he was crazy, but she waited.

The Outsider howled in triumph and raced into the gazebo.

A sound like a thunderclap rolled through the park, and where the gazebo had been, there was an immense bulbous clay pot, the size of a small car, covered all over with sinuous scribbles. Mr. Beadle shouted "Forward!" and his coterie of lieutenants and apprentices raced to the pot. This time, they didn't draw anything, just peered at every bit of the scrawl-covered pottery, then nodded, one by one, stepping back. "We have full integrity!" Beadle called. "We're good!"

"What," Marla said. "The ever-loving *fuck*?"

"We knew it was going for the gazebo," Nicolette said. "So we just gave it a different gazebo: basically the kind of jar you trap genies in, but *big*. We covered it in illusions so strong they almost became real, to make it look like the old gazebo. Took about twenty illusionists working non-stop. I knew the illusion was good when even Bowman here couldn't see through it."

"You put the outsider in a *jar*?" Marla said.

"Ha. It looks like pottery, and it started out that way, but it's indestructible. We're going to bury that jar like nothing's ever been buried before, and we won't let any stupid death cultists get near it."

"I noticed it, right at the end." Bradley nodded. "That it wasn't the real gazebo. Not because the illusion wavered, though, that was amazingly solid—the fake gazebo is just a foot or so to the left of where the real one used to stand." He frowned. "But where's the real gazebo? That's, like, how I get *home*."

Nicolette waved a beefy hand. "We disassembled it. Don't worry, Beadle numbered all the pieces, he's going to put it back together just like it was, down to the last nail. I like having the entryway to the ruler of your realm in my city. You owe us a favor, now, right, Bowman? Because we stopped this monster for you?"

"I will take that question upstairs, but my inclination is, for sure." He shook his head. "Damn, Nicolette, what got into you? You used to just fuck stuff up. Now you're ruling and schooling."

She kicked at the dirt. "You know how it is, movie star. I'm finally where I belong. I figured it out. All this time, I've been about the hating, the wrecking, the revenge. Don't get me wrong—doing what Marla failed to do warms my cockles and lots of other places, and if you're miserable about it, Marla, I'm even more glad. But… I've got a purpose, now. A place. I'm the witch queen of Felport. This is my city, and my people live here."

Marla took a deep breath and then held out her hand. Nicolette stared at that hand like it was leprous, but then she took it. Marla gave Nicolette's hand a single shake. "You did good," she said. "I was wrong about you. You're a worthy adversary—and you're a hell of an chief sorcerer."

"I need your approval like I need pubic lice." Nicolette's voice was as sneering as ever—but Bradley could tell she was pleased. She turned and cupped her hands around her mouth. "Hey, all you chickenshits! Good job looking terrified and running away—I was totally convinced! You're natural cowards! Afterparty at the club for everybody, and get medical attention for the ones who were too dumb to avoid getting injured in this little pantomime!"

"Were the ghosts fake?" Marla said.

Nicolette snorted. "Hell no. Those were the actual founding families of Felport. I was happy to get rid of them. Parasites. When I went all Fisher King I trumped their magical connection to the health of the city anyway. Fuck the past. This is the new Felport. Welcome to the Age of Nicolette."

"Long live the queen," Marla murmured. She glanced around. "I have to go talk to Regina."

"Yeah, send Nanook on back north." Nicolette watched Marla leave, then grinned around at the others. "The rest of you toadies, Marla's bootlickers… you're welcome in Felport anytime. I love reminders of my ultimate victory. See you at the party."

She ambled off, shouting at her people.

"Damn," Marzi said. "Last time I helped save the world, nobody threw me a party."

"Say what you will about Nicolette," Rondeau said. They looked at him expectantly, and he shrugged. "Nah, that's all. Say what you will. I don't care. She's something else, though."

THE AFTERPARTY WAS A RAGER, but Bradley drifted away from the crowd toward the office where Nicolette was hanging out, keeping herself occupied by drinking very good whiskey and being magnanimous. She was back in her tattooed body, behind a desk, legs kicked up. Perren and Hamil were there, and Crapsey and Squat, and Pelham and Rondeau, the latter two sitting in a corner playing cards.

"Bowman!" Nicolette called, sounding drunk and delighted. "What's the word from on high?"

"I went and talked to myself in the mirror for a while, and the big me says, it's all good. The Outsider is contained so thoroughly he can't even sense the monster's presence anymore. Beadle does good work."

"Wisdom of the ancients with a modern twist." Nicolette shrugged. "And also my leadership. Can't forget that. Crapsey, pour this man a drink."

Rondeau's dark doppelganger dumped a couple fingers of something old and brown into a glass, and after only a moment's hesitation, Bradley took it. Falling off the wagon was bad, but screw it, he was getting re-integrated into the collective pretty soon anyway—the over-Bradley had told him to enjoy the party first, so why not take him at his word. He took a sip, and the familiar burn was delicious. A little binge wouldn't kill him.

He sat on the couch beside Squat. "Hey, man. I keep hearing how terrifying you are, but no offense—you don't seem so bad."

The toadlike entity on the couch shrugged. "Nicolette's got me in therapy. Fixed my eyes this morning. She thinks she figured out a way to keep the strength and invulnerability but get rid of most of the worse effects of the curse. I'll never be tall again, but screw it, I'd have to buy all new clothes anyway. You know, for a while there, I thought I'd made a bad mistake—that Nicolette had played me, sweet-talked me into turning on Marla."

"Well, she did." Crapsey dropped to the couch on the other side of Rondeau. "She totally played you, man. It's just, after that, she *reformed*."

"Marla probably never would have cured me, though," Squat said.

Bradley nodded. "Maybe so, maybe not. She's not a bad person, Marla, and she's trying real hard to get better, but… she sees the things she wants to see, sometimes, and other stuff, she never notices at all."

"Speak of the deposed leader." Crapsey nodded toward the door. Marla came in, trailed by Regina Queen.

"I thought you sent the ice queen packing?" Nicolette said from behind the desk. "Pretty sure I didn't invite *you* to this party, either, Marla."

"Perren, you might want to move away from your boss." Marla's voice was grim.

"Nonsense," Regina said. "I am very precise." Regina waved her hand—and another icy globe formed, this one encasing Nicolette, the desk, and the chair. Perren stumbled backwards, and Crapsey and Squat leapt to their feet. Bradley just stared at the blue-white ice. His heart felt frozen in his chest.

Perren moaned. "Marla, no, all the people of Felport, they'll freeze, they'll *die*."

Marla shook her head. "No they won't." She turned to Regina. "We're done."

"Mmm. A pleasure." The ice queen turned and left, as elegantly as if striding down a catwalk.

Perren reached her hand toward the globe of ice and then winced when it got within a few inches—the ice was that cold. "What did you do, Marla?"

"Yeah." Bradley couldn't stop staring at the ice, which was so much more than *just* ice, the crystal threaded through with all sorts of peculiar magic. "How did you do that? Nicolette should have been impervious to all harm—wait. She's not harmed, is she?"

"She's safer than she's ever been." Marla kicked the block of ice with one cowboy boot. She seemed tired. "I got the idea from the Pit Boss, actually. He wanted to put Rondeau in a medically-induced coma, because if Rondeau dies, the Pit Boss might die, right? So I thought—why not put Nicolette in that kind of stasis? And when it comes to putting people on ice, nobody's better than Regina. Tweak the ice magic a little to make it more like a cryosleep, suspended-animation deal, and bang. Problem solved. Nicolette will live forever, invulnerable, so her psychic link to everybody in the city doesn't matter."

"Marla." Bradley shook his head. "I… she was doing good. Nicolette."

Marla turned on him, clenching her hands into fists. "You're giving me that shit? She could never do enough good to make up for the bad she's done. She doesn't get to *win*. I can't have that." She looked at Perren. "You want to be chief sorcerer?"

"I—what?" The woman tore her eyes away from the block of ice.

"I'm not giving it to Hamil, that fucking collaborator. But you had some backbone. I've bested the chief sorcerer of Felport in combat, more or less, and right at this moment I rule the city by right of conquest. I'll give you the job if you want it, though, if you promise not to give it back to the Chamberlain. She's nothing without her ghosts, anyway. You can become Fisher King if you like—maybe Hamil can find a way to transfer the spell from Nicolette to you. I honestly don't care."

Perren nodded slowly. "I'd… better inform the rest of the council. You might want to leave town, Marla." She left the room.

Marla turned her gaze elsewhere. "You two lackeys have objections?"

Crapsey and Squat exchanged a look. Squat sighed. "Fuck it. I'm used to being ugly. I won't make a fuss about this if you don't come after me for helping Nicolette escape in the first place."

Marla considered for a moment, then nodded. "All right. We're square, Squat. Bygones and all."

Rondeau, in the corner, lifted his hand. "Hey, boss? I'm having a little trouble reconciling things here. You put Nicolette in suspended animation because her crimes were too vast to let her walk free, right, even though she was in the midst of majorly redeeming herself. But in order to stop Nicolette, you agreed to free Regina Queen, a woman who murders people completely without remorse, and is no more interested in redemption than a cookie-cutter shark would be."

Marla nodded. "Yes. I made a deal with the devil, or the icy equivalent. And that sucks. In the circle of binding, I very specifically said that I, Marla Mason, would not try to stop Regina. I was very specific. Really quite specific."

"Oh, sure, so someone *else* is free to stop her—" Rondeau stopped and stared at her, frowning. "Wait. Like *who?*"

Marla just looked at him, entirely expressionless.

"No," he said. "No, no, no. Me and Pelly? Hell, no."

She shrugged. "You've got experience dealing with her."

"Hey, you're rich again, right?" Crapsey said from the couch.

Rondeau narrowed his eyes. "Uh. Yes. But I'm not looking to hire an evil body-double, thanks."

"No, stupid-but-handsome. Me and Squat are out of work all of a sudden. I think we've proven here that we're morally neutral, yeah? Pay us enough and sic us on a bad person, and we'll be the good guys, at least comparatively."

"Sure," Squat said. "So why not hire us to go kill Regina Queen? We should probably get out of here, anyway. We're not real well-liked by the supernatural populace at large, me because of stuff I did for Nicolette during the takeover, and Crapsey because... he's Crapsey."

"It's an idea," Marla said to Rondeau. "Worst case, they succeed and get rid of Regina. Best case, they fail and she kills them. It's one of those no-lose situations. But whatever you decided to do, Rondeau, I'm making Regina your responsibility. It isn't right, but." She shrugged. "It's necessary. You're who I trust. "

Rondeau stood up, swaying. "Come on, Pelly. I've lost my stomach for celebrating." He looked at Marla and shook his head. "You know I hated Nicolette. Hated her up one side and down the other. But what you did here... I don't know, Marla. I don't think it was right." He left the room, Pelham drifting after him.

Marla put a hand on Pelham's shoulder as he went by. "Do you think I made the wrong choice too, Pelly?"

"It is not my place to condemn you, Mrs. Mason." He bowed his head and left the room.

"Ha," Marla said. "But if it was his place, he would. He disapproves of violent regime change. Even though this really wasn't all that violent. I wonder if Nicolette has enough loyal partisans around for me to worry about reprisals? Word's gonna get out soon that she's an ice cube."

"Yeah." Bradley nodded. "You might want to leave town. I guess we should pick up Marzi—she's at the hotel. She didn't want to party, just pack up to leave for home. I'd hate for this... thing you did... to blow back on her."

Marla held up the key. "We can go straight to her room from here."

Bradley shuddered. "Tell you what. I'll walk."

"I can walk with you."

He held up a hand. "How about I just meet you there. I... need a few minutes to process all this."

Marla leaned against the wall by the door, tilting her head back. She seemed so exhausted. "Did I fuck up, B? Should I have left Nicolette in charge? Forgotten all her crimes and just let her run this city, *my* city?"

"What's that tattoo on your wrist say?"

She didn't answer. They both knew.

"You didn't give Nicolette much of a chance to redeem herself," he said. "She was trying. She was *changed*. People don't often really change."

"Some things are beyond redemption." Marla's voice was stiff and unyielding.

"Okay," Bradley said. "Good thing we have you to make those decisions for us."

Marla opened her eyes, looked at him for a long moment, and said, "I did what I thought was necessary. I'll see you at Marzi's hotel." She opened the door with Death's key, and stepped through, pulling it closed after her.

After a few minutes spent gazing at the frozen globe, trying without success to see some hint of Nicolette's shape in the cloudy ice, Bradley left the office, and the party. Sierra was waiting at the curb, all upright and repaired. She offered him a ride to the hotel, and on the way they talked about a few things. When they arrived, he went into the lobby, and then into the men's room. He knocked on the mirror over the sink, and his own face appeared, but different.

"Little B!" the man in the mirror said. "What's up?"

"Can I get a little longer on Earth? I want to get Marzi safely back to the west coast, and I am done takign shortcuts through Hell. I was thinking me and Marzi could take a road trip in Sierra. Maybe take Marla, too, if I feel like I can put up with her that long."

"Huh. You aren't going native on me, are you? We miss your wisdom and perspective up here."

"Yeah, sure you do. If only you had a billion minds almost exactly like mine to talk to."

"You know, since you're there in a body, and that universe is part of the multiverse again, your current incarnation is actually multiplying and splitting throughout the realities... which means you're making the collective more robust. We're not infinite, after all, and having more of us in the multiverse isn't necessarily a bad thing. We can always call you guys up later if we need you, after you've multiplied a while longer. So sure, stay a while."

"Huh. You mean after more than thirty years of being gay, now I'm a *breeder*?"

"Basically." The man in the mirror shook his head. "That's some shit with Regina, huh? Freezing Nicolette like that. Can't say I think it's a bad idea—in most of the universes where Nicolette is still wandering loose, she's a force for awful things."

"Yeah, I know. But in one of the few universes where she *wasn't* terrible, she got frozen in a hunk of ice. That's fair?"

"Ha. Well, Marla Mason, right? Look up 'unforgiving' in the dictionary."

"Yeah. Thanks, Big B. I'll be in touch."

Bradley went to the elevator and rode up to Marzi's room. She greeted him effusively, wearing a fluffy bathrobe. "Hey! I thought you'd be partying."

"It wasn't much of a party. How you feel about heading home tonight instead of waiting until morning?"

"Oh. Sure. I miss Jonathan. Are we flying?"

"I was thinking we could ride in Sierra. She can drive non-stop, so it'd only take maybe a couple of days, maybe a little longer since we'll want to eat and pee and stretch our legs occasionally. I mean, we could get a plane, but you said you wanted to talk to me about some stuff anyway, right? We'd have plenty of time to talk on a road trip."

Marzi nodded. "I wanted to ask you about some things, for sure. Magic. Being a sorcerer. Maybe setting up a meeting for me with your old teacher, Sanford Cole? I'm a little nervous about just cold-calling the guy, if I decide that's what I want to do."

Bradley smiled. "Yeah, I can definitely do that." He looked around. "Marla's not here? She took the shortcut through Hell, I was sure she'd beat me."

Marzi shook her head. "No sign of her."

"Huh," Bradley said. "Maybe she's sulking. She did something... I'll tell you about it later. We'll give her a little time, let you get ready, and if she's not here when it's time to go, we'll leave her a note. She can always catch up with us—she can pop right through Sierra's passenger door any time she wants."

Marzi put her arm over him. "Road trip with a dead movie star. Look at me coming up in the world."

"Oh, you could go far," Bradley said. "In fact... I was going to leave town, but maybe I'll stay in California for a while, and teach you a few things." He liked the idea. He'd never been a teacher—he'd always felt like he still had too much to learn himself, whether it was acting or magic— but helping Marzi along... that would be doing good in this world, a kind of good that might ripple out through all the possible worlds that sprang from this one.

They ended up waiting a long time, into the wee hours of the morning, talking in Marzi's hotel room, but Marla never came.

Epilogue:

The Dread Queen in Her Realm

MARLA STEPPED THROUGH THE OFFICE DOOR, leaving the icy hulk of Nicolette and her disapproving ex-apprentice behind. Her mind was a seething mass of misgivings, doubts, and even a treacherous thread of something that might have been regret—

But when she stepped through the door, cool serenity descended as always, and the part of her that fretted about the opinions of mortals receded into a tiny unilluminated portion of her mind. Her intellect became cool, vast, and not even remotely amused. She was the dread queen of the underworld, now, the bride of death, and it was just a shame there was still time left on her mortal month in the world, because there was so much *work* to be done here below—

The queen paused in the foyer that wasn't really a foyer at all. The walls were cracked, the ceiling a moldy ruin, the floor pitted and splintered. She'd noticed the disarray the last time she passed through, but hadn't thought much of it—the place's appearance was just a convenience, after all, because it had to look like *something*. Now, though, without the distraction of those *living things* in her presence, in a place where they did not belong, she could sense a deeper wrongness. Something about her realm was… broken.

She looked around, and the walls dissolved, shimmered, and became her throne room, a cavern of obsidian, onyx, and black marble. There were two chairs there, carved of sapphire and emerald. Once upon a time, one chair had been smaller than the other—the smaller chair belonged to Death's consort, a mortal raised to godhood to rule aside a creature more purely divine—but the queen had put a stop to *that* nonsense. She and her husband were co-regents, halves of a whole….

But he wasn't here, now, and his emerald chair lay toppled on its side. She reached out for him, tried to sense him, which was normally as easy as sensing the position of her own left arm.

Nothing. Where could he be? Was *he* out, walking the Earth?

She realized the compulsion to return to Earth, normally so overwhelming when it was time to spend her month as a mortal, was gone. She felt no pull toward the mortal realm at all—as if the bargain she'd struck to spend six months of the year on Earth had been broken. The bargain she'd made with her husband, Death. But what could break that arrangement?

"Marla."

The queen spun. There was another god here. That happened, sometimes: they could reach this place more easily than mortals, by passing through certain places that would mean death to humans. Volcanoes, trenches in the deep oceans, miles-down caves teeming with blind monsters. The other gods came for favors, or to socialize, but Death and his queen routinely turned them away, too busy with their business overseeing the cycles of death and rebirth—without which there would have been no gods at all.

"I don't have time," she began, and then recognized him. "Wait. You are Reva."

He bowed his head, not that he had a head, exactly. "I am. I was… not friends with your husband, exactly… but acquaintances, certainly."

"You *were*? You aren't any more? Did you have a falling out?"

Reva shook his head. "Marla. The Outsider… when Death opened a door from this realm in the Outsider's presence, on that beach in San Francisco, the monster could sense the path. The Outsider could find the passageways, and pry them open, and pass through. After I encountered the Outsider I could sense his actions, you see, because he was an exile himself, one of *my* creatures, as far from home as it is possible for anything to be. I felt him come here, and I pursued, to warn your husband, but I was too late." Reva sat down on the stony floor and put his head in his hands. "I'm sorry."

The rings. In Felport, fighting the Outsider, she'd noticed its ostentatious rings. The monster hadn't been wearing them on the beach, but when the rings appeared later, she'd thought they were merely an ornament, a refinement of its human costume. Her own husband, when he chose to appear in human form, often appeared wearing rings, each holding a precious stone from the wealth below the surface, each imbued with strange magics. The Outsider's increased power, in the final battle… He'd stolen it from Death.

"He is dead?" she rasped. "My husband is dead?" She touched the necklace at her throat, where her wedding ring hung.

Reva didn't raise his head. "You're the only god of Death, now, Marla. I'm so sorry. This realm is yours alone, now… and it's incomplete. I don't know what happens next—if you should take a mortal consort, or if another Death will rise, or—"

In the back of her mind, the mortal part of Marla, the part that still longed to do good in the world, to care for her friends, to make amends, to make a difference, to kill monsters, to *do better*, howled in agony at the loss of her husband, and in fear at what the uncertain future might bring.

The greater part of her, the part that was now the only ruler of the land of the dead, howled in agonies of her own.

The agony of being cut in half, and left alone, to reign in Hell.

Acknowledgments

THANKS, FIRST AND ALWAYS, to my wife Heather Shaw for her love and support, and to my son River for putting up with his dad spending all those hours writing about monsters. Thanks to my artists Lindsey Look (who did the cover) and Zack Stella (who did the interiors)—if you need great art, hire them. My appreciation to Aislinn Quicksilver Harvey for suggesting the title of this novel. Many thanks also to John Teehan of Merry Blacksmith Press for his continued support.

And finally, thanks to all the readers who supported the Kickstarter that made this possible: @atleb, A Anthony James, Adam Caldwell, Alex Moffatt, Alexa Gulliford, Allen L. Edwards, Alpha Chen, Alumiere, Alyssa Ritchie, Amy Kim, Andrea Leeson, Andreas Gustafsson, Andrew Hatchell, Andrew J Clark IV, Andrew Lin, Andrew Wilson, Angela Korra'ti, Ann Lemay, Anton Nath, Arlene Parker, Athena Holter-Mehren, Atlee Breland, BattleVark, Ben Esacove, Ben Meginnis, Beth Rheaume, Beth Wodzinski, Bethany Herron, Betsy Haibel, Bill Jennings, Brenda Hovdenes, Brittany, Bruce F Press, Bryan Sims, Bryant Durrell, C.C. Finlay, Caleb Wilson, Casey Fiesler, Cat Rambo, Catie Murphy, Chad E Price, Charlie Bast, Chelle P, Chris McLaren, Christian Decomain, Christian Stegmann, Christine Chen, Christine Maia-Fleres, Christopher Kastensmidt, Christopher Todd Kjergaard, Christy Corp-Minamiji, Chuck Lawson, Cinnamon Davis, Claire Connelly, Claudia Sadun Muzi, Cliff Winnig, Colette Reap, Colin Anderson, Colleen LeBlanc, Collin Smith, Courtney Ostaff, Craig Hackl, Cynthia Anne Cofer, D-Rock, D. Potter, Dan Percival, Dan Walma, Dana Cate, Dani Daly, Daniel and Trista Robichaud, Daniel Brady, Daniel Lyon, Danielle Benson, Danielle Ching-Yi Kong, Danielle Church, Dave Lawson, Dave Thompson, David Bell, David Bennett, David Martinez, David Rains, Dean M. Roddick, Deanna Stanley, Deb "Seattlejo" Schumacher, Denise Murray, DoorGirl, Douglas Park, Duck Dodgers, Ed Matuskey, Eduardo Tubert, Edward J Smola III, ejhuff, Elias F.

Combarro, Ellen Sandberg, Elsa, Emily Agan, Emma Bull, Emma Larkins, Emma Marston, Emrya, Enrica, Ferran Selles, Fred Kiesche, Gann and Constance Bierner, Gary Singer, Gavran, Glenn Seiler, Glennis LeBlanc, Glyph, Greg Levick, GrumpySteen, Guillaume, Gunnar Hagberg, Hathway, Heidi Berthiaume, hipployta, Hugh Berkson, I.Z. aka IDzeroNo, Ian Mond, Iysha Evelyn, J Quincy Sperber, J. Croisant, J.R. Murdock, Jacqueline H. Kessler, James Burbidge, James M. Yager, Jamie Grove, Jasmine Stairs, Jason D Wilson, Jay G, Jaym Gates, Jean Marie Ward, Jeannette Lane, Jeff Huse, Jeffrey Krauss, Jeffrey Reed, Jen Sparenberg, Jen Warren, Jen Woods, Jenn Ridley, Jenn Snively, Jennifer Berk, Jennifer Howland, Jennifer Theis, Jeremy Rosehart, Jim Crose, Jim Lewinson, JM Templet, Joanna Fuller, Joe Rosenblum, John Blankenship, John Curley, John Dees, John Devenny, Jon Eichten, Jon Hansen, Jon Lundy, Jonas Wisser, Jonathan Duhrkoop, Jose Rafael Martinez Pina, Josh Lowman, Juli McDermott & Rob Batchellor, Justin Morton, Justine Baker, Karen Tucker, Kate and Andrew Barton, Kathlyn Luliak, Katie Douglas, Keith Hall, Keith Teklits, Keith Weinzerl, Kelly A. Hong, Kendall P. Bullen, Kenn Luby, Kerim, Kevin Hogan, Kevin Tibbs, Kiara Pyrenei, Konstantin Gorelyy, KorieK, Kris Downs, Kristin Bodreau, Laura A Burns, Laura Hobbs, Laura McIntyre, Lavendermintrose, Lexie C., Lianne Burwell, Lilly Ibelo, Logan Waterman, Lori L. Gildersleeve, Lori Lum, Lukas Bürgi, M.K. Carroll, Magentawolf, Mara Jade Smith, Marc Carnovale, Margaret Klee, Margaret Taylor, Marie Jones, Marius Gedminas, Mark "The Guitartist" Loggins, Mark Rowe, Martin S. Hesseling, Martin Wagner, Matthew Sheahan, Matthew Wayne Selznick, Max Kaehn, Maynard Garrett, Melissa Tabon, Michael "Maikeruu" Pierno, Michael Bernardi, Michael D. Blanchard, Michelle, Mike, Mike Bavister, Mike, Jen, Keira & Rowan Schwartz, Miles Matton, Mitch Anderson, Morgan McCauley, Mur Lafferty, Natalie Luhrs, Nathan Bremmer, Nellie, Nicole, Nicole Dutton, Ori Shifrin, Paul Bulmer, Paul Echeverri, Pedro Arjona, Philda, Philip Adler, Phillip Jones, Poppy Terwilliger Lammergeier, Rachel Sanders, Ragi Gonçalves, Reed Lindner, Renee D. LeBeau, Rhonda Parrish, Richard Leaver, Rick Cambere, Ro Molina, Rob Steinberger, Robin in Vermont, Robin0, Rodelle Ladia Jr., Rodrigo Martin, Roger Silverstein, Ron Jarrell, Rosie, Rowan A., Ryan Rapp, Ryan Spicher, S. Nasiri, Sally Novak Janin, Sam Courtney, Sarah Kingdred, Sarah Livingston Heitz, Scott Drummond, Scott Serafin, Sean Brennan, Shadow, Sharon Wood, Sheryl R. Hayes, SJ Elliott, Skyler Spurgeon, Smith Roberts, Sophia Fisher, Stephanie Langdeau, Steve Dean, Steve Feldon, Steven Desjardins, Steven Saus, Su Lem, summervillain, Sy Bram, T.Thaggert, Tamara L. DeGray, Tania Clucas, Tara Rowan, Tara

Smith, Tara Yoshikawa, Ted Brown, Thomas Zilling, Tim & Meredith Hines, Tim Uruski, Timothy Moore, Tina Kirk, Tom Bridge, Topher, Travis M. Dunn, Trey Wren, Vincent Meijer, Von Welch, Yoshio Kobayashi, Younjee Shon, ZenDog, Joey Shoji, Armi Guerilla, Evan Ladouceur, Richard Ludwig, Heather Richardson, Keith Garcia, Edward Greaves, Cailtin Savage, Michelle Bourne, Lucinda Bromfield, and Duncan McNiff.

Made in the USA
Middletown, DE
19 July 2024

57581912R00133